The Magpie's Bagpipe

Selected Essays
of Jonathan Williams

Selected and Edited by
Thomas Meyer

North Point Press
San Francisco
1982

Copyright © 1959, 1960, 1961, 1962, 1963, 1964, 1965,
1967, 1969, 1971, 1973, 1974, 1975, 1976, 1978, 1980, 1981, and
1982 by Jonathan Williams
Introduction copyright © 1982 by Thomas Meyer
Jacket photograph, *F102*, copyright © 1957 by Aaron Siskind
Printed in the United States of America
Library of Congress Catalogue Card Number: 82–081474
ISBN: 0–86547—092–8 (cloth)
0–86547–093–6 (paper)

Acknowledgments

For permission to reprint part or all of these essays here sometimes in different versions, the author and editor are grateful to *Conjunctions* for " 'Bottom of the Forty-fifth . . . Coming In to Pitch:' "; to *Parnassus* for "Am—O"; to the Jargon Society and Atlantic Richfield for "Being a Wee Introduction to the Scots Poet/Toymaker/Typographer"; to the Jargon Society for "Publishing Bucky's Epic"; to *Parnassus* for "Much Further Out Than You Thought"; to the Jargon Society for " 'Think What's Got Away in My Life!' " and " 'No Layoff from This Condensery' "; to the *Nation* for "Things Are Very Far Away"; to the *Texas Quarterly* for "Edward Dahlberg's Book of Lazarus"; to *Lillabulero* for "The Roastin' Ears Are In and Vida Pitches Tonight!"; to *Arts Review* for "A Poet's Profile of John Furnival"; to *Margins* and *Open Letter* for "Country Joe and the Fission"; to the Jargon Society for "O. L. Bongé of Biloxi, Mississippi"; to *Paideuma* for "Eighty of the Best"; to the Jargon Society for " 'Better Git It in Your Soul' " and " 'Surely Reality Is More Interesting' "; to *De La Rue Review* for "My Time Will Yet Come . . . Said Some German"; to *Parnassus* for " 'Anyway, All I Ever Wanted to Be Was a Poet' "; to the Welsh Arts Council, the Southeastern Center for Contemporary Art, Special Collections of Kent State University Libraries, *Travelling Light,* and the Arts Council of Great Britain for "The Camera Non-Obscura"; to *Aperture* for "Lea, the Place Where Light Shines," "Aaron Siskind at 75," and "The Shadow of His Equipage"; to the Jargon Society for " 'They All Want to Go and Dress Up' "; to the Victoria and Albert Museum and Gordon Fraser Gallery for "Some Speak of a Return to Nature"; to the *New York Times Book Review* for "A Walk in Wales"; to *Parnassus* for "St. Bees Head to Robin Hood's Bay"; to the *New York Times Book Review* for "Further Adventures While Preaching the Gospel of Beauty"; to Coburn Britton for "Bashō and the Blue Rider"; to Simpson Kalisher (*Railroad Men,* Clark & Day), Buffalo State University, and Gnomon Books for "A la

Recherche du Sud Perdu"; to *Cultural Affairs* for "The Arts—a (Finger-Lickin') Southern Experience"; to *Craft Horizons* for "A White Cloud in the Eye of a White Horse"; to Ellsworth Taylor and the University of Kentucky for "Beauty? Beauty My Eye!"

For aid and shelter special thanks are due to SUNY at Buffalo Libraries (Poetry Collection) where the Jonathan Williams/Jargon Archives are housed and to Wake Forest University and the Aspen Institute for Humanistic Studies.

Contents

A Note

Guy Davenport, a writer with his words at the ready—and precisely the words to knock your socks off—likes to say that my writing is "paratactic, peripatetic, and cathectic." Well, that sounds about right—and I don't want to have to blush, and jump about on one leg, and exclaim "gosh all hemlock," like Shuffle Shoffer (sp?) on radio's own *Ma Perkins*.

Having written it all down once, I could never face the medusa-like task of pruning and improving it. If one writes a big piece on crafts in the Southern Highlands in 1966, some of the information dates in 1982. It has to, for there is no way for me to take the time to head for Blenko and Penland and the John C. Campbell Folk School, etc. Essays date from when they are written and I can't see a thing in the world wrong with that.

Thomas Meyer has taken on the task of editing and ordering all that *The Magpie's Bagpipe* contains, and he is due admiration from anyone who realizes just how much work that involves. A book like this is to be read at random, on whim. When it's the shank of the evening and a particularly good version of "St. Louis Blues" is on the stereo, I hope a few will join me in pondering Edward Dahlberg, and other caitiffs of the Republic who will not be on HBO tonight or on any television screen ever again.

I'm not the kind of writer who ever employs an agent—they don't like to live on air. The majority of pieces in *The Magpie's Bagpipe* were written "on spec" or for magazines and papers that paid either little or nothing. The motivation and attention of editors were welcome, and I thank them for both.

For JW, prose is to order. Poetry just happens, like dandruff and what some call inspiration.

Jonathan Williams
January 15, 1982

Introduction: *Ach, Du Liebe!*
Mein Herr Williams,
Du Bist Buddhist!

"Mr. Wilde, do you like music?" the Great Man was once asked by a Chelsea hostess. Having accepted her invitation to tea, he was now amidst a very long recital, youngest daughter at the Bechstein, in *his* honor. "Oh, no. Not at all!" he confessed, "But I like *this*." Just so, I expect one day soon to be asked if I like essays, and my answer will ape darling Oscar's: Oh, no—but I like *these*. What extraordinary dinner companions Jonathan Williams and Oscar Wilde would have been, they could have enjoyed each other immensely. Nineteen eighty-two is the centennial of Wilde's American tour. Off the *Arizona* he stepped, and passing through customs in New York, when asked if he had anything to declare, replied: "Nothing but my genius." Richard D'Oyly Carte was about to launch *Patience* on these shores and the backers knew that its success depended upon us colonials knowing what an *aesthete* was. So they sent over a ripe one. Art in the Newfound Land would never be the same. Almost halfway through his visit, Wilde felt compelled to prepare a second, completely different lecture, "House Decoration." He told his Yankee audiences, "Having seen fifty or so cities I find that what your people need is not so much high imaginative art, but that which hallows the vessels of everyday use."

"The old Puritan doctrine, that art is sinful, has been roundly repudiated, as it ought to have been," Washington Gladden declared in the *Andover Review* before Wilde hardly had time to get out of the country. And: "No subtler or more dangerous foe of civilization is now abroad than the moral indifference which infests so much of our art, and which accustoms us to look coolly and curiously on the plastic forms of human character. . . ." American aesthetics had been invented, crown of thorns and all. Here we are, still trying to make that leap from Walter Pater to Henry Thoreau. God only knows what pressure in the next hundred years Jonathan Williams's diatribes on food and drink, here and abroad, in public and in private, will exert upon the course of some Republic's poetry, or photography, or jazz, or indeed, democracy. Classics of an as yet undeclared Confucian school?

"How splendid it is to have a day out with Jonathan," observed a friend whose houseguests we were in Dorset last autumn during the first hard frost of the season. He and JW were just back from Abbotsbury, the Benedictine swannery there, and an auction sale. "Most people don't see anything," our host went on, sorting out bread and jam and tea, "but Jonathan notices everything." Or perhaps (as Mr. Wilde might've put it) what he notices, is everything. No periphery allowed. So fierce is the attention, that his already catholic taste seems to effervesce, engendering entire worlds whenever he addresses a subject. A man is most eloquent—Dante proclaimed in *La Vita Nuova* (I think it is, though it sounds more like *De Vulgari Eloquentia*)— who uses the speech of ordinary men: To raise the common to the estate of the uncommon by the grace of language is Jonathan Williams's passion as an artist. His prose crackles with that determination. *Odi et amo* is written between every line. I hate and I love . . . I'm in a hurry but won't be rushed . . . People must have good manners and I don't care whose toes I trample saying so . . . Since they're no damn good anyway, what the hell am I going to do without society in this greedy nation whose plenty delights me so? His style is a champagne of contradictions: the wit *brut*; the satire *mousseux*. The "floundering eloquence" Carlyle found in Bartram's prose moved the old essayist far more than he knew, as it did Coleridge and Wordsworth, because it was fresh, direct, and unflinching. And that Philadelphia Quaker ("The Flower Hunter in the Fields") William Bartram—who discovered Appalachia and was its Adam—is our present author's dear master.

Williams quotes a breathtaking passage from Bartram's *Travels* (1775) in "A White Cloud in the Eye of a White Horse." It describes Cherokee maidens by a stream bathing, picking strawberries, cradled in Eden, a premonition in all its indolence "à l'ombre des jeunes filles en fleurs." Then JW cuts in quickly, as Bartram's vision closes, to tell us today these girls work in a pink plastic curler factory polluting that very same river. Such is his craft— on he goes, and now unfolds the sad and dire consequence the region suffers 200 years later. As in Bartram's *Travels,* primary devices throughout these essays are descriptive catalogs and sharp contrasts, but Williams's genius is exquisite timing. The prose is breezy, then driven, hectoring and suddenly tender, an "eloquent floundering," indeed.

The secret, Dante knew, of the vernacular was its informal, sensual tone (its vowels actually). This provided a coloring not possible in Latin with its modulation, its rhetoric (its regular quantities). A motion more like the heart's could be made from a common tongue. Something similar is true in English. Compare any passage of Jonathan Williams to one of Edward

Dahlberg (another of JW's mentors). Dahlberg's is a homemade classic English, beautiful as it is eccentric, but it needs wide open spaces to turn the same corners Williams can manage in a burp. Never as interior or involved, this skilled pacing allows him to wield a prose whose nimble form, despite scale, casts the same silhouette as Proust's. Both men are *flâneurs des mots* whose shared obsession for details, place names, and human foibles are nearly erotic in their intensity. Each's attention—relaxed, acute, close to pedestrian and always omnivorous, constantly refocusing—never alerts us to its real object or purpose until it comes to rest. Only suddenly do they take shape, essay after essay, episode after episode. "Bashō and the Blue Rider" unexpectedly switches from a rambling daybook into a report of political upheaval, personal threat, and human grief just upon conclusion. Or "The Shadow of His Equipage," which starts and finishes a tribute to the surreal photographer Clarence John Laughlin, is, in the meantime, a dressage on artistic frailty and very real vulnerability. The anecdotal again and again takes on the strength of myth without pretension, without strain, but with a little *bon ton:* and that, my friends, is art.

A glance at the acknowledgments will give an idea how fugitive a first appearance these essays made, but what isn't clear is the abundance from which they were culled. Reading through the heap of material that there was, outlines of three or four books came to mind, and I could only imagine this one after sketching the others: a collection of interviews JW has made with, for example, Basil Bunting, Stevie Smith, Ian Hamilton Finlay, Paul Kwilecki, Guy Mendes, and Dan Rice, including those of himself that have appeared in places like *Gay Sunshine* or Martin Duberman's study of Black Mountain College; a publishing memoir of the Jargon Society and its titles, to describe its founding, direction, and influence as a writer's press; a generous selection of JW's letters is already long overdue—anyone who has ever written the man will know what a remarkable epistolary style he commands; and a "looking at photographs," modeled on John Szarkowski's book of that title, a gallery of camera work encompassing the art's history, JW's choice, his comments *en face*.

What didn't fit roughly into any one of the above I realized was a piece of the book at hand. Jonathan Williams is a latter-day Marcus Valerius Martialis, gentleman farmer and amiable grouch. I think my selection will do justice to the concerns and sentiments this Jeffersonian dandy is capable of ranging. He takes potshots at, bemoans, weeps for, or sees fit to celebrate almost anything. Post-modern Crèvecoeur, he is our most elegant spokesman for that unique American fancy, the democratic elite. My editing therefore has mostly been a matter of compiling and arranging. Much of what belonged in an initial gathering of JW's prose was obvious—his pieces on travel, by foot or interstate; the encomiums and eulogies; something about jazz; a lot about photography; certainly the essays on the South. No attempt has been made to "undate" dated material; linguistic currency is capital to our author's *élan* and *éclat*—so, we have here Negro settlements, black communities, Eisenhower "cool," Nixonian "heavy," the Monkees, Herman's Hermits, Metrecal, and the *New York Herald Tribune,* to name a few.

Some gentle pruning was called for, though, to keep favorite anecdotes, words, and phrases from overworking themselves as touchstones, yet some "tone rows" remain; they include Uncle Iv Owens, Anton Bruckner, *Eine Messe des Lebens,* Roark Bradford, bloodroot and wood thrush, Bashō, rowans and the winter wren's song. A few times the occasion a piece was commissioned for was too specific, yet it might yield a paragraph or passage I couldn't let go. These I felt free to clip out and paste down in a felicitious context elsewhere, as elaboration or epigram.

Sifted and sorted, the essays suggest a peregrination along which JW is our guide. Although he may lead us over hell and half Georgia, we never stray far from that confluence of the brooks, trickles, and ice-water springs of his personal enthusiasms and peeves, his *odi-et-amo*'s. Of the many things it may be, this book isn't dull. Nor is it for the dull. Letting you go your way on these pages, I close and quote Henry W. Grady, president of the J. Gordon Coogler Fan Club of Atlanta (the Bard of the Congaree numbers Jonathan Williams among recent converts): "There must be something in the writing of a man who can attract attention and win applause when corn is thirty cents a bushel and potato bugs have become a burden."

Thomas Meyer
Highlands, North Carolina
The Fierce Winter of '82

"To ensure freshness, all foods are cooked from scratch, which is subject to run out."
Dip's Country Kitchen, West Rosemary, Chapel Hill, N.C.

"I sincerely believe that the best kind of criticism is that which is amusing and poetic; not that cold and algebraic kind which, under the pretext of explaining everything, displays neither hate nor love."
Charles Baudelaire

"When I say boogie-woogie, you shake that thang!"
Clarence "Pine Top" Smith

Portraits

"Bottom of the Forty-fifth . . . Coming In to Pitch:"

We're three minutes into the fourth quarter. The meanest man in town, Jack Lambert, has dogged on second down; Brian Sipe has coughed up the ball. We're in the NFL playoffs and Terry Bradshaw has just nine minutes to bring the Steelers back from a nine-point deficit. James Laughlin is smoking his pipe in the Connecticut hills, eyes glazed. CBS is the still point of the turning world; a whole season has come down to these exquisite seconds.

And the telephone rings! It's either Kenneth Rexroth or Merle Hoyleman—poets so maverick and unworldly they don't have a clue their suave publisher at New Directions is a Pittsburgh sports freak and goes quite funny when you talk about Maz and Roberto and Franco and Big Willie. I get calls during football games too, and the World Series, and the Masters, and the NCAA finals. Only at such ineffable moments do J. Laughlin and J. Williams wish that poets were more like other people.

I am delighted to blame JL for much of my literary madness. (The sports mania I owe to early exposure to the likes of Slingin' Sammy Baugh, Bill Tilden, Ben Hogan, and Lou Gehrig.) The first New Directions book I read must have been Henry Miller's *The Air-Conditioned Nightmare*, back in 1944, when I was fifteen. *Time* magazine didn't like it. Which meant one's father wouldn't like it either—if he happened to stop listening to Fulton Lewis, Jr. on Mutual Radio, or reading Westbrook Pegler on FDR in the newspapers. Obviously, a book to buy. Miller led to Patchen and Rexroth. By the time I'd dropped out of Princeton in 1950 (and confirmed my poor father's worst fears), I was up in Old Lyme, Connecticut, typing a book of fables for Patchen, who was having a bad siege with his back. Everything tended to be legendary and pleasantly unreal at the Patchens' cottage, nestled in amongst clumps of early blossoming paranoia, red trees, and little green deer. Sir James Laughlin seemed to be a scion of the Sitwell-Gatsby-Laughlins. One day it was thought he was going to buzz the cottage in a monoplane

3

and dip his wings twice if he was accepting a manuscript of Kenneth's, possibly landing on the Connecticut River later to confirm this. His father was said to give garden parties in Pittsburgh in full armor. (I continue to have a vision of trying to drink a martini through a visor and managing to get the stuffed olive.)

New Directions was the model that I needed in 1951 when I started, just one generation after it did (i.e., fifteen years). Laughlin went to Choate and dropped out of Harvard. I went to St. Albans and dropped out of dreaded Princeton. We both like living in High Celtic/Hebraic countryside. We are both easily satisfied by the very best, a requirement defined by the late W. S. Churchill. New Directions, in JL's words: ". . . an absolutely selfish, self-centered, egotistical undertaking it has always been. I did what pleased me or what pleased my friends and what my friends could convince me was worth doing." Despite the collective ignorance of Ezra Pound, Edward Dahlberg, Charles Olson, Mina Loy, Charles Henri Ford, Alfred Starr Hamilton, Douglas Woolf, Patchen, and dozens more about the prowess of Elroy Face as he shambles forth from the Pirate bullpen, publishing such writers could hardly have been more rewarding or less dull.

The last time I saw JL, Tom Meyer and I drove from a printer's shop in Charlotte, North Carolina, to Rock Hill, South Carolina, where he was to deliver banquet remarks at a writers' conference organized by an institution known as Winthrop College. I knew as little about Winthrop College as they knew about me. I have an ancient horror of blue-haired academics and southern poetry-lovers. An image of linguistic vasectomy flocks to my wary mind. The sacred words of South Carolinian, J. Gordon Coogler, Bard of the Congaree, stand there, written in fool's gold, on the wall:

Alas! for the South, her books have grown fewer.
She was never much given to literature.

So, there we were. JL spoke entertainingly about folks named Ezra and Bill and Gertrude and Fordie. Over the luke-warm pork roast and luke-cold jello salad, I became gloomy as the ladies in their ball-gowns tittered and shifted their thoughts to talk of the Sunday school at the Baptist church two days hence. It takes stamina, good nerves, and good digestion to survive the Rubber-Chicken Circuit of the Muses. Pull down thy vanity and try, try this one more time! Next morning, JL sampled the grits at the local Ramada Inn and was full of enthusiasm for two young teachers who had amazed him with their acumen about John Hawkes and Denise Levertov. He's right: "If one or two are gathered together," then one does make one's small effort. The odds are against us, but so what? Throw the bomb!

At the moments when patience gets exhausted, I look to Laughlin and quietly whistle with amazement—what endurance the man has. Forty-five years amongst the high-culture mavens. He still finds it possible to read both good and bad poems, still has refined manners, still has enthusiasms that smolder and burn quietly like peat fires on the Scottish moors, where Laughlins came from in the first place.

Let it not be forgotten that JL still turns his hand to the occasional, astonishing poem. The American Establishment does not allow one to be good at more than one thing. Laughlin has been a fine poet *also* for all these decades. Let us hope that the University of Nevada at Las Vegas will figure this out by 1995. (JL is nearly as tall as one of their Watusi princes.)

Just today, I had a letter from Simon Cutts, poet & publisher, whose Coracle Press is a generation younger than Jargon Society and two younger than New Directions. His effort is having a hard time surviving in Mrs. Hatchet's Britain. Says Simon: "There are lots of things I'm not putting up with anymore, and all attitudes held by artists must be spectacular, undemanding, and exemplary." Hallelujah! But, none of us has many days like that. Some of us are simply stuck with it. . . . After I recover from the high drama of watching Indiana/LSU and Virginia/UNC in the final four of the basketball tournament in Philadelphia this afternoon, it will be time to lift my shot glass towards Norfolk, Connecticut, and drink a few drams of Glenmorangie single malt whisky to the most remarkable publisher yet produced on our (currently post-literate) continent. It is not his fault that no more than 60,000 folk in the nation read excellent books. Cheers!

Highlands, North Carolina 1981

"I'm bugged mostly by the past. Christ. To get rid of it. To get on. . . Anyhow, I'm bullish—even if at the moment if you waz in this room you'd think . . . it looks like a bear . . . Who wants to do anything but publish what they have written? Selah? Adam? Huzzah?"

That's Olson writing me from Gloucester about eighteen years ago. And it's very much the way I have been feeling for a while—stuck down here at the bottom of the Poetic Augean Stables, having to use a spade that is one-tenth the size needed just to keep each day from turning into a cloaca.

Olson again: "You mustn't mind so much if I don't write you. Ain't I got no credit in yr dept.? I'm still in the throes of shriving myself of the Good Mt—and by god I need letters fr my friends. . . . Besides, I'm guilty. You ask me to do a thing and I haven't yet been able to get my own things done. So there I am failing you. That's too much. You have to give me a break. Or bust me for it."

The editor of *Parnassus*, Herb Leibowitz, the Ineluctable, busts me by telephone, so there's nothing to do but what little I can to give a sense of what Charles Olson was like as teacher, friend, and counselor, back in the time of Black Mountain. I have never said much about the Big O. (What a language we have. Here in 1976 "The Big O" would resonate in most citizens' minds as either (1) Oscar Robertson; (2) the myth of the female orgasm; or (3) a national chain of tire stores.) In print there are comments in taped interviews for Martin Duberman's *Black Mountain: An Exploration in Community*. And there is the "Funerary Ode for Charles Olson" at the end of a sequence of poems in *The Loco Logodaedalist in Situ* (Poems 1968–70)—a work that is too rancorous and diffuse and one I cannot read in public. Reasons for this reticence come to mind: the woods are already full of scholiasts busy making the canon; we came to grief after the publishing of the first three books of *The Maximus Poems* and started playing Lazy Southerner and Imperious

Yankee; Olson and I hardly met the last ten years of his life. Looking, now, over some one hundred letters from CO in my archives makes me feel even worse about the rupture than I did at the time.

When I walked into the dining hall at BMC, one lunchtime early in July, 1951, I knew that the man talking to my friend from Princeton days, Ben Shahn, had to be Charles Olson. A month earlier I had never heard his name. But in Colorado Springs, Emerson Woelffer, the painter, had said: "You're gonna like Charlie. He's a tremendous big guy. Used to be a postman in Gloucester. And he writes and talks in ways you've never heard." So, when he stood up to display his amplitude (six feet nine, 245 pounds) and his courtliness of manner, the first things to strike me were the literal charm of the man and the intensity with which he peered at the human subjects in front of those big, thick glasses of his. The "high energy transfer" he asked of poems was what was already built into his nervous system and physiognomy.

I came to Blk Mtn in my 1940 Lincoln Zephyr, "The Golden Fury," fresh from a month in the West—my first visits with Kenneth Rexroth in San Francisco and Henry Miller in Big Sur. The poetry I brought into Olson's class was a remarkably turgid maceration of strands from Kenneth Patchen, e. e. cummings, Dylan Thomas, Robinson Jeffers, science fiction, and the eldritch H. P. Lovecraft. One embarrassing, blessedly brief example was titled, I think, "Autumnal":

> the fog, falling, came like a gold singing snake
> to bite the heads off anguish . . .
>
> scales dragging through the bloody fruit,
> and silence a rain in the woods

Hmmmmm—perhaps only Orpheus himself knows what adolescent phallic wonderment that is all about? Anyway, Olson gritted his scrimshaw dentures and, for a start, made out a list of people to read: Stevens, W. C. Williams, Pound, Miss Moore, Lawrence, Hardy, Shakespeare, Melville, Dante's *De Vulgari Eloquentia*. And Fenollosa and Chinese verse. Of newer contemporaries in 1951 he selected just four (besides himself). Of experimental bent: Robert Creeley and Robert Duncan. (I already knew two books of Duncan's and had just tried to visit him in San Francisco with no success.) Of classical bent: W. S. Merwin (Merwin was very surprised to hear this when we met for the first time in Charlotte, North Carolina, last month) and a man named Laurence Richardson who had been publishing poems in the *Yale Poetry Review/Poetry New York,* presided over by such editors as Rolf Fjelde, Harvey Shapiro, and Roger Shattuck. It is my recollection that Richardson went into some such study as archeology. I have not seen poems of his since. (One scholar: front and center!)

The marginal comments made scrupulously and magnanimously by Olson on piles of fledgling JW poems give a very clear sense of his care. No blarney and no mush. They amount to a useful guide for any of us, now—including me. Here are some of them, starting in the summer of 1951 and running through spring of 1955.

       ugh   ugh
                                      ugh
ugh   oh yeah?
                        shsssh
                              wow   no!
go on!   you sure?
       triste, triste
               no kiddin?

---

too much description, too RU-MAN-TICK

This is by far the most enjoyable—and surely because it is closer to a single observation AND a feeling, eh?

---

have you added anything of equal force to Vanzetti? if not, why add?

---

aw, ga-wan . . . absolutely separated from what you are—have to offer, whatever

---

too easy—not significant detail: NOT objects, merely materials . . . *here*, is what poem there is.

                 P.S.:

                 Size stays
                 problem #1,
                 these days

                 you shall have to watch
                 (as all of us, these) that
                 the old rugs all
                 been slipped out from

(clearest reason
why so many look
poetic, trying
for the old
stance)

the study is,
to have it in
some new ways, why
one's own document,
at least: no "he"!

---

again (as in *Weeks Hall* poem) feeling of *loss comfort consideration* comes through: these are *yr* emotions/ And so it works—maybe *Elegies* are yr other form (beside the raising of the Low Pun to the High Coup?

DON'TS FOR JW
1) pun
2) compose
3) write *words*
4) give a dam for
others   4a) "we-we"
5) be obscure

DO'S
1) see
2) say
3) straight
4) anything
5) yours

---

this is beating yourself—which is also a form of *negative* feeling! You must know *all* of us are *beat*. So it comes out the blues—to be risen against

---

but *here, surely, much* is *NOT SAID:* why not *SAY IT!!*

---

lovely, without MORE

---

you have yr blood, as another: leave the seasons to what's their's: it definitely, physiologically, ain't blood

a throw-back to yr earlier so poetic style . . . obvious, eh . . . a pumped-up verb—all such bursts with the pin of the reader's attention (fake radicalism)

MacLeish, or somebody: the counters are too large, blown up

& lawd, he always cautions abt literary references—unless egg-zack-tly

---

Jon-a-than:

      first to say, you do
HAVE
    it—that
is, fresh lines: the verbalism
of the trade

      the rest is.
the continued use of the same PLUS
the getting in behind it what
who has words for it except
an amount of what another knows
is the experience of

FIND OUT YOUR OWN CONSERVATISM. Don't at all be uncomfortable in quietness. For it is now a most telling virtue (after all radicalism, and bohemianism—and false conservatism—have shown themselves to offer nobody anything . . .

No, Jonathan:
            i', sure I steer you right to urge you back to yr own inherited, & possessed, quietness
               (yr desire for fine paper, & for fine type, is damned healthy
               And you mustn't, beyond that point, lose the same distinction (by craving too much change, & excitement—drama—in how paper, color, type is used

                    It should be worn like any virtue, not on the sleeve of itself. The professional merely does his job—and lets others find out how to dig it.

Well, I'm sure sounding off, today. But we played a ball game against the town American Legion Juniors last night. And I, for one, missed yr style! The way you play baseball is the way . . .
                    It was wild
how
badly we played. The baubles! And these quiet kids made us look like
dumbheads! . . .

It was sad, it was sad when that great ship went. . .

to the bottom

of the,

highway 70

Have I caught us up on all? I hope so. And please take all of this as over the fence—not at all as complaint, or in any way pressure on you, on the Max:

I think you know me well enuf to know I want the whole fucking job to be yrs—that you have the pleasure of, the jaunt. I only offer you what I know. Luf, O

That final entry was most of a letter, which had branched from poems to beisbol to how to publish. (Someone could make a textbook on typography just from Olson's attentiveness to *Maximus* and his response to what I tried to offer him as an almost outrageous beginner. Between us, and the good offices of Dr. Cantzsche Druckerei of Bad Cannstatt, Germany, there would never again be any excuse to make a slipshod or meagre or ordinary book in Jargon's series.)

As for the poems, there seemed to be Hope. I took another five years to achieve the Personal Voice, something somehow assembled into a bizarre *olla podrida,* containing hunks of Cabeza de Vaca, Bartram, Thoreau, Whitman, Courbet, de Kooning, Kline, Catullus, Delius, Fauré, Ives, Jelly Roll Morton, Lou Harrison, T. Jefferson. That's Democracy In Action for you. And Olson had made it possible. The clues came not so much from those cryptic equations on the blackboard (*typos/topos/tropos*; or, Mechanics + Function vs. Discussion + History) as from seeing him operate in the skin.

The Saturday nights at BMC playing poker—a skill he claimed to have polished on the campaign trains with Roosevelt, whistle-stopping the nation. *Classy,* no matter what lousy cards . . . Watching Charles serve as first baseman so vast that almost nobody could throw the softball past him into Lake Eden . . . Olson dining at the Old Heidelberg on Beaucatcher Mountain in Asheville, with those lovely public airs of his. Wearing his last $125 sportscoat from days in the Democratic party and a salary. Barely intact, but more so than his gray flannels with the gaping tears in them he would try to hide as best his bulk would allow . . . Olson at the Isis Theater one Sunday night in West Asheville. We'd just seen that great flick, *The Invasion of the Body Snatchers.* There were gasps when the lights went up and the great man rose with his traditional wool blanket over his shoulders. . . . Olson at Griffith Stadium the night Big Jim

Lemon hit three off Whitey Ford (in the presence of Dwight David Eisen-hower, as well) and the Senators still lost to the Yankees: 12–3.

There is a lot to be learned from how a man plays poker or softball or treats waitresses in a restaurant. (I keep thinking that, finally, poetry is a branch of manners.) There was a lot to be learned when he confided over a beer one evening: "The only requirement for a poet is to write fresh lines." Olson was neither a barbarian nor Crazy Uncle Heavy. One sel-dom ever has so keen a friend. I go occasionally to the fishermen's ceme-tery outside Gloucester, look at that curious neo-seventeenth-century slate stone of his, and remark it more each time. "Ah, si, hombre. . . ." And the eyes get as wide as his were.

Highlands, North Carolina 1976

Being a Wee Introduction to the Scots Poet/Toymaker/Typographer —That is to Say, Poetoyographer— Ian Hamilton Finlay

Visiting him up in Ardgay, Easter Ross, on his fortieth birthday, he was happiest about the gift he received from his friend Sue Swan: two tons of gravel, for making paths and poems, garden paths to garden poems. To say it simply as possible, for me Ian Hamilton Finlay is both a very rare man and the superb fabricator of an art that works and plays in the most delicious of ways. He brings to mind the refinements and purity of Erik Satie (Scots on his mother's side), Max Bill, Anton Webern, and the other great Scottish designer so far in the twentieth century, Charles Rennie Mackintosh. Note that these solitary companions of Finlay's, digging for white potatoes in brown fields under clear blue skies, are men of music and of "design." Finlay is not a "poet" in the narrow sense most of us have reserved for the poor souls who have to practise this vestigial occupation. Finlay is a "maker"— which is the *real* definition of poet in the Greek, as Buckminster Fuller has reminded us. He makes poems out of letters that have no sound in them, that function as objects to contemplate with eye and mind, and mind's eye. He makes toys for his children and gardens for his toys. All this he does in as quiet and remote a place as possible: at Stonypath, Dunsyre, Lanarkshire, Scotland. He lives on the high margins of an art-less, dour Scottish land where artists are ignored and useless as thistles—which are, likewise, "inventions of the Devil." But, Finlay is still, intensely, a Scot. He reveres wee, dour Scottish things and really thinks that anything to eat but salt herring and tatties (poetatoes) is very "decadent." I once asked him a riddle: If America has affluence, France has ambience, and England has panache, what does Scotland have? He replied quickly: porridge! But happily, this crypto-puritan purist is the most delightful of artists and one of the large forces in poetry today. Though he does not travel at all in his person—he stays at home and minds his own business, that hardest of creative ways of life—his work influences poets everywhere at once. He is a real man of letters

13

in the most exact and useful meaning of the term, and his publishing effort (The Wild Hawthorn Press) is uniquely valuable. For Finlay is *authentic*— which means made with an honest human hand for human needs and joys. I suggest that Ian Finlay is the little white rose of Scotland the poets have yearned for, whether Scotland ever knows this or not. Given time, peace, and quiet, his poems can light up the sky and enkindle a mind in return.

Aspen, Colorado 1967

Publishing Bucky's Epic

4

It was my privilege to publish the first poetic work by R. Buckminster Fuller, *Untitled Epic Poem on the History of Industrialization*. Bucky Fuller defines himself as "an explorer in comprehensive, anticipatory design science." It gains us little to insist that he is, primarily, an architect or a geometer or a mechanic or an engineer or a poet. He is a symbiot—one of the most remarkable men of our age. It also gains us nothing to argue about the nature of this epic. Fuller says, "If you don't think it's poetry, go ahead and call it ventilated prose." Harvard appointed Fuller the Charles Eliot Norton Professor of Poetry in 1962, and I think we can understand why. He finds the poem "the best medium for lucid communication of unfamiliar thoughts and concepts undigestable or incomprehensible in prose." This is what John Cage, the composer who also insists on the right to write poetry without belonging to the Literary Merchants' Sodality, means when he writes: "Poetry is not prose simply because poetry is in one way or another formalized. It is not poetry by reason of its content or ambiguity but by reason of its allowing musical elements (time, sound) to be introduced into the world of words. Thus, traditionally, information no matter how stuffy (e.g., the sutras and shastras of India) was transmitted in poetry. It was easier to grasp that way." Fuller in his epic is going towards the center, towards universe: "The possibility of the good life for any man depends on the possibility of realizing it for all men. And this is a function of a society's ability to turn the energies of the universe to human advantage."

It is a rare pleasure to read a man of such integrity and engagement; an even rarer one to have published him. He gives us in the epic a work "to make the mind of men by the help of art a match for the nature of things." The words are Francis Bacon's, and Fuller's address is to poets *and* scientists—to anyone who cares for livingry and human potential instead of the killingry of obsolete systems.

Highlands, North Carolina 1962

Much Further Out
Than You Thought

I do not suppose that we shall ever
talk as of old, until we come to sit as
cherubs on rails—if any rails there be,
—in Paradise
Edward Lear

I remember once picking up a copy of a faded blue book of poems from the
thirties in Bertram Rota's bookshop in Vigo Street, London. I asked Arthur
Uphill, who was tending the store: so who's Stevie Smith? "Who's Stevie
Smith?" he exclaimed, as though I had failed to recognize Queen Victoria,
Dame Edith Sitwell, Gertrude Stein, Mae West, and Bette Davis all walking
down Savile Row together. "Well, *really!* Well, really, indeed!"

I set about remedying this blushing ignorance as quickly as I could. I
obtained all her books. I paid calls to Stevie Smith's house in Palmers Green
and chatted over tea or sherry with the famous aunt, "The Lion of Hull." I
had her to dinners when I lived in Barbara Jones's house in Hampstead. The
last time I saw Stevie was at lunch at the Old Cheshire Cheese in Wine Office
Court. The date was February 5, 1970. Charles Olson's death was one topic
of conversation that day. Another was my urging Stevie to have a look at
Lorine Niedecker's *Tenderness & Gristle,* then newly published by the
Jargon Society.

Now, two years later, my favorite women poets in America and England
are both dead. But, Stevie certainly gave little evidence of age or illness that
afternoon at lunch. She always suggested some kind of mildly discommoded
bird—perhaps a jackdaw with a touch of *Weltanschauungangst* or *Zeit-
merz.* Anyway, she promised to come to Yorkshire that summer and be the
first poet to inaugurate my sauna bath. She asked: "Won't they burn you for
a warlock in Dentdale if you have such a contraption?" I said: "No, Leeds

17

United and Manchester United just bought saunas from the same firm in Birmingham, so it's ok. What's good enough for George Best is good enough for Dentdale."

In March, 1971, I received word of Stevie's death while I was in residence at the University of Illinois. Arthur Uphill, ever on the job, sent the first clippings: the excellent obituary in the *Times,* plus tributes from John Wain, Douglas Cleverdon, and Neville Braybrooke. The occasion of her death made me ashamed that I had not managed to make a public assessment of her work while she was still able to read it with proper chuckles and chidings.

What I want to do now is consider what her drawings, novels, and especially her poems mean to one poet and reader whose last decade has been made so much more pleasant by knowing this person from—not Porlock—Hull.

The Drawings

Stevie Smith once remarked to me: "It's quite easy with poems because you can carry poems around with you while you're doing housework." So: poems, in the manner of darning socks. When not darning or poeming, Stevie did a lot of doodling (her own word for it), "when not thinking too much. If I suddenly get caught by the doodle, I put more effort into it and end up calling it a drawing. I've got a whole collection in boxes. Some are on tiny bits of paper and drawn on telephone and memo pads. The drawings are not illustrations for the poems. I take a drawing which I think "illustrates" the spirit or the idea in the poem rather than any incidents in it. When I look through a pile of the drawings, I often am inspired to write more poems. Lately [1963, that is] I like the drawings and I would like to gather them up into a book of just drawings with only captions," as in *Some Are More Human Than Others* (Gaberbocchus Press Ltd., 1958).

The drawings, I must confess, are the aspect of Stevie's work that moves me the least. I can't find a cat in all of them to put with Mr. Lear's faithful Old Foss or one of Monsieur Grandville's curious felines. They're not even in a class with the stuffed pusses in Dr. Potter's Museum of Humorous Taxidermy, Bramber, Sussex. Nor can I find a single gawking female in terrible clothes and lethal hat to compete with those of Mr. Thurber. I don't even yearn to possess a drawing by Stevie in the way that would make John Berger suspicious of my capitalistic, bibliophilic lust. The "Look Ma(tisse), No Hands" approach to art rarely pays dividends in the hands of the amateur. Often Stevie Smith walked a tightrope in a poem where the eye could see no wire at all—and got away with it. I think we will just have to put up with the doodles, albeit wishing the memo pads had disappeared in the fire. (At this point a champion should rush to the fore, shouting: "For Christ's sake, the lady liked to have pictures with her poems. Let it go at that and don't be rude.")

The Novels

Confessing to a further, mild rudeness, I say, well, they're better than the drawings, but I do not think Stevie Smith is going to eat much asphodel pudding on the basis of the three novels she left behind. I can't possibly imagine how they read at the time—the early reviews were impressive. Stevie, herself, confesses to an overdose of Dorothy Parker at about the mid-30s. I was going to Tarzan movies at the time and have never rejected them in favor of Miss Parker, so I wouldn't know. The style seems very much the Old Interior Monologue, come home to daydreaming on the Piccadilly tube-line to and fro from Wood Green Station, London, N. 22.

Novel on Yellow Paper (Jonathan Cape, 1936) is the first, and the only one people seem to know. Over the Frontier (Cape, 1938), the second, defies finishing. The Holiday (Chapman & Hall, 1949) is the most conventional. I used to think that Penguin ought to reprint The Holiday, but I don't anymore. Of course, this is where literary "criticism" gets so deadly. I reread those three books in five nights last week. Ian Hamilton Finlay was appalled when I told him this. He said: "Wait a wee minute, Jonathan, you must read only one Stevie Smith novel every five years—very slowly at that." He is probably right. In a triple-shot, they seem like nothing but chatter, chatter, chatter. There is no relief, and the prose runs through the ears like the salts of Epsom.

Still, if you can stand being the thrall of an art deco chatterbox for some considerable number of hours on end, do be Stevie's guest.

The Poems

Last March I wrote to Basil Bunting about Stevie's death. He was in a snowbank in the wilds of Binghamton, New York, i.e., caught in the usual penal servitude of the academy. ("I'm sick of universities—students and faculty!") He wrote back: "So sorry to know I shant hear Stevie Smith again: little stuff, but honestly done, worked on." Mr. Bunting is not being haughty or dismissive when he permits himself to say only those few words about Stevie Smith. He is equally laconic about himself and gives us (somewhere in a reference book from Detroit about poets) a wry, five-word autobiography: "Minor poet, not conspicuously dishonest." Bunting abhors "criticism" of poetry, and so do I. Out of curiosity I've looked up critic in the recent two-volume microbiotic OED that is to be read only by stoned, myopic hawks. I like Thomas Dekker's warning in Newes From Hell: "Take heed of cricks: they bite, like fish, at anything, especially at bookes." (An even more scintillating remark has been made by André Gèdalge, the teacher of Darius Milhaud: "Critics make pipi on music and think they help it grow.")

Before I have my brief say about Stevie Smith's poems, let me quote the very best thing that has yet to be said about her. It comes from an essay by Kenneth Cox entitled "Three Who Have Died": "Our own Stevie Smith, an English eccentric, ridiculous and terrifying, aunt and prophetess, her voice between giggle and scream crackling the provincial vicarage, declaring again and again: There is no formula for poetry, no school, no authority, nothing but the spirit that moves and the wit and the nerve to give it utterance."

The operating word there, for me, is *nerve*. One might acquire benefits from exploring the technical mastery of the baroque imagination of Edith Sitwell; or the etiolated, raspy line of Marianne Moore; or the backyard concision of Lorine Niedecker. The only interesting thing about Stevie Smith's technique is her cheeky, audacious lack of *any*. Granted, this legerdemain in legerdemotic style is very calculated and she comes out *original* instead of silly or stupid. (I can remember, to my discomfort, first hearing the Bruckner Seventh and wondering how anybody but a complete oaf could write a first movement with such an initial tune in it. Redon used to put me into fits of schoolboy laughter. Pride goeth before destructions, etc.) In the Stevie Smith poem there is usually a touch from the Anglican hymnal, a miasma from Colonel Blimp Land, something from under the stairs, something out of a ballad or the nursery. While Edward Lear—lovely and amiable man that he was—would welcome the company of Stevie Smith, it is not to be assumed that Robert Creeley, J. V. Cunningham, or Louis Zukofsky would welcome her to the regions of their mordant, saber-toothed, strangulated poems.

I have tapes of Stevie Smith reading some of her poems, singing crazily, intoning in her own way. That she had no "voice" is obvious and of no importance. It was the fire underneath that counted—she was no Laodicean, lacking a hearth. Professional readers invariably have too much "voice" for poets whose poems are based on common speech or on popular ways of singing, like Stevie's. We like Lotte Lenya and Marlene Dietrich and Mabel Mercer and Mae West and Billie Holiday because of the way they sound and make a song, not because they are vocalists with a great repertory. But, this is not to say there is only Stevie's way to do her poems. William Carlos Williams had a peculiarly flat way with his poems, Marianne Moore with hers. They all give us something authentic, a special guide for our own efforts. If Hermione Gingold and Cleo Laine and Annie Ross can handle Sitwell's *Façade,* advocates of "Do Take Muriel Out," "Le Singe Qui Swing," "One of Many," and the others will emerge.

Florence Margaret Smith, 1902–1970: quietly desperate, always saving, always drowning. Toward the end of her life she said to Neville Braybrooke: "People think because I never married, I know nothing about the emotions. When I am dead you must put them right. I loved my aunt."

I trust that the Death of Stevie Smith keeps a spectral cottage near Kingston Bagpuize, so she can go to the pub where the Windrush meets the Thames and drink black velvets with Wordsworth, Coleridge, Pope, Shelley, Thomas Hood, and Dr. Sterne. Meantime, her cats, Brown and Fry and Hyde, will doze on their tombstones, while in the old woods there will be a "roaring peace."

Dentdale, Cumbria 1973

"Think What's Got Away in My Life!"

About one poem, like the frailest peony blossom, drops from Lorine Niedecker's typewriter every year. It is the nicety of her work, the discretion. It does not insist on being The Best Female Poetry Almost West of the Mississippi, and calls no notice to itself at all except for the most primary reasons—that it gives absolute clarification and concentration to its words, that it is local and personal in the ultimate way that leads to its becoming "classic" and included in the anthologies. Mina Loy is her peer; and Elizabeth Bishop and Denise Levertov some of the time—few others occur to me.

Louis Zukofsky, Miss Niedecker's mentor and champion, once remarked that one test of a poet is his, or her, stick-to-it-iveness. It is now some thirty-five years that the poems and peonies have been flowering in Fort Atkinson, Wisconsin, a town thirty-four miles southeast of Madison. She has never fled to pre-beat or de-beat San Francisco. She's not on LSD or a Wisconsin Pen-Woman either. Nor is she a snarling caitiff, feeling despised by Gross Middle America. I know because I've been there to see. Miss Niedecker, I guess in her fifties by now, lives in a tiny, green house out at Black Hawk Island, three miles from town. Right out in back is the sparkling Rock River, on its way to lake Koshkonong. No phone, almost no neighbors—I'm sure none with whom she can talk about poems, about the latest book from Louis Zukofsky off in Brooklyn Heights. August Derleth is about the only writer in those parts and he lives due west of Madison in Sauk City, so they almost never meet. The river is a major fact in her life—lying there sparkling and running, often flooding and worrying the people. It's in the poems. The October day I stopped for lunch I found her reading some of Lawrence's letters, which she compares with Keats's. Miss Niedecker lives in terms of the communications from Zukofsky and a few others. Besides her writing and her extensive reading, she works at the local hospital for support. She is a frail person, like the poems, but sturdy as they also are.

I write about the peripheral things because the poems are so damn good there's not much else to say about them. They say it, it's there. Let's see two examples, first:

> My friend tree
> I sawed you down
> but I must attend
> an older friend
> the sun

That has a lovely sound, put together with hand-tooled pegs. And how good she is in this next poem about the weekly washday—how much Lorine Niedecker gets *in* there:

> The clothesline post is set
> yet no totem-carvings distinguish the Niedecker tribe
> from the rest; every seventh day they wash:
> worship sun; fear rain, their neighbors' eyes,
> raise their hands from ground to sky
> and hang or fall by the whiteness of their all.

This is a world that still matters, in which care may rule, as in Thoreau's meadow where so *much* was going on—if you looked. Like the blazon of peonies, sprung up seemingly overnight and amazing in their whiteness, are her poems; and almost too good to be true.

Aspen, Colorado 1962

"No Layoff from This Condensery"

On January 2, 1971, the Madison, Wisconsin, *Capital Times* ran a brief obituary. The salient points of this notice were the following: "FORT ATKINSON—Funeral rites for Mrs. Albert Millen, 67, a well-known Wisconsin poet, who died Thursday [December 31, 1970] in a Madison hospital after a brief illness, will be held here Sunday. . . . she wrote under her maiden name, Lorine Niedecker, and had written a number of books of poetry that were published internationally. . . . Mrs. Millen had been a contributor of poetry to many newspapers in the United States." Pretty damn hopeless. A Wisconsin cousin (her closest friend) has still never read any of her poems. The report goes: "Hell, I didn't even know the woman," said one of Ft. Atkinson's prominent citizens. "But I heard she had kind of a negative personality." Secondly, she wrote very few books indeed. And third, she was not a blue-haired lady who poured treacle into columns of newspaper verse. Basil Bunting, who was visiting Wisconsin at the time of her death, wrote the *Capital Times* a letter suggesting their words might be more savory and accurate than they, in fact, were. I presume he told them his opinion, that Lorine Niedecker was the best contemporary poetess. "No one is so subtle with so few words." In any case, the newspaper did not publish Mr. Bunting's letter. To my knowledge, the *New York Times* printed no obituary at all, despite letters from myself and others, and, I am told, telephone communications from Louis Zukofsky. There is not much to say, really, except that she died much as she had lived: in privacy.

It took a month to hear of Miss Niedecker's death when I was in North Carolina last winter, and over two months to hear the news in England of August Derleth's—which was on July 4, 1971. It all seems more and more like the 19th century, with everybody locked up in the attic or too callous to care. I don't venture that August, Lorine Niedecker's nearest literary neighbor, was a "great" writer. But I do know that he was a man who did enormous amounts of hard literary work, who wrote useful reviews, and behaved like a true man of letters. He was a writer who truly felt "at home"— that in itself is a regional oddity. I corresponded with Derleth from 1944, when I was in my H. P. Lovecraft frenzy, and, ever since, have admired his energy as the publisher of Arkham House. On my visits to Place of Hawks at Sauk City, Wisconsin, I also liked his zest, the largeness with which he did everything from wrap books and talk and drink to the mandarin way he'd order Chinese food in the culinary wilds of the town of Baraboo. So, at the end of this note to observe Lorine Niedecker's death, this added salute to Augie. Let others not forget that Miss Niedecker's *T & G* (Collected Poems 1936–1966) received only two reviews in the United States which examined the book with any amplitude of spirit and perception. August Derleth's was one of them. Perhaps some of those who consider themselves his literary betters would have a world less snide, less pathetically minimal, and less tenuous if they had half his generosity and ability to respond.

Dentdale, Cumbria 1971

Things Are Very Far Away

About ten years ago I ran across an essay by Kenneth Rexroth in *Circle* (1944) entitled, "Les Lauriers Sont Coupés." This, one of a series, concerned Mina Loy. The others, for the record: Robert McAlmon and James Daly. It began: "At one time it was common to couple the names of Mina Loy and Marianne Moore. Pound treated them as equals, said they both wrote something called logopoeia. . . . There is no question but Mina Loy is important and should be reprinted. No one competent and familiar with verse in English in this century would dream of denying it. . . ." Or as he said elsewhere: "Mr. Laughlin, the 'Five Young Poets' are still Eliot, Stevens, Williams, Moore, Loy—get busy."

Jay Laughlin, of New Directions, was undoubtedly busy enough, coping with the grisly competitors of the American avant-garde and the ladies with three names and three-pound manuscripts *sans* postage, but one of his annuals soon turned up some recently dated poems of Mina Loy, and I wrote him in surprise that Miss Loy was alive and active. Laughlin wrote back that he had happened to see her in Aspen, Colorado, during a skiing expedition. Miss Loy was advanced in years, living quietly with her children. My recollection is, I wrote two letters to Aspen, investigating the matter of a book. Neither was returned, but neither was answered. This was about 1955. In May, 1957, I found myself in Boulder, Colorado, in the midst of a seven-month tour of the country by station wagon. The Pontiac was loaded with Jargon Books, City Lights Pocket Poets, Bern Porter Books, Divers Press, portfolios by Kenneth Patchen, New Directions, and Evergreen books. I was reading poems, selling books, talking about "the underground," etc. I wired Aspen and received one in return: "CAN YOU MEET ME HOTEL JEROME THE NINETEENTH?" The night of the eighteenth, eight inches of snow fell, obliterating the cherry trees in blossom and blocking all access to Aspen. I drove south into New Mexico and had to phone Miss Loy that I'd try again on the return across the country a few months later.

Hiking with Rexroth in Marin County, California, that summer, talk turned to Mina Loy and he reaffirmed his belief in her eminence. So, when I'd finished hawking my wares in the great renaissance center, San Francisco, I drove east for two days and arrived in Aspen, with the gold aspens properly quaking and lots of overweight humanists digging scenery and seminars. I was pleasantly installed by Miss Loy's family in a Swiss-type inn and went to see *La Strada* at the old opera house. The next day at noon I was to have luncheon with Mina Loy's daughters, to present credentials, etc. I found them as attractive as their legendarily attractive mother. Joella, now married to Herbert Bayer, the artist; and Fabi, married to Fritz Benedict, the architect. Both daughters had been brought up in the world of the international avant-garde. There is an extraordinary painted head of Joella by Dali, as well as portraits by Tchelitchew, Campigli, and Man Ray. Fabi resembles very strikingly one photograph of her also legendary father, Arthur Cravan. (For information about this robust figure, see *The Dada Painters & Poets*, edited by Robert Motherwell for George Wittenborn, publisher.) A book on Cravan remains to be written. Suffice it to say here that I learned from Fabi the true facts of Cravan's disappearance in Mexico: "It was testified that a corpse answering his description (and there are not too many men six feet four, sandy-haired, in the tropics!) was found; obviously he was killed and robbed of his money belt—how prosaic!" At any rate, meeting the daughters I felt that, with considerable justification, they wanted the details and legends very carefully scrutinized regarding Mina Loy and her tragic life. (I found it fairly incredible later, for instance, that one of her grandsons, nearly thirty, did not know his grandmother wrote poetry.) Over lunch, then, I had to dispel all suggestions of being simply a skeleton-rattler.

Later in the afternoon I went to call on Mina Loy (the family name was Loyd), still a distinguished and handsome woman at nearly eighty, and impeccably dressed. Her very few manuscripts and mementos she carried in a net shopping bag. Of her one book, *Lunar Baedeker*, published by Robert McAlmon's Contact Press in Dijon, 1923, she had not a copy—or of the later anthology published by Contact in 1925. (She had had no news of Pound or Dr. Williams for years and was delighted to hear they were still alive.) She did have some manuscripts of recent poems and of a novel that awaits a publisher to this day. The new poems Miss Loy agreed to have typed, and so, in a day or two, I went on from Aspen back to North Carolina with the project relatively set. A few months later I was doing some reading at the Library of Congress and prepared a typescript of Mina Loy's earlier work in the rare book room from the two Contact editions, from *Others*, from *The Little Review*, etc., having also consulted the staffs of the New York Public Library, Yale, and UCLA. There were, undoubtedly, some fugitive poems unseen, but nothing, we hope, of major importance. A number of corrections had to be made. McAlmon was a marvelous publisher (the University of Nebraska Press, by the way, publishes Robert E. Knoll's excellent study of him), but conspicuously no proofreader at all. Even *Lunar Baedeker* was misspelled. Miss Loy and her daughters went over the new script. And so did William Carlos Williams, Kenneth Rexroth, and Denise Levertov. I asked each poet to contribute an introduction to the book, thus giving judgments from three generations and heralding the republication of Mina Loy in the most intimidating fashion possible. Besides that, the back jacket bore testimony from Alfred Kreymborg, Louis Zukofsky, Henry Miller, Edward Dahlberg, and Walter Lowenfels. There was the danger of making it all sound like the panhandled plugs on an Exposition Press book by a budding Denver housewife, but, as Rexroth said, it was to mark "a real EVENT, like the opening of King Tut's tomb."

Lunar Baedeker & Time-Tables was published December 17, 1958, and I marked the occasion with a big cocktail party at the Martha Jackson Gallery in New York. Mina Loy telephoned from Aspen and some of her old friends, Bob Brown, Kay Boyle, Romany Marie, spoke to her. The book had been most handsomely printed by William Loftin of Heritage Printers, Charlotte, North Carolina. Emerson Woelffer drawings of birds, nesting and in flight, graced the cover and the title page. Next to Zukofsky's *Some Time*, I am more fond of the Mina Loy book than any of my other typographic designs. The usual fifty or so complimentary copies went out to magazines and newspaper reviewers. How is one to take it that not one of these people reviewed Mina Loy's book?

In April, 1959, through the instigation of Marcel Duchamp, an exhibition of Mina Loy's collages was shown in New York City. The event was at least *noted* by the *New York Times, Art News,* and the *New Yorker.* Robert Coates of the *New Yorker* said: "Mina Loy, now showing a set of— well, she calls them 'Constructions,' but Marcel Duchamp, in the catalogue, calls them 'Haut-Reliefs et Bas-Fonds,' at the Bodley Gallery, was a flashing figure of the resurgent nineteen-twenties. She was a poet then, and a highly original one; the difficulty in defining her current work should attest to its originality, too." Whatever the case, the poetry critic of the *New Yorker* seemingly felt no need to pay respect to Mina Loy by the simple act of public notice. (Apparently it will be a very cold day in hell before the *New Yorker,* the *New Republic,* and the *New York Herald Tribune* review any of Jargon's titles. It seems curious that none of the books of Charles Olson, Robert Creeley, Robert Duncan, Louis Zukofsky, Irving Layton, Kenneth Patchen, Bob Brown, Denise Levertov, myself, et al., have even been considered worth abominating in these august journals.) And no other member of the critical fraternity felt any responsibility. However, Kenneth Rexroth devoted a whole broadcast on station KPFA, Berkeley, California, to *Lunar Baedeker*

& *Time-Tables,* thus keeping intact his position as Miss Loy's only critic in America for thirty years. Since the publication date, between the efforts of friends of Mina Loy in Aspen and my readings from the book in public, the edition has dwindled away. Already it commands a good price from the dealers in modern first editions.

A shrug of the shoulders may be the only healthy solution, but there are days when I feel that celestial wrath should descend on the keepers of the sacred word—these lackluster ladies and gentlemen with spirits as benign as bookburners and draft-board members. I don't know—maybe their Metrecal is drugged? But maybe Mina Loy, herself, is right? She wrote me in June, 1959: "*Time* sent their representatives from Denver to interview me about two weeks ago. Nothing. . . . I was given some devastating remarks from the *Times*—but about my pictures only, I think. . . . How carefully you have counted the reasons for disliking a poet. My advice to you, dear friend— the best way to conquer is to wear as helmet: *a smile.* You *do* let yourself look too severe—I don't agree that there is no winning in this country. Change from *Persona Non Grata* to Persona Good Grinner—now don't hate me!!! I hope you will visit here again *soon.* And we can discuss the right design for your face-armour. Now don't let this seem merely an encouragement to relax—it is entirely for friendliness between poetry and the world. Yours, M.L."

Highlands, North Carolina 1960

> And I said, "O defiled flock, take a harp, and chant to the ancient relics, lest understanding perish." Then I labored for the miracle of seeing and knowing, and thought I heard murmuring Euphrates, and perceived the first-born leaves of Eden whose savor of apple, elm and hazel-nut garnished the lips of Jehovah. But it was nothing, and my spirit was a mute tomb.

The preceding inscription is the most concise statement of Edward Dahlberg's position I can find. It occurs in that sedulously ignored little volume, *The Flea of Sodom*. It is because of such ignoring that I undertake the celebration of his work. God knows, I do not have the prodigious knowledge of classic literatures clearly necessary. Nor the cast of mind of a Talmudist. Edward Dahlberg in his sixty-third year can say, with Robert Burton: ". . . confined to the company of the distinguished, I have spent thirty-seven full and fortunate years." Which is a lot of reading and experience. Yet, the work insists. I only hope it will lead others to a thorough job of explication. But let this be said at the outset about Dahlberg, and I again quote Burton, in *The Anatomy of Melancholy,* who is himself quoting Agrippa: "He speaks stones and let his readers beware lest he break their heads."

> And he will be a wild man; his hand will be against every man, and every man's hand against him; and he shall dwell in the presence of all his brethren.
>
> Genesis 16:12

Edward Dahlberg calls himself Ishmael and dedicates *Do These Bones Live* "to the memory of my Mother, Elizabeth Dahlberg, who, as sorrowing Hagar, taught me how to make Ishmael's Covenant with the Heart's Afflictions." As Ishmael, then, he is a wild man, a loner. This is the Dahlbergian secret since the beginning and I do not think I wrong him by quoting Robert Burton again, on solitude: *"Solitude* prompts us to all kinds of evil; this solitude undoeth us, 'tis a destructive solitariness. These men are Devils alone, as the saying is, a man alone is either a Saint or a Devil; his mind is either dull or devilish; and, in this sense, woe be to him that is so alone! These wretches do frequently degenerate from men, and of sociable creatures become beasts, monsters, inhuman, ugly to behold, *misanthropes,* they do even loathe themselves, and hate the company of men." It *is* man-killing to look at one's doom and say simply: "A poem or a book that does not make the reader toil for his fate deprives him of energy, which is his most tragical and valiant weapon against the cosmos, and without which man is neither epic nor universal. A book that weakens human will is inartistic, for all writing is heroic feigning, imagining that though everything perish, a book will be perdurable. Knowing that death is always brushing our backs, we write to forget death." (From "A Long Lotus Sleep," *Poetry,* February, 1953.) By this fierce standard Dahlberg judged his novels symptomatic of the disorders and in no way curative. "Remembrance is a torn, placeless ghost, raw and wandering, unless we bury our griefs and pains in one specific ground, region, and sod. Ghosts, too, must be seeded like fruit, rains, and despair, if they are not to return to make of our hearts, their Acheron, for hell is going to and fro in the earth, and having no landmarks, or country, or epitaph to define our souls."

Do These Bones Live is, simply, a ranging attack on the Modern World, on you, on me, on every disintegration and blight of American civilization, on the superstitions of Totalitarian Man—his machined logic and the sterility of an armature with no flesh. This testament is delivered with a prose authority of the most formidable density, and consequently is not a "simple" book. It demands times to live with, respect, and humility. The author excoriates himself in the process. Elsewhere (in a section of the current autobiography-in-progress, *Because I Was Flesh*) he writes: "Let me now say that I have not the least respect for my moral nature. I do what I am, and though I would do otherwise, I cannot. I do not say this easily, but with infernal pain in my heart. Perhaps after many years in libraries, I can prattle better than I did. Had not Addison or Steele asserted that no one was any better for beholding a Venus done by Praxiteles?"

Beyond this, *Do These Bones Live* cultivates the entire heritage of Western literature and morale. One imagines that Dahlberg operated the factory where David bought his slingshots. He even quarried the stones. For Plato is quoted as saying over and over that knowledge is reminiscence. One of the chief arguments is that in America the refusal of memory has given us a religion of place and a subsequently enfeebled batch of writers crawling with localist nostalgia and adolescence. "American civilization is 'deanimated,' 'metronomic,' a grotesque enlargement of that 'gap between touch and thing,' as William Carlos Williams writes in *Jacataqua*."

The title essay is a series of examinations of our chief writers: Melville, Poe, Whitman, Thoreau, Emily Dickinson, Sherwood Anderson. The native, aboriginal intelligence is not treated piously—Whitman just barely proving more cosmically useful than Mary Baker Eddy's hygiene course. "The fetish of originality is our curse. Dante took a guide!" Puritanism is considered in all its deadly detail. "Purge the flesh and you canker the spirit." Dahlberg remembers Thoreau's episode at Walden Pond of wanting to eat a muskrat to stifle his flesh repulsion. And we have the legend of Miss Dickinson's starving in her father's garden, though Jay Leyda's new book may have news for us. Dahlberg writes: "In almost a hundred years of American Literature we do not have one feeding, breeding, sexual male, not one suffering, bed-pining Manon Lescaut or a Shulamite. There are no ripe women here. . . . We have spectral essences, odorless and hueless. . . . When you deny the male and female, as they are, eating, sexually throbbing and giving off dense physical emanations, then you have the great STINK. Our misanthropy comes from one thing only, not man's poverty, politics, government, but from the revulsion from his own ordure." (It is true that if one is really hip to Modern America he can learn to stop only at those motels whose johns are antiseptically "presealed.")

Yet, I wonder if this indictment, as the author suggests elsewhere on another subject, is not casting out devils and entering the swine? It is a dangerous doctrine if one is going to take writing as canonical scripture. The charge is: sexual confusion—starvation, disembodiedness, sodomy. "To damn sensuality, laughter and irony, Cotton Mather had turned woman into a witch; Poe took the infernal witch, begot by Mather, and buried her alive; Melville exorcised her! Lady Dickinson hid in Christ's bosom." If this is to be the measure of a writing man (and literary style *is* the man), then one has to ask questions: should poor Melville have been allowed to work in that customs house for those ruinous decades? He would have been a security risk to the state if he really thought *those* thoughts about pale Nathaniel Hawthorne. Certainly, Walt Whitman should not be allowed to ride streetcars or visit army hospitals!

I make this purposely mocking and ridiculous because the human animal (which, as Mr. Dahlberg says of himself, does what it is) has *every* right to defend its privacy. Maybe I misread the intention of this attack, for in another section of the book we find: "To deny evil is to deprive the bones of penance and to shed forever the cry of Abel's blood, the existence of Saul, Sodom, and sin of Lot's daughters, Judas Iscariot. However man may come to Being and Deity, the poor, panting Word, or absolute suffering atheism—to refuse What Is in man, his most perfidious whoring tumults, is to steal his

grace." Exactly—and that I, for one, accept, though, perhaps not every
definition of what is Good and Evil. "Good and Evil are inseparable; beast
and man are sewn together with threads of heaven."

The chapter on Randolph Bourne, "In the Saddle of Rozinante," is a
wonderful, restorative act. How few writers and readers there are who know
anything of Randolph Bourne. One of the first things a devoted reader of *Do
These Bones Live* will do is procure a copy of *The History of a Literary
Radical & Other Papers* (which, I hope, is still in print, having been repub-
lished by S. A. Russell, New York, 1956). Dahlberg is right to point out that
Bourne's attack on the state is the strongest in our literature since Thoreau's
essay on civil disobedience. This chapter is joined by others exposing the
visions of Dostoevski, Shakespeare, Christ, and Cervantes. Edward Dahlberg always begins and ends as a quixotist: "Man pursues a desperate
philosophy of gallant idealism and lives and hopes and cankers with a defiant
flourish. With inextinguishable fervor he ceaselessly creates his cycle of
sonnets, music, art, ethics, and then with a chivalric irony wraps the worms
in the Golden Fleece of Colchis."

Sir Herbert Read says of *The Flea of Sodom*: "A book like Nietzsche's,
for all and none; a book, also, for all time." To me it is Dahlberg's most
unsatisfactory, provocative work. He notes that

> if this little book appears opaque, the reason is easy to know: the line is
> gnomic, pulsing with Ovid, Livy, Strabo, Suetonius, Herodian, Plutarch,
> the Book of Enoch, the Apocalypse of Baruch. The similes themselves are
> definitions of ancient rituals, which are a bucolic physic for men who feed
> and gender upon our macadam meadows. This volume is a prayer for a
> FABLE, and a jot of piercing knowledge regarding Aristotle is that in his
> old age he found his greatest solace in mythology. Myths are sanctified
> customs, without which men are morose and slow-witted, and lack the
> learning to garb themselves suitably, or to bake a good loaf, and build a
> savory town,—for a people who do not know how to make pleasant
> bread cannot brew Pramnian wine or amatory verse, as any one who
> understands the ritualistic occupations of Demeter, Bacchus and Venus
> may know.

In the midst of a welter of modern, arcane parables, there is a central chapter,
"The Rational Tree," wherein the book receives any redemption it needs. It
is a veritable *Works and Days* in the most ancient tradition, and some of the
most resonant language of our time. Just one of innumerable beauties:
"Empedokles rests in Asphodels for putting the ass's Bladders in the hills to
catch the Etesian gales; Speusippus, inventor of the Twig Basket, frolics with
the sea-trulls of Neptune who found the vetch. But Anaximander is in
Tartarus tethered to his maps, clocks and gnomon. Who would hesitate to

be Virgil or Chaucer rather than Aristotle or Plotinos? Proteus's shells smite
the mind more sweetly than Anaxagoras's kosmos, and the Vedic Heifer
yields more than Plato's Philosophy."
    "Be primordial or decay"—this is the final instruction in Edward Dahl-
berg's latest work, *The Sorrows of Priapus*. As it was in the beginning, the
Paradise of literature, it is a *Works and Days* that evokes a theogony from
the writer. But this is Hesiod informed by 3,000 more years. "Grass and
rivers are the pleasures of men which pass away, but the ravines and hills
mineral the will." The prose is put together like a rock wall—one oracular,
declarative sentence put firmly against another. The result looms above the
boneyard of contemporary slovens like the vatic batholith it is. The lichens
and stains it bears are exotic ones—Greek natural philosophers, Hebrew
prophets, Hakluyt, Monardes, de Vaca, and innumerable mythographers
and discoverers. We have a pamphlet of lore from two worlds and five
millennia.
    Section I, "The Sorrows of Priapus," is an urbane, witty encyclopedia
on the physiognomy of a salacious anthropoid *Homo sapiens* as he is beset
by the ridiculous appetites of his reason, his stomach, and his phallus.

> Most men of considerable intellectual strength have a conspicuous nose
> resembling a potato, a squill, a testiculate cucumber, for the nose is the
> second phallus in the male. Beside that, it is the messenger to the testes, for
> virile olfactories not only take much delight in the *Analects* of Socrates or
> in the *Dialogues* of Plato, but they also revel in good weather, inhale the
> seas and fruits, and are very quick to capture the fragrant skin of Nicarete
> of Megara or the adulterous uterus of Clytemnestra. . . . Far worse than
> the human nose, often well-made, and the tongue, are the testes, the most
> ugly and ill-shaped member. The phallus is a slovenly bag created without
> intellect or ontological purpose or design, and as long as the human being
> has this hanging worm appended to his middle, which is no good for
> anything except passing urine and getting a few miserable irritations, for
> which he forsakes his mother, his father, and his friends, he will never
> comprehend the Cosmos.

Dahlberg concludes his melancholy but droll prosecution by saying: "Man
is at present in a misshapen stage, neither possessing the gentler customs of
the beast, nor the faculties of the angel. . . . Since man is not going to be
different for a thousand millenniums he should select certain animals to
teach him to be just, eat and gender at regular intervals, and blush. . . . What
is man that he should imagine he is more than a goose?"
    In Section II, "The Myth Gatherers" (dedicated to William Carlos
Williams of *In the American Grain*), Dahlberg states four postulates for
Thermonuclear Pale Face:

[1] Let no one assume that the fables of the red races of the three Americas do not invigorate the intellect. The legends are vast energies to be domesticated; the continent is a prone mongol Titan, with the jaws of Osiris.
[2]The American intellect is a placeless hunter. It is a negative faculty which devours rather than quiets the heart.
[3]The Indian, or American, mind is primal rather than domestic because it is new. . . .
[4]Man is at the nadir of his strength when the earth, the seas, the mountains are not in him, for without them his soul is unsourced, and he has no image by which to abide.

Edward Dahlberg's is a tutelary muse. His books seed the mind with desire for other instructive books. Some that come to mind in various ways: Crèvecoeur's *Letters From an American Farmer, The Travels of William Bartram,* Henry James's *The American Scene,* D. H. Lawrence's *Studies in Classic American Literature,* Sherwood Anderson's *Many Marriages,* William Carlos Williams's *In the American Grain,* Charles Olson's *Call Me Ishmael,* Josephine Herbst's *New Green World,* and Wright Morris's *The Territory Ahead.* Consciousness is the first problem. Once you've got it, these books suggest where to put it.

Amidst a plethora of oak, maple, streams, hummocks, Pale Face is famished for a tree, a little hill, a foal, a clump of sod; utterly sterile, he begs for the Nature he has warped and killed. He cannot be a thinker, a moral animal, until he returns, as a lover, bringing the peace calumet and the grains of tobacco, as a votive offering, to the cliffs and the wilderness which he threw away.

The Sorrows of Priapus

Aspen, Colorado, 1967

The Roastin' Ears Are In
and Vida Pitches Tonight!

If there is any such fiction as "good ol' homefolks," then Paul and Nancy Metcalf are it.

I first drove up to their cabin in Skyland, North Carolina, on a winter evening early in 1954. All I knew—from Charles Olson—was that Paul was a Melville from Cambridge, that Nancy was a genuine Southern Belle from Spartanburg, that he did some clandestine writing (though he never showed up in Olson's class at Black Mountain College, some twenty-five miles across Buncombe County), that he currently was operating as something called a Dianetics Auditor, that he was fiercely independent and preferred delivering oil and driving the local school bus and farming a little to hanging around universities or enclaves full of bohemians. Skyland was on my run from home (Highlands) to Black Mountain, so when I got a note from PM, commenting nicely on receipt of *The Maximus Poems* and inviting me to stop in, I decided to do it. The infant daughter I saw crawling on the floor that night is now a statuesque bride in Lenox, Massachusetts. During all these avuncular years there has never been any real vexation with Paul Metcalf, as publisher or friend. I think that's worth pointing out at the first, now that literary behavior becomes as lethal and cranky as all others in the disappearance of crafts, services, and readers.

Skyland, North Carolina, was one of the suburbanite vestiges of the Asheville boom of the late 20s. Log cabins or congealed bungalows of dark red brick—lots of tacky shrubbery and little or no grass, set some hundreds of yards off the main highways on unpaved roads signposted Camelot Lane, Buena Vista, etc. A population of rattled, semi-retired outlanders; poorish locals with the aspiration to have a picture window, a blackamoor hitching-post, a mirrored-glass globe on a pedestal out front; a garden here or there; chickens; car dumps; a country grocery store with a beauty parlor stuck on the side; filling stations; and beer joints.

By 1972 much of Skyland will have yielded to Jim Walters prefabs, surrounded by mesh fences; and elaborate mobile homes, some featuring leaded windows in the latest Tudor styling. Maybe, in one of the remaining cabins tucked way in back, there will be the naevoid alcoholic and his boozy, bewigged wife, who used to work for the big schlock furniture store in town, if they haven't burned themselves up by now. Next door will be the piggy girl who likes to rub dog shit in the hair of her smaller playmates in the seventh grade. It's all very familiar—meaning, it's familiar to those of us brought up in the shadow of rednecks, the Bible Belt, all those nobodies trying to be somebodies at the expense of just about everybody else of whatever color. Jest so long's yer money's green, we got no problems atall, friends. Put'er thar.

Anyway, about the time I met the Metcalfs, Skyland and its grotty folkways were beginning to get close. They moved out into a remote valley near the old Asheville airport called Merrill Cove. Here they could see no one's smoke and hear no one's axe; they could do their gardening, build a pond in the woods, keep a horse or two, piss off the front porch if fancy dictated, and stay clear of the Plastic Hydrangea People. (I do not exaggerate: Asheville's Woolworth's has the finest display of plastic hydrangeas I have seen anywhere. The electric orange ones at two ninety-eight are particularly engrossing.) You don't often find people thoroughly set in their ways who also have the flexibility to cope with one's unsettled self. I seemed always to be driving into the Cove from the ass-end of nowhere, just having read poems at some bastion of the Muse like Western Piedmont Community College, and demanding food, rye old-fashioneds, gin rummy, Monopoly, and sleep. The Metcalfs are the only people I know (except for Professor G. Davenport, of the bluegrass, who says if God had intended us to ride in automobiles, He would have provided us with wheels and put a tailpipe in our ass) who are *always* home. This is because there was always a schoolbus for their imperious and beautiful daughters, Anne and Adrienne, that came at an ungodly black hour like 7:15—in all weathers and over seeming decades of time. And because there were farm chores to do. The simple point I am making is that they thrived on "routine" and took pleasure in being "at home." Those were days when we'd all rock on the porch, sipping the wine of the country, mulling over the words of L. Ron Hubbard, N. Wiener, C. Olson, E. Dahlberg, J. H. Rodale, or some of the Black Mountain bards I'd bring by en route to Highlands: R. Creeley and R. Duncan.

Not that there weren't occasions out. There were and maybe one remembers them all the better for their rarity. A trip to Nacoochee Valley in North Georgia to see a cousin of Nancy's, Lewis King, who has lately figured as the main character in Jim Dickey's novel *Deliverance*. The night we all went into Asheville with Olson to see *Moby Dick* at the Imperial—the film version with Gregory Peck we got to calling *The Man in the Gray Flannel Whale.* The night Paul got me to read poems for a coven of scientologists at a house called Points of View, near eldritch Moonville, South Carolina. (Whew.) Then, there were the days in Asheville when Nancy was doing the big weekly shopping at the Tea Store. Expeditions to the two second-hand bookshops (before they got torn down to make parking lots) which produced the occasional odd score: a set of the first edition of John Lloyd Stephens's *Travels in Central America, Yucatan, etc.,* for five bucks. The investigations were preceded by the only likable food in town, save for the WASP-infested S&W Cafeteria. It was a choice between a greasy spoon on a corner of the Triangle that served an honest hot dog, all-the-way, for twenty cents; or, the Cosmos Grill. The latter featured a Greek salad, the pride of the suffering Athenians of Haywood Street who mostly dished up meat-and-tater, country-boy, blue-plate specials to local tire salesmen.

Allow me, please, a further brief digression on the mediocre desolations of Asheville, North Carolina (where I am told I was born, though I have insisted there must be a mistake, it was Krypton, or Munchkin Land, or Swallowdale, or Lothlorien). Cities, according to a superb Shakespearian phrase used by Olson, are to provide "awe, night-rest, and neighborhood." It is difficult to think of a place of 60,000 souls that provides less than Asheville. And I'm talking about even back in the days of the Andrews Sisters and such personifications as Faith, Hope, and Charity; before the American Dream became completely besotted with color television and ceased to be dreamed at all. Asheville seems the perfect geographical example of what John Keats is talking about in his Detroit book, *The Insolent Chariots:* "The automobile did not put the adventure of travel within reach of the common man. Instead, it first gave him the opportunity to make himself more and more common." Asheville's setting—as fine as Stuttgart's, or Edinburgh's, or Avignon's—just makes it more depressing. Today, the place looks like a bomb had hit it and the only civic thought was to rebuild the freeway, the motels, and the standard aluminum bank building. Out there, surrounded by acres of earth and demolition, stands T. Wolfe's ancestral boarding house, Dixieland. But there are only so many times you can drive wistfully by, or go down to his grave in the cemetery by the French Broad River. Asheville doesn't even have a good cigar store, or newsstand, or an "adult bookshop." In the South these are the only possible amenities that can salvage necropolitan spots like Biloxi, Mississippi, and Gainesville, Georgia. I think you see more cripples in Asheville than anywhere else, more people who look too old to die, more tough old nurses in white stockings up on the Square, more desperate farmers skulking in and out of the ABC stores for their bottles.

Having registered a disaffection that could be used against most gathering places of 60,000 citizens on earth, let's be fair. Paul Metcalf and I used to sit through a lot of night games at McCormick Stadium to see the awesome Asheville Tourists in action. We ranged over enough years to note, with satisfaction, that the black players no longer got called "Shine!" automatically when they came up to bat. Even rednecks are gentlemanly enough to applaud the likes of Willie Stargell on his way up to the Pirates. He lost a lot of fastballs in the kudzu patch over the signboards in dead center field. And most important of all: the Sondley Reference Department in the Pack Memorial Library. This is where Paul did research for his first two books. Ida Padelford and the other librarians treated him warmly and professionally. This must have kept the Metcalfs around Buncombe County longer than not. They outlasted Black Mountain College by six or seven years. I continue there in my holy quest for the Ideal Deathburger and room-temperature Beaujolais—an eccentric to the end.

One can only imagine how Paul Metcalf made the move from Cambridge life and the spell at Harvard to a farmer-writer in the Blue Ridge, and, later on, in the Berkshires. From a man who'd been subject to tuberculosis in his youth, he developed himself into a physical workhorse. The Metcalf calves and feet are built to stand firm—a pair of trunks with taproots. *Metcalf* means Middle-Hill in Yorkshire, where the name comes from. Accordingly, he plants himself. His approach to reading and writing is precisely the same as doing the daily chores; nothing to jabber about: do it. He doesn't cultivate literary gents. The few who get lip service date to his early days: Conrad Aiken, Henry A. Murray, Charles Olson, Wharton Esherick, and DuBose Heyward. Paul liked to work in an outbuilding away from the womenfolk—some old chickencoop or woodshed he'd converted and put a stove into. He worked to a schedule, with time out for pipe smoking and visits to the outhouse in the woods near the pond. The Metcalfs had things like indoor plumbing and home freezers but, simply and without self-conscious whimsy, they preferred the old two-holer and canning their own produce in Ball jars. They lived the quiet life and made sure not too many people came around to make it unquiet.

Nancy Metcalf is a wonderful woman. She escaped being finished by her finishing school in Manhattan; she escaped her Spartanburg heritage and comes out an original, the kind of person that makes the USA interesting in spite of massive efforts to the contrary. Poor thing, she married a Yankee and a writer to boot. But (one hears the sighs of relief emanating from Upper South Carolina) at least he was white, gentile, and non-political. . . . Nancy deserves to have a peak—make that *two* peaks—in the Grand Tetons named after her. She looks like the real thing in those family photographs: the Budding Corn Goddess, smiling coyly behind the shucks. (Whether she really dances in the altogether by her forest pool when the wild lily-of-the-valley is in flower and the moon is full is not verifiable.) She's a lady with a lot of gumption and savvy. God knows, she's cooked and washed and canned and cleaned house to a degree that would make the current crop of land-romantics turn pale. She definitely deserves better tipple than her regular tankcar rotgut sherry from the A&P with which she relaxes on the sofa before dinner while reading *Good Housekeeping* or *Lillabulero*. Let it be known to potential visitors to Wild Thymes near Chester, Massachusetts, that Miss Nancy will cook them all the turnip greens and fatback they can eat in return for a bottle of Apricot Brandy. . . . There are always fresh herbs in the Metcalf salads; turnip or collard greens never far away, plenty of sorghum, plenty of garlicky dill beans, and, in the spring, plenty of poke salad to tone you up. She does a mean, liberating chili. . . . The Metcalfs are clearly not fancy people. They don't eat fancy, or dress fancy, or live fancy. They live in old wooden houses, listen to old 78s of "The Lark Ascending," and "Appalachia," and Roy Harris's Third, and Howard Hanson's Second, and the "Concord Sonata." They buy overcoats at the next-to-new shop in Pittsfield; read good, old copies of Dreiser and Sherwood Anderson and WCW and Grandpa Herman. There are comfortable old dogs sleeping all over the furniture. Mitzi is my favorite. The Master of the House reads the sports pages of the *Berkshire Eagle,* dreaming of a new dynasty at Fenway Park, sips his bourbon, while the part of the self that writes those dark, peculiar New England books tiptoes into the cellar of the mind to see what devilment is brewing.

I propose to say nothing at all about *Will West, Genoa,* and *Patagoni,* except that I am proud to be their publisher. I've loved helping get them out of the writer's cedar chest—where he might well have let them bide—and out into the world. As sure as God made little green apples, Paul Metcalf has made these clearings in the geography of ourselves with an axe both literal and real. What was that you thought you spied at the edge of the circle of firelight? Whatever it was, it was not comfortable. Metcalf's great-grandfather once said flatly: "We are the last First People." Ecology comes too late.

Dentdale, Cumbria 1972

A Poet's Profile
of John Furnival

11

John Furnival is here now at Corn Close making his annual visit to Dentdale. We meet approximately every six months—in the Dales or in the Cotswolds—to drink the Wadsworth's, Theakston's, Marston's, Hartleys, and Yates and Jackson's bitter and to see if either of us has become even more internationally unknown. I have no trouble figuring out why an aging, acerb, and hulking mountaineer from the North Carolina Blue Ridge, who writes both rude and "funny" poems, might be ignored in the Land of Stodge; but, it always puzzles me that someone as invigorating, affable, and imaginative as John Furnival remains on the shelf with the Urchfont tracklements, the Scottish Powsowdie, and such a congeries of oddments as Edward Lear, Stevie Smith, Mervyn Peake, Ronald Firbank, and Lord Berners.

This week I have required of J. Furnival a drawing of "Mr. Lear, Looking Severe, and Surrounded By Some Of His Creatures"; a drawing of "Fred Delius, Dreaming Of The Western Dales"; a drawing (from life) of another houseguest, the venerable bard of the Tyne Valley, Basil Bunting, as he nods over a biography of E. M. Forster and occasionally rouses himself in the pale light to mutter, "great bloody bore." And then there have been discussions of a new folio about the weather called *St. Swithin's Swivet*; and vague thoughts about an old project, *Corbel and Misericord,* I can never seem to put words to. For that one, the draughtsman had to travel three times to the borders of Wales to the Norman church at Kilpeck to draw the Sheela-na-gig and her stony friends; and to Beverley Minster on Humberside to crawl about under the choir stalls in the dark. This is what I meant about his affability.

If I needed the visage of a be-jocked, soft-core ephebe en route to a tea dance on Fire Island, I would ask David Hockney. Otherwise, for almost anything else I would ask John Furnival. R. B. Kitaj is the only artist in England I know with the encompassing literary intelligence and sheer drawing skills of John Furnival. But, again, RBK is not a man interested in other people's requests for images. He is this very heady, very sombre cat who is into his own thing, as they used to say in various art-loving cities of the Western world. Both Kitaj and Hockney are imperiled now by their vogue. When each is shamelessly imitated in the color supplements and life becomes a color movie, it is best to ask them for nothing, wish them very well, and a speedy retreat to the studio, where the private lines to the collectors and dealers have been ripped out. Furnival has escaped all this danger by staying home in Gloucestershire to weed his drawings, manure his ideas, entertain his friends and students, and be his own chuff combo: "one-sixth Dutch, five-sixths French, 100 per cent Cockney and 7 per cent Poshwold-Fuckall. The important thing is not to grumble."

It will be interesting to see how long it takes the public collections in Great Britain to grow eyes and come to Rooksmoor House in Woodchester. They'll find the gaffer producing good spuds in his special imported legume-boots, and practising the crafty arts, carts and rafts, and afts and crarts. Erik Satie whistles there from an upstairs room, pleased that he has an aire-apparent.

Dentdale, Cumbria 1978

Country Joe and the Fission

12

Hey Joe, mach die Musik von damals nach!
Bert Brecht

The point I am (perhaps) making in the title is that Joe Tilson now lives in the country, either at Christian Malford in Wiltshire or down the hill below Teverina in the Provincia di Arezzo. The ultimate urban *coup de grâce* in our time was delivered by Mr. W. C. Fields in *The Fatal Glass of Beer*. Sophisticates of the agora, please note: "City ain't no place for a woman, though a lot of pretty men go there." One need not be an eremite, misanthrope, or rube to come into conjunction with this word *country*, which the dictionary tells us is simply the land lying opposite or before us. The Old Rectory and Casa Cordeto, both lovingly restored by the Tilson family, become granaries filled by a new husbandry, a new fission of care. (Wiltshire, a few miles east and west, produced Richard Jeffries, Francis Kilvert, Ralph Vaughan Williams, and Geoffrey Grigson, to name only four fellow countrymen.)

"Our bodies are our gardens, to the which our wills are gardeners; . . . either to have it sterile with idleness or manured with industry," said the Bard of the Warwickshire Avon. So, a man who paid as much attention to things, to poetry, to philosophy, to history as Joe Tilson would eventually have to bed down in nature with bee-loud glade and mini-Walden Pond close at hand. Close enough to blot out Concorde, buzzing in and out of Fairford, where it does God knows what to the medieval glass of the Church of St. Mary the Virgin. Few artists read Heraclitus or like to talk about Herr Doktor Professor Jung, Giordano Bruno, Renaissance logics and rhetorics, etc. It should hardly be held against Tilson, since who is to say it has stood in the way of his inspired carpentry. Joe collects thoughts and sifts and dries them in the way one would make a pomander for putting into winter closets. The Old Rectory is full, not only with charts and maps of the mind, smoldering

43

wooden eggs, labyrinths to a promised land, angelic ladders, but also full of tins, bottles, drawers with labels. We await either vintage bottles from the thistles of Casa Cordeto or coverlets dyed with these same attended plants. The Tilson family is in the middle of a cultivated world. "Birds make their nests in circles," said Black Elk, shaman of the Oglala Sioux. Not strange to find English people, worried about overpopulation within a hundred miles of London, reading Black Elk and tending to their ecological business. Joe Tilson's is a redolent mind at work. I love sweet-corn thoughts.

Highlands, North Carolina 1975

O. L. Bongé of Biloxi, Mississippi

13

Father Orcenith Lyle Bongé, courtly citizen of Harrison County, God-Hep-Us-Mississippi, is the signal representative of a wild-eyed, smooth-talking tribe who could charm the skin off a snake. I know several others: Billy Bob Dunlap, the Delta artist, and the deliciously named V. E. G. Ham, down-home scholar and mystery man.

A columnist for the *Times Literary Supplement* recently found a sentence for his Reviewer's Hall of Fame from a British review of the 1930s on *Mein Kampf*: "It lacks tact, but is filled with Hitler's abounding vitality and fascination." There are some urbane critics, including neo-Marxists and structuralists, who frown, jog, diet, and strain at stool, who will find Bongé's photographs very, very suspicious and much too rich for their blood. I have been looking at OLB's prints for nearly a quarter of a century. They endure, touched by the same aesthetic gumbo (magic, stuff and nonsense, genius) that operates for Cousin Clarence John Laughlin over in New Orleans.

Bodacious, surely, is the first adjective that springs to mind when I think of Lyle Bongé. If I were to pursue *bodacious* to its roots in the manner of Robert Graves instead of H. L. Mencken, I might let my ear hover on the sound of *Boadicea,* the queen of the Iceni, the Celtic tribe in eastern Britain in the first century A.D. We have Dio Cassius's portrait of Boudicca (Boadicea in the Latin): "She was huge of frame, terrifying of aspect, and with a harsh voice. A great mass of bright red hair fell to her knees: she wore a great twisted golden torc, and a tunic of many colors, over which was a thick mantle, fastened by a brooch. Now she grasped a spear, to strike fear into all who watched her." Hmmmm. Father Lyle ain't no Celtic Queen but the description is pretty damn close, even though the red hair has grayed somewhat.

Dentdale, Cumbria 1981

45

When a man reaches fourscore, it is assumed that he has outlived Wisdom; or is given to the curse of Old-Fartism; or has forgotten most of what he remembers. Since Basil Bunting does not set up as a sage and since he has made himself very clear on the subject of literary criticism (i.e., there is no bloody excuse for the stuff), what is one to do with him on the page, with the subject here at Corn Close for a visit and more or less obliged to follow my literary whims?

I have asked him more often than he likes for anecdotes about the time he addressed the Fabian Society as a young man and was congratulated by a man with a long beard called G. B. Shaw. One can also invoke the Webbs and a heavyset woman in black by the name of Annie Besant. But, maybe there is a less ponderous way of getting at the man without delving into the dim past. One time, in discussing Chopin, the name of Artur Rubinstein came up. "What happened to Rubinstein?" asked Basil. "I remember in the 1920s painting his arse gilt for the *Bal des Quatz-Arts* in Paris." Mr. Rubinstein, posterior unstuck to his piano bench, continues to explore Chopin. Basil Bunting also continues in 1980, so I propose to ask him eighty questions. That's not easy, to make the questions lively enough for the victim not to feel dull and considerably fazed. The substance should be somewhere between *Hollywood Confidential* and the famous questionnaire in the last issue of the *Little Review,* in which Mina Loy admitted that her greatest weakness was compassion and Man Ray stated that he liked his hot dogs all the way, with a little sauerkraut if possible.

(1) *Basil, what do you dislike most?*
Personal questions; also gentlemen. Not just English ones.
(2) *Where do the best kippers come from?*
Craster, Northumberland.

(3) *Novalis is reported to have said: "Not only is England an island, but so is every Englishman an island." What do you make of that?*
Probably true. Three hundred years ago it wouldn't have been. This reserve, such that even a working-class man won't tell you what he is thinking, must have come from the Whig aristocracy.

(4) *This reticence, is it also something to do with the origins of the Saxons versus the Angles versus the Celts? Poets such as MacDiarmid have managed to keep an unbridled tongue.*
Aneurin was a Celt; the author of *Beowulf* was presumably an Angle. Reticence did not arise until much later. You might say that they were "reticent" in that they paid no attention to themselves in their work. Yet, the author of *The Seafarer* talked about nothing else. Very sorry for himself. . .

(5) *I can't quite leave the word* gentleman *alone. George Bernard Shaw defined* gentleman *as someone who treats everyone the same. Doesn't that take the curse off the species and rid it of all class consciousness?*
Certainly; but the kind I'm talking about is some son of a bitch with a Kensington accent, who thinks he's a lot better than the bus conductor. The opposite is usually true.

(6) *You give little evidence of liking London or the south of England these days. Where would you prefer to live if you had your choice? Can you narrow it to a particular village or valley or river?*
Between Wark and Bellingham, on the North Tyne.

(7) *John Martin (Haydon Bridge) and Thomas Bewick (Ovingham) were men of the Tyne Valley. They make me want to ask you of their comparative virtues. What do you make of Martin's grandiloquence and excess? And, on the contrary, of Bewick's small scale and straightforwardness?*
Bewick was obviously the greater artist. I don't think much of Martin except as an historical amusement. . . . My stepgrandmother would be disappointed to hear me say that. She had two enormous Martins on her walls.

(8) *That answer makes me want to pry a little further into the notion of pattern. Would you say that Domenico Scarlatti was more of a composer than my lumpen favorite, Anton Bruckner? Bruckner has architecture, God knows, but what is it that you so miss?*
I think that Bruckner and his contemporaries were far too pretentious. Beethoven's Fifth Symphony may have done a great deal of damage. Scarlatti was not just frivolity or music without personality. It is very beautiful but pretends to be nothing more than it is. It serves no moral purpose. No one is required to write an "Ode on the Intimations of Immortality" every day of his life. Short as he is, Scarlatti gets to a very great depth. Purcell and Corelli

could simply change the key and do more in two bars than most of these nineteenth-century behemoths.

(9) *What are your favorite wines?*

Chateau Mouton-Rothschild, about fourteen or fifteen years old . . . Of course, I love the millionaire's port and the millionaire's Madeira, but I'm not a millionaire. God got the destinies mixed up a bit.

(10) *What about bitter beer? Theakston's, Wadworth's, Youngs, Boddingtons, Hartleys—they seem tasty enough when kept well. Any recommendations?*

No. None brewed now is particularly good, compared to what they were.

(11) *What are the local specialties of northeast England you most like to eat? And are there public restaurants that serve them?*

Potpie. You can't get it anymore. It was a big basin lined with suet pastry into which you put steak and kidneys and mushrooms and some onion. Then steamed. It just disappeared. Followed by apple tart and with bitter beer to drink, it was very, very good. I would gorge myself.

(12) *What's the best pornographic novel you know?*

The *Anti-Justine* of Nicolas Restif de la Bretonne.

(13) *In some notes on Schoenberg's String Quartet no. 1—to which we've just been listening—I see that Heinz-Klaus Metzger says:*

> The Quartet was written during that constructivistic but late phase when the radical romantic idiom which he had developed by applying a rationalized Brahmsian methodology to Wagner's limitless material was already drifting towards expressionistic gestures. . . . This state of affairs, taken in conjunction with the inexhaustible contrapuntal combinations, leads one to think of Freud's concept of over-determination, in which case the compositional economy of the work could also be interpreted as a criticism of this compositional economy; perhaps the most fruitful aspect of a dialectic whose task, according to Adorno, is to break through the constrictive nature of logic with logic's own means.

Would you agree?

I don't think even Hegel could be so meaningless.

(14) *What book are you reading at present?*

Dante, over again.

(15) *You've mentioned that you have seen two social revolutions in Britain in your lifetime, under Asquith and under Attlee. Any thoughts on the current regime under Mrs. Thatcher?*

It shows an intention of being the worst government since 1906. And the people in it seem as bad as those in Lloyd George's 1919 cabinet.

(16) *I've never heard you express yourself on jazz. I'd think a man with a limitless ear for the European dance music of Scarlatti, J. C. Bach, and Haydn would have feelings for Scott Joplin, Clarence "Pine Top" Smith, and Art Tatum.*

It's really too limited. The Elizabethans did better in what they called divisions. However, I like some of it, but not enough to remember the names, that's the trouble. I do also like pop music now and then. The Beatles were very good.

(17) *What's the best question anyone ever asked you?*

A four-year-old little girl in Washington New Town stopped me outside a shop and asked me: Are you God? I said, No, my dear, I'm not even Santa Claus; but perhaps I should have admitted the charge.

(18) *This is the centenary of Frank Bridge, John Ireland, and Cyril Scott. Is this inspiriting news? Will it make you refresh your ears with their music and that of Roger Quilter, Granville Bantock, Balfour Gardiner, Percy Grainger, E. J. Moeran, and Sorabji? I'll bet you didn't know Cyril Scott turned from music to Theosophy and occultism and finished up writing books with titles like* Cider Vinegar *and* Constipation and Commonsense?

Well, I'm damned. . . .

(19) *What are the ten finest sights to see if a pilgrim comes to the Basil Bunting country and wants to travel in Northumberland?*

The moors; Durham Cathedral; Briggflatts Meeting House (and Dentdale in passing); the Bewcastle Cross; the Farne Islands, seen from Bamburgh to Seahouses; the Roman Wall between the Twice Brewed and the Mile Castle public houses; the two churches at Bywell; the valley of the North Tyne; the beech avenue at Capheaton; and the Isabella pit heap at Throckley.

(20) *I've been reading an essay of John Piper's called "Gordale Scar and the Caves" about the limestone country of the The Three Peaks. He quotes Wordsworth's phrase about the "stationary blasts of waterfalls." What force is your favorite in the Dales?*

Cautley Spout in the Howgill Fells.

(21) *Would you like a cup of tea?*

Yes. Always.

(22) *Can you call to mind one meal that sticks in memory—as opposed to craw—more than any other in your life?*

Yes indeed. During the War I drove up to dine with some Bakhtiari in the mountains of central Persia. We began with alternations of tea and whisky and little sweet cakes for nine or ten hours. About nine o'clock in the evening we sat down to a large plate of porridge, followed by half a turkey per man, smothered in rice, followed again by a leg of mutton per man. Then we were allowed to retire to bed; a good thing, since I was half dead.

(23) *Persia makes me want to ask you what you make of the latest holy man to darken the horizon, the Ayatollah Khomeini?*

An exemplar of the very worst breed of political reactionary, from which one can expect nothing whatsoever. He's a bloody priest.

(24) *Can you say how you define a poet's place in a society like this one? Are you an unacknowledged legislator of the race, an ordinary bloke with a job of work like any other, a vestigial craftsman, an oligarch, a democrat? It often seems to me that it requires more confidence than one can afford to find a* place *nowadays, so maybe you don't even think about these things?*

There is no provision made for poets in this society. I try, under very difficult conditions, to maintain the art.

(25) *What was your favorite childhood book? Someone was suggesting that perhaps it is only in childhood that books have any deep influence on our lives.*

Grimm's Fairy Tales. And there were a whole series of books by E. Nesbit; and a few things like "Two Bad Mice" by the lady from Near Sawrey.

(26) *That question makes me think of another. In a current issue of* Origin *there is a nice saying:* I fanciulli trovano il tutto nel nulla; gli uomini il nulla nel tutto. *Children see everything in nothing; grownups, nothing in everything. . . . No source cited. Do you know it?*

No, I have no idea. It's a reasonable generalization of the sort that tends to suggest the truth, but isn't.

(27) *The Greek poets were fond of asking each other: When you die, what will you miss most? Praxilla became famous by saying, "sunlight, bright stars, the moon's face, ripe cucumbers, apples, and pears." What do you say?*

The income tax demand.

(28) *I was asked a bizarre question by someone in Australia the other day. Namely: have there been any real advances in poetry since Dada? I have been too dismayed to answer. Would you?*

There are no advances in poetry. Only changes. There's no stopping them. Every chap who works by pen or typewriter rings changes. Zukofsky made many. Tom Pickard is firmly making a few in his latest poems.

(29) *What's the funniest book you know in English?*

Ulysses, by James Joyce.

(30) *The John Simon Guggenheim Foundation gave a fellowship recently to a scholar exploring the topic, "The Growth and Marketing of Muskmelons and Cantaloupes." Does this make you apprehensive or resigned?*

It makes me laugh.

(31) *When you read the Bible, which translation do you prefer?*

The Great Bible of 1648, which is Coverdale; or, Coverdale revising Tyndale.

(32) *Which is your favorite malt whisky?*
Glenfiddich.

(33) *On what occasions would you prefer a Dog's-Nose as a tipple?*
When I'm worn out.

(34) *Wouldn't you rather have that elusive brandy of the* épuisé *gastronome, Marc au Vipère? The one where they pickle an entire viper and leave it in the bottle, causing half the dining room to collapse from shock?*

I once had a student in Santa Barbara who had eaten rattlesnake in all but one of the fifty states, but my interest was not excited.

(35) *Let's try Chopin. The other afternoon I heard Andrei Gavrilov at the Royal Festival Hall, playing the Etudes opus 25 with a marvellous cantabile line, but at speeds that would have bemused passengers on the Concorde. Is there anyone around these days whose playing seems right to you? And, in a word, what is the key to playing this music?*

Gieseking, in about 1925 or 1926, is the best I can remember. Nowadays I don't get out often enough to know the names. The problem, of course, is: what speed? But few pianists can keep the rhythm carefully shaped at slow tempo. This is true of readers of poetry and actors as well. . . . Chopin is mostly dance music and the effect of his rubato is to make a slight syncopation ahead of the notes. They ignore this.

(36) *The dreaded Ayatollah Khomeini in the papers this morning, saying: "One of the things that still drugs the brain of youth is music. Music makes the brain inactive." O tempora, O morris dancing! It sounds pretty terrible in Tehran, does it not?*

The man is as bad as St. Bernard.

(37) *One of your most precise recognitions, to me, is the statement that you only expected to be read by "unabashed boys and girls." Are they still being produced in numbers sufficient to constitute an "audience"? Or, are poets being reduced to that "Ideal Reader" that Robert Duncan goes on about? In his case he imagines a little old lady in a flowered hat, holding a watering can and a cat. She loves the considerable everything he says. She is never seen in the flesh.*

The right boys and girls are about all right, but they're not being schooled to read anything. In fact, they often can't.

(38) *A research fellowship at Queen Mary College, University of London, is advertised in the* Guardian *this morning. The subject is "Laser Measurement of Bovine Spermatozoa Motility." What should be done with old poets who are unemployed?*

They might become subjects for research. Or, perhaps, turned into cat's meat.

(39) *Time to play "Superlatives"—the bests and the worsts . . . Let's play a shortened version of "Desert Island Discs." If you were cut off by floods in the North Tyne Valley by a leaky dam in some monstrous new*

52 THE MAGPIE'S BAGPIPE

hydroelectric scheme, what four or five pieces of music would you most want with you on your portable gramophone?

The Monteverdi bit out of Ariosto . . . Some Dowland played by Julian Bream . . . A concerto grosso from Corelli . . . Any of D. Scarlatti's 500 or so harpsichord sonatas played by Ralph Kirkpatrick . . . And maybe Stravinsky's *Petrouchka.*

(40) *Some go to Colmar to the Isenheimer Altar of Grünewald; some go to Arezzo to see Piero's frescoes. Where would you go to see your favorite paintings in Europe?*

To Paris to have another look at the Impressionists and Postimpressionists . . . Ravenna, to see the mosaics at Sant' Apollinare in Classe Fuori . . . I'm always glad to see the Turners at the Tate.

(41) *Please name me five pieces of architecture that would cause you to make a pilgrimage. Norman Douglas said that he would cross an Alp to see a village idiot of quality. I'd agree, but it might really take the existence of the Certosa di Pavia on the other side to make me go in fact.*

The Masjed e Juma'a at Isfahan . . . The Omayyad Mosque at Damascus . . . Pisa Cathedral . . . San Paolo Fuori le Mura in Rome . . . And Durham Cathedral. . . .

(42) *We know you're fond of sailing, but I don't think we know whether you have either played or followed other sports. That would be the question, with a slight fillip on the end: who's the greatest athlete you've ever seen?*

I used to swim reasonably well, but not competitively. . . . I've never seen a great athlete. I won't count what I've seen on television.

(43) *Who have been your favorite comedians? Any northern ones like George Formby, Max Miller, Stan Laurel, or Frank Randall?*

Cockney comedians: Charles Chaplin and Nellie Wallace. Marie Lloyd . . . Ella Shields . . . There was the Australian who caricatured the concerto. Damn, I can't remember the names.

(44) *Can you think of five films that seem to you genuinely memorable or works of art?*

Broken Blossoms, with Lillian Gish, for the invention of the close-up . . . *Birth of a Nation,* by Griffith . . . A film of the 1920s which introduced a vast feeling of space: *Over the Hills to the Poorhouse* . . . *A Nous la Liberté,* by René Clair . . . The central portion of *Blow-Up,* by Antonioni, before it becomes a bore . . . *Modern Times* (or nearly any other of Chaplin's films).

(45) *What are the five ugliest places you've seen? In our conversations,* Descant on Rawthey's Madrigal, *you surprised us with the three cities you found most livable.*

Dusseldorf; Middlesbrough; Canton, Ohio; Gary, Indiana; and perhaps Wolverhampton—it's bad enough.

(46) *Is it merely a myth that pejorocracy is the rule of the day and that everything gets worse by the minute? Are there instances of improvement in English society that you can enumerate?*

Not since the 1950s. . . . Perhaps in the 1960s the miniskirt was the one improvement. I remember thinking how benighted the United States was in 1968. The miniskirt was at least four inches lower than Britain's.

(47) *Do you agree with the old Brazilian proverb: "When shit becomes valuable, the poor will be born without assholes"?*

Yes.

(48) *Is there anything better about being eighty than sixty-three or forty-seven or fourteen?*

No! What the hell. . . .

(49) *Your five-word autobiography ("Minor poet, not conspicously dishonest") implies the virtue of modesty and honesty. What other Quaker virtues do you hope for from yourself and from your friends?*

I'm not convinced that I have any virtues.

(50) *If you did have virtues, which would you want?*

Inconspicuousness, combined with enterprise. That's about it.

(51) *When's the last time you had a singing hinny? I never have had one yet, but I enjoy the name.*

It's donkey's years.

(52) *It being some sixty-seven years since you first came down from the rail station up Dent to visit Briggflatts, are the changes in the landscape or the meeting house very conspicuous?*

Hardly any. The horses have vanished—that's the big change.

(53) *Are you a member or merely an attender at Briggflatts Meeting?*

Attender.

(54) *Is speaking against your nature in Meeting?*

Hard to say why I prefer silence.

(55) *Chomei at Toyama, in your version, ended by saying: "My tongue clacked a few prayers." And he quoted Buddha that "none of the world is good." In modern times he might have agreed with William Steig, the cartoonist, whose hero sat in a doghouse smaller than the Hojoki and intoned: "People are no damn good." You're not that definitive, are you?*

I keep the condemnation for myself. I don't know people—only myself, in passing.

(56) *Would you have enjoyed sharing Dove Cottage with Dorothy Wordsworth? Having someone around the house with that lapidary prose style might have driven you to the extremes of John Lyly.*

She's probably better than I think, but she's too anecdotal for a man like me.

(57) *Why is it your answers are tending towards absolute brevity?*

I suppose the limit is absolute zero, and we must be approaching it.

(58) *Does the idea of travel still interest you? Edward Dahlberg got to the point that he paid so little attention to anything outside himself that he said: "The only reason we travel is because there is no place to go." Edward Lear would have scoffed at that, infirm as he was.*

I'd like very much to travel (for instance, up the Amazon, to Persia again, and to the south of Italy), but so much of what it requires to keep the niggling ills of old age at bay is tied up to things in the home, moving very far becomes impossible.

(59) *I don't remember seeing Herbert Read or Hugh MacDiarmid lift a hand in a garden. Contrarily, Delius had to be restrained from using the secateurs into the night. Has the garden ever held much interest for you, as more than a place to snooze and read books?*

Yes, indeed. When I went to Wylam, for some years I worked hard in the garden.

(60) *Can you imagine there are only twenty questions left? They can't be worse than sitting through a late Bruckner adagio? What we need is a modicum of* sprezzatura *and* brio *to ward off the effects of the gray, muggy weather. I can put on an afternoon's worth of late Haydn symphonies if all else fails.*

[Exclamation point.]

(61) *One literary question that sneaks in because I happened to think that the painter, Balthus, might be a good man to illustrate a selection of Bunting. Does the strain of eroticism in your work (unbawdy as it is) contribute to making northern hackles rise? Or, is any poet considered by the middle class as disreputable and a wastrel because he fools about with high art and fanciful language?*

No problem in my case, the work is so little read. The working class isn't bothered. You could be a Chinese mandarin.

(62) *What's the state of the long poem you thought you might have it in you to write last year when you read a beginning section?*

Stuck. S-T-U-C-K.

(63) *Talking of long poems makes me smile that a young cousin of Henry Wadsworth Longfellow was named Ezra Pound. Maybe he was even a great-nephew? And wouldn't it have been something if Ezra's father had married Ella Wheeler (Wilcox) instead of his mother Isabel? Like Charles Ives sounding like Victor Herbert, maybe?*

I dare say Pound would have managed to be even more optimistic than he was, though he would also have managed to avoid the imbecilities of Mrs. Wheeler Pound.

(64) *I remember one time your going through a list of poets you considered absolutely world-class, as one might say. The Masters of the Art. I recall*

I had read almost none of them and had scarcely heard of half. Would you do that list again for those who might be feeling smug and decided in their reading abilities?

Homer, Ferdosi, Manuchehri, Dante, Hafez, Malherbe, Aneurin, Heledd, Wyatt, Spenser, Sidney, Wordsworth . . . That's about the lot.

(65) *So, if an aspiring bard was going off to attend Paideuma U, would you limit him or her to these great dead or allow in some fairly good country writers like Sappho and Catullus and Buson and Bashō and Li Po and Hölderlin and Miss Dickinson? Is there a simple program for training a poet, beyond suggesting reading and correcting writing?*

Make them learn English grammar—especially syntax.

(66) *I ran into a quotation from D. Scarlatti that I think you will agree with: "Show yourself more human than critical and your pleasure will increase." Do you?*

He's probably right, but one of the functions of criticism is to point out defects in the work that keep it from being more human.

(67) *What do you make of the story of the two stone heads from a shrine of Maponus near the Roman Wall? They were sent to the home of Dr. Anne Ross, the Celtic scholar and archaeologist. On three occasions she and her daughter observed a dark figure, half-man, half-animal, that raced through their cottage and made the sound of a creature landing on pads as it lept away. Has Maponus long since departed? The coolly rational Dr. Ross is convinced it was an instance of haunting. She got rid of the heads.*

Bloody nonsense. I think that's really all there is to say about it.

(68) *Basil, if you see the Corn Close Ghost, I hope you'll be skeptical but polite. It always appears benign but some react to it more than others. I never see all of it, just a portion as it leaves the library.*

I think that's all you'll ever see of it.

(69) *You wrote me that there had been a plethora of obscure eighteenth-century English composers on the BBC, plus a careful selection of the worst pieces by J. C. Bach and nothings by Frederick the Great. Why do you think they do this to us?*

Sadism.

(70) *Can you estimate the amount of whisky you have consumed since approximately 1916? A non-Quaker resident of Sedbergh is interested in this statistic.*

Only a few barrels.

(71) *What are the cheeses most to your taste? Mr. Eliot once called Wensleydale "the Mozart of cheeses," to which Ludo Read replied: "Nonsense, Tom, it's Handel, of course." You may rhapsodize if you feel the need.*

Take it all around, Blue Wensleydale is as good as you're likely to get. . . .

[Postscriptum from JW: Basil, if you're ever in the vicinity of Otley, Lower

Wharfedale, do go to the Farnley Farm Shop, up on the north rim of the valley. They age the Wensleydale they buy at Hawes and keep it until it has a texture as smooth as the best Roquefort. It's outstanding.]

(72) *Do you hear anything from British composers these days that elates your ears?*

Can't recall hearing anything at all from British composers. The last good ones were the Beatles, as I mentioned before.

(73) *I forget who said "only emotion endures" (it may have been Pound). Do you agree? Duke Ellington was of the opinion that "it don't mean a thing, if it ain't got that swing." Hard to know what G. Fauré would say to that. Some emotions don't tread very hard on the dance floor.*

What endures is a combination of shape and invention or observation (they're both the same thing). People say Shakespeare invented Falstaff. He didn't. He saw him wandering around Southwark.

(74) *I don't know if anyone has ever found The Ideal Pub in England— something as good as the Saxon church of Escomb or the Norman church of Kilpeck, or Raby or Pendragon as a castle? But, the search always goes on. What's your pick?*

Once upon a time, the Ferry Inn, Dittisham, Devonshire.

(75) *What century would have been the one in Northumbria for poets and players of catgut in season?*

From 650 to 750 A.D.

(76) *You mentioned over dinner that there was something about W. B. Yeats's epitaph that had always put you off. What was that?*

The *horseman,* for reasons of common sense and of rhythm, both together.

(77) *It's been suggested that literary folk are considerably nastier than peasants—and quite a nasty one seems to have made the suggestion. Have you met literati who were preposterous, silly, vile, etc., etc?*

Surely. Most of them are.

(78) *Does the intellect have much to do with writing a poem?*

What the hell is the intellect?

(79) *Have you ever written letters to the editor of the* Times*—and have they ever been published?*

Yes, one or two. One on the habits of the Arts Council of Great Britain.

(80) *Isn't it time for a Dog's-Nose?*

High time.

Attentions

Reading Mingus's *My Audience* my eye hit the word *poppalopper*, and if I may swing it like Robert Duncan would, I'd figure Mingus puts this as the double to what Americans allegedly do to their mothers. The first poppa-lopper was Cronos (an old crow god), who used his flint sickle on Big Daddy Sky somewhere above Cape Drepanum. Jim Crow is one of his extant cousins, cutting people apart. At any rate, poppalopping seems like a score to me—Americans are notoriously without reverence for their beginnings, live in terror of Big Daddy, and cop out with no rites or care for the land of their inheritance.

One of the Great American Questions continually asks: What is the baleful spirit of the place that turns the poets into sages, mages, and rocks of ages? Because it does happen so often. Maybe Americans love only their grandfathers? Even Ezra Pound now grazes in asphodel and Kentucky blue-grass on the strength of his mandarin chin whiskers, deified to the Pantheon of the Gray Beards and Cracker Barrels by Richard Avedon of *Harper's Bazaar*. But, the game is usually up for the poet by age thirty—he is sour and dry, gone to his niche in the monolithic world of buying and selling. On the other hand it has been obvious for a long time that the jazz musicians and the big city painters are more fortunate in withstanding a term in the national boneyard. They are more convivial and friendly, despite the fact they now have a prestige product to sell in Texas (the painters do) and have to perform in underground fishbowls for the noisy and sodden pleasure of *Playboy* readers (the musicians have to). So it is, the only solace for a poet in New York is the occasional spirit in painting and jazz—the "opening out/of my countree," the projective flash that Charles Olson sees operating in much of the greatest American art: Ives, Ryder, Sullivan, Melville. In the winter of 1959 this spirit radiates for me from the paintings of de Kooning, which seem the best landscapes since the Land of Oz, and the sessions of the Charles

Mingus Jazz Workshop (Mingus, bass; John Handy, alto; Booker Ervin, tenor; Horace Parlan, piano; Danny Richmond, drums). I have heard this quintet more than thirty times in three months, increasingly rapt by the presence of those worn but inevitable words "nobility" and "love" in the music.

One night at the Half Note, Mingus stopped in the middle of his memorium for Lester Young called "Goodbye Porkpie Hat," and left the bandstand. Some lizard was destroying the piece with all his drunken yak. This is the root of "the communication problem." Mingus tends to read White Citizens Council on every pale brow, whereas the swine was probably slumming from Music Corporation of America. Meantime it remains incredible that Mingus can dredge out of the slough such miracles as "The Fables of Faubus" and "Wednesday Night Prayer Meeting." His music sits there, far beyond the Communication of Nothing and all palaver of merchandise men, for anyone with straight connections between ears, eyes, head, heart, and gut. It is, in a word, a vulnerary for those outraged.

Which reminds me twenty-two years ago I used to carry a hik-o-meter provided by sending a quarter and some Wheaties boxtops to Jack Armstrong. I now find I used it to measure the same Blue Ridge country that Vachel Lindsay charted in *A Handy Guide for Beggars*. Moral: each man must save what he can from inattention and all destruction.

New York 1959

16

The large armadillo-like lady who rattles her bracelets and clicks her com-
pact two minutes before the end of *Das Lied von der Erde* is not my friend.
It is from her million-headed inattentions and carelessnesses that I have tried
to remove myself by going to Carnegie Hall to hear Gustav Mahler's song-
symphony. Yes, "I too know that the blackbird is involved in what I know,"
said Wallace Stevens, and I'll add armadillos, but that is something quite
different. The lady, then, must be a friend of John Cage's, who once told me
he hated all music except his own, and who now tells me that perhaps the
noises of the environment are more interesting than the sounds of music,
including the indeterminations of his own. The idea is so "cool" that it has
been bugging me for many weeks, particularly since an evening at the Living
Theater in January when I heard Cage and Tudor, the pianist, perform
"Indeterminacy," the stories and the sound barrier employed to irritate the
ear into sharper attention. I have found myself additionally irritated because
as a poet I am forever writing statements of "purpose," planning, making
determinations—"ideas of order, or we die," to invoke Stevens again. What
I must fear in John Cage's work is the submission of all these activities before
chaos and chance—which seems alien to the American world in which we
live. I mean they are alien, if one is going to produce "purposeful" work.
Cage seems more interested in auditioning the world, instead of making
relationships in it. He writes: "My intention in putting 90 stories together in
an unplanned way is to suggest that all things, sounds, stories (and by
extension, beings) *are* related, and that this complexity is more evident when
it is not oversimplified by an idea of relationships in one person's mind."
That is the way Mr. Cage states the major principle, if I am aware of it.
Perhaps I should interpolate that I regard Mr. Cage with the greatest respect
and curiosity—I've been buying the records for thirteen years now and
expect to continue. However, back to "coolness" and that Zen monk who

found out a bereaved woman was weeping over the death of her only child, and then he hit her with a stick a bit triumphantly, declaring that'll give you something *really* to cry about. Passion is a factor—what do you do with that? The cheek cannot turn to stone. If one were sitting or standing, black or white, in a Woolworth's in Winston-Salem, North Carolina, this week, one could not solve the ridiculousness of the world with little gems from D. T. Suzuki, Meister Eckhart, or somebody's hip mother. . . . But again, I can say I enjoy Cage's stories (which are moral preachments from the lives of the composer and his friends, and tales about mushroom collecting, monks and sages, and the processes of making music.) I just hope it all simply isn't much too cool. Ah well, as Robert Duncan observes, one of the distinctions between us and the artist is, we can be entertained by what he suffered.

Highlands, North Carolina 1960

My Time Will Yet Come . . .
Said Some German

17

It was Nietzsche; and, then, Gustav Mahler quoting Nietzsche. And if you die long enough it's liable to happen. (But, I've been asked here to speculate on what's going to happen in literature for the next fifty years. Rather than bore you with the details, it seems much more modest to talk about my own plans for that period and let such speculation at least pay for one month's rent in London—that much is for real.)

What is going to happen? "Certainly if writing is to have a future it must at least catch up with the past"—that's William Seward Burroughs in a piece, "Censorship," in the *Transatlantic Review*, No. 11. Burroughs calls for experimentation and new techniques to enable the novelist to move forwards and backwards in time and space. He is being termed a cosmonaut of inner space, and says he sees no point in exploring areas that have already been thoroughly surveyed. In another magazine I was reading last night *(Down Beat)*, the pianist Cecil Taylor was being called an astronaut, because he, too, was busy charting vibrations from another area of psychic process. Well, every artist his own cipher, to keep up the technical lingo. But, "The Kingdom of Heaven is within"—that's a good thing to remember before you blast off. (If you've got to go, remember Paul Potts's poetical offer: "If you're walking to the moon, I've got clean socks for you.")

I frankly don't want to go—there seems to be enough of a mess here as is. The artist or non-artist will have his hands full making the "cell of good living" that Eric Gill spoke of. The artist, like Lord Acton, has got power troubles. Because *power* is what *words* are. I'll try to stick to words. The first thing to remember about Orpheus, king of poets, is that his song could melt stones and tame the beasts. What lyricist, bard, or *vates* doesn't still want that endothermal control? Namely, a voice to move the spirits of others. Forget the brain damage and the cracker-barrel confusion. Remember the Confucian chin whiskers and Pound's great use of the ideogram of character—a man standing by his word. You can't run a clean state with dirty words. Politics begins at home, in the mouth. The uses to which poets put words are all for other human beings. Not to con them, not to sell them, not to denigrate them; but to move them by the free play of the mind, the eye, and the ear. Which means, simply, to remind them of their own selves, to light *their* eyes, to feed *their* imaginations, to warm *their* hearts. Millions die yearly in the modern world from hearts that are cold and hard. Words are clear about that.

The construction of a piece of writing like this sets the mind to making combines and isolations from all one has read and from everything one has lived. You use everything and hope to come up with something viable. Louis Kahn calls on this metaphor when he writes of the purpose of the true architect. It is to create meaningful spaces. As a maker of language the poet devotes himself to the structures he coaxes from his syllables—to reorder the world, to make it a little more viable for some one or two or some one or two millions or billions. The process is terribly difficult for a poet himself to discuss, for his heart is moving in upon the task to which he has staked himself and it is futile to measure himself against the past (which leads to odious comparisons, often) or against the present (which leads to vanity and venal competition). Yet, one must seek to know the best measure of the past and present, and the critical faculties that have thrown light on both. Elizabeth Sewell, in her singular book, *The Orphic Voice: Poetry and Natural History* (Yale University Press), creates an image of Goethe "bedded down into nature like a huge thinking tree." Because, it seems, that the poetic process is nature's own—a fusion between the mind of man and nature's movements. Ralph Waldo Emerson writes: "Nature will be reported. All things are engaged in writing their history. . . . The air is full of sounds; the sky, tokens; the ground is all memoranda and signatures; and every object covered over with hints, which speak to the intelligent. . . . Nature conspires. Whatever can be thought can be spoken. . . ."

The communication problem, to use a dull phrase for it, arises because each human being is new, and nature is "new." And one must wander on. Thus we come to some of the physic areas and inner spaces that W. S. Burroughs spoke of, and also we come to an unfamiliar way of chartering nature. Again, I have to call on my culture (which Pound defines as whatever the hell the informed people of a particular generation are hot about) to clarify the point. So, I quote S. I. Hayakawa writing in *The New Landscape in Art and Science* (Paul Theobald, Chicago): "Our basic knowings are no longer of 'things' and their 'properties,' but of structures—usually implied structures. In other words, events at the level of nuclear, atomic, and molecular levels, cosmic ray phenomena, and events at the level of the extremely large, as in astrophysics, are not visual experiences, but logical and mathematical derivations from instrument-observations and hypotheses. The inferred structures and events, then, are never directly experienced. . . ." Hayakawa then writes of a war waged with radioisotopes in which people would be doomed to death by particles and have no direct knowledge of contamination by them until shortly before the painful end.

Still, of the future and literature, it seems firm to say that the writer will be exercising his faculties abroad widely and freely, as he always has. His business will be to get his perception down in words and to bridge the gap to those who want the information. Trance has much to do with it. One is "entranced," one is "enchanted" by song—by the primacy of love as sung by the mind's music. To peg it more tightly down than that is to risk killing it—the classic Chinese parable of the sage who tore the wings off the dragonfly to see what made it fly.

Since the beginning of language every generation has been told: let each man save himself as best he can. *Salvation,* then. It is accomplished by love— what else to call it? At this point all dichotomies go. There is no I *versus* what is out there; no subject *versus* object; no form *versus* content. In order that this state be available to the poet, he must be in a condition of grace before his muse, his tongue. The attunement to the language permits the transfer of its total force of sights, sounds, and intellections. I take it that poetry may become a division of ecology. The need, as in all relationships of all the animals, vegetables, and minerals on the planet—and the signs that stand for them—is for awareness of balances, the spaces between them, reverence for what goes next to what, insistence on equality and allowance of differences; all of which are conditions to make viable connections. Most poets, surely, sense this already, but many readers will want to examine the work of a number of extraordinary generalists who prefigure the world's next phase. The message is very plain: "Only when love takes the lead will earth, and life on earth, be safe again. And not until then"—Lewis Mumford.

Whether there are enough voices to enable us to have a future is always in grave doubt. I spent a weekend in Worcester and Birmingham talking with two young poets who felt nothing was possible in Great Britain without an entire social revolution. One day I received letters from three distinguished men of letters on this island. One spoke of the day-to-day, year-after-year difficulties and neglect that have finally made his work "extinct." The second spoke of London—"It is cruel, big, and ugly; the old megalopolitan dump of nihilism." The third spoke of the snobbism and mental flatulence of the "impenetrable density of this country against which I have broken my knuckles all these years." Though they seem to be about ready to tear down his birthplace in Soho, the visionary spectre of William Blake still radiates in some English hearts—and some Russian, American, and Madagascan. One never knows; or, perhaps nobody ever wins anything. I think it is the writer's

duty to try. I have my friends, the cottonmouth and deadly nightshade to
think about. We shall build bomb shelters for them all the time against our
emotional armor. And that's what it's about isn't it? Coda:

> the nightingale is singing
> on Hampstead Heath
>
> 141 years after the death of Keats
> tradition is in us
> like the sun
>
> "sin is
> separation"

London 1963

Colonel Colporteur's Winsome-Salami Snake Oil (JW to His Students)

18

Let *B* stand for *Barbarian*. There have always been a lot of them around, hammering at the gates of language. Poetry is very tough; it is also very fragile—there are never very many people who can defend it by writing it well or reading it with attention. (If the biggest problem in America is getting rid of trash—and treating people like they *were* trash—then the next biggest is that so few people can bring any concentration to bear.)

———

Writing is a cottage industry—one of the last—approximately like what the women in the Hebrides do: weave sheep's wool into Harris tweed that is dyed with a mordant of male urine and lichens collected locally. It has to do with privacy and the quiet of the hearth. The desk and the hearth are sacred places to the devoted writer and reader. Note the multitude of warming particles in the word *hearth: hear, heart, ear, earth, art*. They are what it is all about.

———

Poets are, after all, the "Boys and Girls of Summer." I mean: poets are persons who continue to play the language games of childhood. Gustav Mahler remarked that he never drew upon his experience (his "head" as they say these days) beyond the time when he was ten. There is a child in every man and woman who wants to play—that's approximately the way that the enchanted German poet, Christian Morgenstern, put it. So, poets are operating as "players" and this is one of the reasons that people who have to work for other people from nine to five, in jobs they usually despise, often resent artists of all sorts. Artists don't seem to do any "work," despite any amount of production of poems, or pots, or pictures, or pieces, or plays. Aging tire salesmen love to see George Blanda playing pro ball against

67

youngsters and scoring, but they think that adults should *really* be "serious," like selling tires at Sears and contributing daily to the gross Gross National Product. (As Herr Freud so kindly pointed out for our benefit: the reason that jobs done for money are almost inevitably so boring is that money is not a childhood desire.)

———

The world has been around awhile (they just found a bone in Sarlat in the Dordogne region of France that is engraved with "art" by a burin tool in a human hand—Marshack flew over from Harvard to confirm this). Perceptions have changed very little since then, and our ability to murder other people more effectively is one of the few technical improvements. "The truth was known already long ago," Goethe noted. Remember Confucius: Make it new! Sappho is just as interesting *now* as she was to the poets on her isle of Lesbos in the B.C. Greece of her day. *Because she got the words right.* Every generation with eyes and ears has been retranslating her fragments into the language and light of its day. Sappho is more interesting than any man or woman now living, *probably*, even though she is older than your 1970 Dodge Polara and never got it from the Colonel or Burger-Chef.

———

One of the things that makes poets like myself scream in the night and make uncouth noises is the (apparent) fact that a whole body of traditional reference is going out of currency. One constantly runs the risk of overloading the circuits and expecting "too much" from readers who have been fed vast amounts of commercial swill and venal junk, but who, for instance, have never read the Bible *for its language,* if nothing else. I am not calling for scholars, but what used to be called The Average Reader. Not just poets are being deprived of their audience; a humorist like Roark Bradford loses out as well if the listener has no childhood memory of the tale retold in "The Adulteration of Ol' King David."

———

Tradition could be defined as (1) what you care to remember; or (2) what you simply cannot forget.

A *tradition* is what the making of poems is celebrating. I'll enumerate some of what goes into my own. The point about "caring" is that it is inclusive. As a poet one does not divide the world up into its innumerable factions: white, black, male, female, old, young, good, bad.

So one remembers fishing trips with grandad to a marvellous place called Sweetwater Creek in the country west of Atlanta. Undoubtedly, all of it is now at the bottom of a polluted reservoir, but no matter. There were summers spent playing with white and black kids on my great-grandmother's farm near Cartersville, Georgia. *Everybody* was poor; the geraniums in the empty lard can and the dirt yards swept clean looked the same at the white tenants' (people named Chitwood—straight out of *Tobacco Road*) as they did at the black.

Books: *Uncle Remus; Ol' Man Adam* and *Ol' King David and the Phillistine Boys* (both Roark Bradford, a white New Orleans newspaperman); and even *Lyrics from Cotton Land* by a North Carolinian named John Charles McNeill. The University of North Carolina Press still sells it by the thousands every year.

Update all that by a generation: lots of time in New Orleans listening to local black musicians (1949–1952): George Lewis, Slow-Drag, Creole George Guenon, One-Eyed Babe Philips, Emile Barnes, Kid Thomas, Jim Robinson, Lawrence Marrero; all the Bessie Smith one could find; Jelly Roll Morton's Library of Congress twelve LPs; Bop, and the two North Carolinians: John Coltrane and Thelonious Monk, the man who spells his first name like an adjective. (I won't list all the Mahler and the Chopin and the Elgar and the Satie—we're sticking to the locale.) And, not until very lately, a willingness to pay close attention to the likes of Earl Scruggs and Doc Watson.

It is our friend Zukofsky's statement that the test of poetry is the range of pleasure it affords in matters of *sight, sound,* and *intellection.* Few poets are strong in the latter department, but one who is word-blind and tone-deaf seldom interests me in the least.

Consider the moon, an object in the sky traditionally sacred to poets. By organizing a level of sonic motion, Sir Philip Sidney (1554–1586) is able to move us in turn:

With how sad steps, O moon, thou climb'st the skies!

Which is, is it not, *mimesis*—what everybody sharp from Aristotle to William Carlos Williams has been insisting on: not to copy nature but to imitate her moves in the mind's music. (I'd not read the Sidney on the page in so long that when it came to looking it up I went searching in Keats and Shelley. This demonstrates not only private ignorance, but also that the poets' feelings for the moon changed little over three plus centuries.) It, in fact, becomes almost impossible to find a new music for the over-commercialized, astronauted moon, i.e., after Johnny Mathis, Bing Crosby, and Casa Loma Orchestra, etc. The last good song I know about the moon is the Kurt Weill/Bert Brecht "Alabama Lied" in *Mahagonny.* It's not just the kitsch world that has despoiled Diana's sanctuary, but poets like Robinson Jeffers:

A night the moon was like a drunkard's last half-dollar shoved across the polished bar of the eastern hill range, Tamar Caldwell rode her stallion. . . .

Pretty embarrassing image. So it behooves us to consider other ways to *look* at the moon:

    mOOn Over tOwns mOOn
    whisper
    less creature huge grO
    pingness . . .

e. e. cummings there begins to see that there is more to words than using them to convey abstract thoughts; that there are *things* in the substance of letter forms—that the looming shape of the moon is conveyed in its pair of Os.

A further development of this way of concentrated seeing is Ronald Johnson's:

            O
        MOON

The poem is all silence, with a stray moon somehow detaching itself from the word and rising (or setting) in blank paper space. Very beautiful.

————

A pseudo-translation of mine from the Chinese says: "*Fox* plus *razor* equals the *eye*—get sharp, or you're dead!" Accordingly, please don't let the world turn you into a Gadarene, a Midianite, or a Laodicean (see the New Testament).

Do not *over*estimate yourselves. Remember Delacroix's remark: To be a poet at twenty is to be twenty; to be a poet at forty is to be a poet. Write poems for the most passionate of reasons and beware the Rational Mind; i.e., *Celebrate*. Bruckner said the thing wrong with Brahms was that he could not *jubilate*. A curious remark, in the light of those four symphonies. One man's epiphany is another man's easy chair.

Eyes&ears, and a *place* you stand on. Go easy on imported nightingales, if you don't know what the wood thrush sounds like. Be down to earth. Be *earthy*. Be at home where you are. Make the things in your rooms sacred by paying them attention, space, and quiet. Be silent more often before the loom of the world. Be nicer to rattlesnakes and trout lilies. And know what things are called.

Be more on your own; go your own way more often. Stay away from crowds of poets with all their hustling and envy and backbiting. Stay away from Big Mac and Whopper. Learn how to cook a hamburger worthy of Orpheus.

Read everything by some really absorbing "minor" or fifth-rate or ignored writer, like M. P. Shiel, or Arthur Machen, or Mervyn Peake. You can get into an anthology edited by W. B. Yeats if you can write one poem as good as "The Sunflower" by William Force Stead, late of Baltimore, Maryland.

Be more *responsive*. Or, as Tina Turner would have it: "Rub it on us; turn it loose!" Get the hots over *words*. Give things a break, including rattlesnakes, trout lilies, and even the androids who purport to run the United States. *We are responsible for what they do.*

Be both *elite* & *elate*. Discover why Rachmaninoff's performance of Schumann's *Carnival* reveals mastery as opposed to the mere competence of most other readings. Persons are equal before the law and the folks are as good as the people, but Earl Scruggs is better than most fireless poets. Listen for that *enkindling* difference and adhere to it and measure yourselves against the best as you find it. Your "best" will change as you explore the world.

Charles Ives said: "Stand up and use your ears like a man!" Picasso said: "Have balls. Look into the sun!" Macho statements, I suppose, and, anyway, if you write poems you will be considered a fruit-and-nut case for life. Better advice would be: don't be cussed about your poems all twenty-four hours of the day. Walt Whitman, in an amazing line, said that what he aspired to do was make companionship as thick as trees by the rivers of America. *We are all here together.*

Winston-Salem, North Carolina 1973

"Anyway, All I Ever Wanted to Be Was a Poet," Said Leon Uris, with a Smile, as We Strode Together into the Vomitorium . . .

19

Poetry, like the Road of Death, according to the old Yorkshire lore, is a "greate launde full of thornes and furzen." If you have never given charity— if only in the form of one pair of worn, discarded shoes—you will walk forever barefoot in hell.

But reviewing living poets (or even despising venal hacks) all too seldom brings forth charity from my breast. Mr. Auden says that loving thy neighbor and earning one's living are much more important than poetry. He could be right, though the villainously low estate of poetry has recently been improved by the news that Colonel Harland Sanders paid 7,500 smackers for the first copy of *Poems About God,* the posthumous volume of a cancer victim from Salt Lake City named Ila Hunt Crane. Anyway, what a hard time I have not relishing vile, insolent, illiterate, now-and-then-correct reviews of some of the big competition, since gents like Mr. Ferlinghetti and Mr. Dickey are so remarkably competitive themselves. Yes, Christian charity is much harder than poetry. Besides, as Adrian Mitchell points out, every poet wants all other poets to write like he or she does—except *worse*. As for the neighbor-loving part of Mr. Auden's injunctions, I try to stay far out of the picture. In neither North Carolina nor in Yorkshire do I live where I can hear the sound of an axe or see smoke from another chimney.

Whatever my reluctances, Herb "the Junkman" Leibowitz, the genial editor of *Parnassus,* who was brought up on all those trash-pitchers toiling in the New York Yankees' bullpen, has tossed me a very peculiar assortment of stuff, designed to get me talking about "popular" poetry Not even Berra would have swung at three of the five books. However, "Bring all you got!" suggests Bob Gibson. Good advice, whether pitching fast balls around a subject or just throwing high, hard ones in general. So, first thing, I went into training—off on the North York Moors, the Hambleton Hills and the Lyke-Wake Walk to hike forty miles and give the typewriter a rest. What refreshment there is in surveying places like Hagg Hall, Bungdale Head, Cock Flat, and Snotterdale, with a stop by Fatlips Castle on the way home. Also, in today's mail I have received a royalty statement from the University of North Carolina Press indicating that my *An Ear in Bartram's Tree* earned me $39.00 this past accounting period. Since I bought $27.60 worth, I get $11.40. That's what I call popularity.

So, after two weeks' brooding on the enormity of it all and on the hopelessness of finding the clearest way into the topic, the thing to do is start. One way in would be to note my sadness at the death of Paul Goodman and the further distress that so few men like him are left. Two paragraphs from Michael T. Kaufman's obituary of PG keep coming to eye here on the desk:

"Mr. Goodman went on: 'One reason I haven't learned anything in 40 years is that the political truth is so simple that a boy can see it: Society with a big S can do very little for people, except to be tolerable so we can go on about the important business of life.' "

"For Mr. Goodman, the more important business of life was creativity, play, love, and sex. Characteristically, he went about these pursuits outside traditional forms."

For *Society*, substitute *A Public*—it can do very little for a poet, except to be tolerable. Here in Dentdale, I assume that my neighbors and I can tolerate each other in the old cautious Dales way. An accomplished knitter over in Wensleydale, Molly Kirkbridge, was saying: "Remember, we were nobbut browt up like bullocks." Wise to remember, when you meet an elderly shepherd driving an automobile as though he were Lord of all creation, or when you try to make sense with a local over this newfangled thing, the telephone. These are not skills given to remote country people. On the other hand, I cannot make a Wensleydale cheese, or shear a sheep, or dream of the promenade at Blackpool. I can write poems for a few people outside the Dales to listen to and look at. I would never try to turn this x-number of devoted readers into some commercial nonsense called A Public. We entertain a certain number of friends with poems, with food and drink and conversation, because we enjoy their company and they ours. The thought of the misery of entertaining The Public is quite terrible. That poem there, why doesn't it suffer more? The mayonnaise there, why does it have those garlic cloves in it?

We all know the thing about "without great audiences, there are no great poets" (coined by that old matinee idol, Walt Whitman); and the fact that nobody reads anymore. Marshall McLuhan would like to read but hasn't the time. We ought to know that we are plunk in the middle of the new Dark Ages that Pound and many others ("The best lack all conviction, while the worst / Are full of passionate intensity"—W. B. Yeats) were predicting decades ago. Pejorocracy is here. Colonel Sanders and McDonalds—and

Much Worse—are here. Out of the cradle of California, endlessly rocking, come names like Nixon, Reagan, and Manson—who could have guessed? We know that the unofficial poet laureate of this same California is Ruth Forbes Sherry, of Laguna Beach, where she wears a tiara; and we know that the poet laureate of Pampagna, Philippines is Brigido B. Sibug, who wears plastic laurel leaves—at least they look like plastic in his paid-for photograph in *International Who's Who in Poetry 1970–71*.

The following sober truths deserve also to be known:

> I know not thy works, that thou are neither cold nor hot: I would thou wert cold or hot.
>   So then because thou art lukewarm, and neither cold nor hot, I will spue thee out of my mouth.—The Revelation of St. John the Divine 3:15–16

All the arts are plagued by charlatans seeking money, or fame, or just an excuse to idle. The less the public understands the art, the easier it is for charlatans to flourish. Since poetry reading became popular, they have found a new field, and it is not easy for the outsider to distinguish the fraud from the poet. But it is a little less difficult when poetry is read aloud. Claptrap soon bores. Threadbare work soon sounds thin and broken backed. . . . There were mountebanks at the famous Albert Hall meeting, as well as a poet or two; but the worst, most insidious charlatans fill chairs and fellowships at universities, write for the weeklies or work for the BBC or the British Council or some other asylum for obsequious idlers. In the Eighteenth Century it was the Church.—Basil Bunting

_____was incredibly bad. Stoned out of his mind, mumbling inaudibly, chain-smoking through the reading, begging drinks, ignoring all of us save for an occasional leer at some cunt upon whom, no doubt, he was endeavoring to put the make. Most of us got up and walked out, a gesture of which he was altogether unaware. I'm told he grosses something like 90 thou a year for this sort of performance.—Paul Metcalf

In the wide society, also in the restricted society of letters, the lucky thing is to have enough mature or maturing authors whose loyalty, let these authors be various as they may, is evidently and always to the best; and whose reputation and influence are such as to compel that powerful club, which can't be eradicated, to something of an identical sense of worth.—Geoffrey Grigson

90% of American poets do not exist. They are androids, manufactured from Randall Jarrell by the lost-wax process.—Kenneth Rexroth

Everybody is trying to convince people that kids are interested in ecology, that kids are interested in politics. That's bullshit. Kids are interested in

the same things that have always interested them: sex and violence.—
Alice Cooper

What *Time* ought to have said about the state of American poetry is that
it is extremely diverse, bouncing and healthy, and that the public who
might buy it and read it is so dismally stupid, sheepish, and tediously
ignorant—I mean the less than 1 per cent of the population that buys
books and the fraction of them that read them—that it is a kind of bless-
ing that we have a single poet in the country.—Guy Davenport

If you keep straight you will have no friends but catgut and blossom in
season.—Basil Bunting, *Chomei at Toyama*

Golly. That assemblage is so dour that I must find you something to
indicate that all is not totally lost. Back to Paul Goodman—part of one of his
last poems, printed in a Canadian gay lib paper:

> Thanks to a couple of rational
> decisions by the Court
> that struck down censorship
> and—brr—its chilling effects,
> I get by mail a gentle stream
> of booklets of poetry
> by young men in love with each other
> good news I read with pleasure
> though naturally wistfully.
> I used to write the same myself
> a hundred years ago.

So, warmed by the thought of a husky reader or two—or at least the prospect
of a volleyball game when I next venture onto a campus to read—it's finally
into the batter's box to take a few swipes at the books to hand.

(1) *in someone's shadow*, Rod McKuen (Cheval Books, 1971). The
publisher's notes tell us that "Mr. McKuen has recorded more than forty
albums of his own songs; his more than nine hundred compositions per-
formed by other artists have sold a total of fifty million records. . . . *Stanyan
Street and Other Sorrows, Listen to the Warm,* and *Lonesome Cities,* the
author's first three books of poetry, have sold nearly two million copies in
less than three years, making him the best-selling poet today. . . ." It is very
embarrassing—like having to tell 80,000,000 avid readers that Richard
Nixon has Dragon's Breath—to reveal that Mr. McKuen is another nogood-
nik, just right for those who, in mildly more literate days, used to go to
church, heaven, bed, wherever, with Kahlil Gibran, Anne Morrow Lind-

bergh, Walter Benton, Gloria Vanderbilt, and nameless denizens of the Beat
Generation. Mr. McKuen is moody, vacuous, abstract, uninteresting, slow-
eyed (sloe-eyed?) à la Robert Mitchum. He dedicates poems to Frank Sinatra
and to Mike Wallace, and such machismo will really put hair on your pussy,
if that's what you like, kiddo. Example: "I'll spread a blanket on the ground
/ and make a picnic of your body." . . . "Your perfume's not as dangerous /
as your shoulders." . . . "Hurry. / Sunday will not wait, / even for a woman."
. . . "The waves are clumsy but they're kind." Gee, Rod, you got to be kidding, right? Right! In the midst of all this mass-media miasma, there'll be a
line like, "It will be a Charles Ives winter." Gosh, what's that, a "Charles Ives
winter"? The atmospheric conditions in Charles Ives always register summer
and autumn up to, and including, Halloween. I suspect Mr. McKuen of
crossing cultural circuits and trying to think of Currier & Ives. Not that it
much matters. The poem is not edifying in either case. Another diary entry,
August 27, contains four lines:

> I got through one more night
> of jacking off and late late shows—
> and sleeping pills
> your doctor had prescribed for *you.*

Strong stuff, that, rather like catching Bing Crosby screaming *motherfucker*
through a dead microphone.

I have such total doubt in McKuen's powers of invention that I think
the following—from a poem called "Did You Say The War Is Over?"—is a
delicious error, compounded from author to lazy proofreader to careless
linotyper:

> The acne of perfection now must be
> to punch the teacher in the nose
> who gave you F instead of D.

"The acne of perfection"—terrible in any context, but surprising none the
less in the sad, minimal world of Rod and his eager, know-nothing millions.

I conclude my melancholy recital of the woes of this bestselling cowgirl
with this, dated and titled "October 3":

> If you had listened hard enough
> you might have heard
> what I meant to say.
>
> *Nothing.*

(2) *A Weeping Eye Can Never See,* Lois Wyse (Doubleday & Co.,
1972). This time the publisher tells us that Mrs. Wyse, author of *Love Poems*

For the Very Married, which sold 100,000 copies, will give us poetry to be read, poetry to be shared, poetry to be cherished. There are also "evocative" photographs by one George Elliott. The whole production looks fabricated by a pharmaceutical house to help sell a new vaginal spray; or, something you'd find in *Vogue,* a magazine that considers itself so far into Women's Glib. In any case, the poems are terrible, though this declaration loses me many votes amongst the Non-Intellectuals of Shaker Heights, Ohio. A short dose is "You See It in My Eyes":

> The glow of afterlove
> Is the outward reflection
> Of the inner lights
> That only you turn on.

That, gentle readers, is pure and simple crapioca. It smells like poetry but it *ain't* poetry, anymore than what you eat in the French Provincial Room of the Red Carpet Inn in Charlotte, North Carolina, is real. Veal "Cordon Bleu" simply does not have a piece of tinned ham, a slice of Velveeta, and a chili sauce on it. And, no, waiter, we don't want Bordeaux straight from the refrigerator—please take it back and call the manager. Ah, how tiresome we people are, who pay attention to food, and drink, and poems. How much sweeter to be relaxed about them and let the world turn into shit before our very eyes. The ultimate trouble with poems like these by Lois Wyse is their tendency to drive people's attention away from decent work. There will be now in the United States just that many fewer citizens who will waste a few dollars on Lorine Niedecker, Denise Levertov, or Diane Wakoski because they've blown $4.95 on Lois.

(3) *Rommel Drives On Deep Into Egypt,* Richard Brautigan (Delta Books, 1970). There is less here than meets the eye. So now it's time to lose votes with the Bolinas crowd that thinks Richard is right on.

Richards tend to be peculiar and losers by name. There were those English kings; there was Herr Wagner and Herr Strauss; there's one named Nixon and one mayor of Chicago; there were two fucked-up Richards at Black Mountain; I had a personal-Richard who had me in endless despair. One could make an interesting list. Anyway, Richards seldom give much away. Brautigan's as goofy as McKuen—another child of the Muses, with a sweet smile. He's read some Patchen, he's read some Creeley. He writes for kids who eat macrobiotic food and (don't) know where it is. Like I say, you'd starve to death on these no-cal poems. E.g.:

"April 7, 1969"

I feel so bad today

that I want to write a poem.
I don't care: any poem, this poem.

Or, "Nice Ass"

There is so much lost
and so much gained in these words.

Or, "Negative Clank"

He'd sell a rat's asshole
to a blindman for a wedding ring.

I'd like to say, Gee, wow, oo-ee-oo, landsakes, that's just very nice. I feel
more like Dr. Benway about to operate: "What son of a bitch has cut the
plasma with Sani-Flush?" It's too thin. Off to a Vic Tanney gym, words! And
a few months at the knee of Mr. Rexroth wouldn't hurt you either. Then, if
you insist on coming on quite so simple, do it in a way that might interest
people who have listened to the beautiful clarities of Scarlatti and Schubert
beyond the Bay Area and the sunshine campuses.

(4) *Transformations*, Anne Sexton (Houghton Mifflin Co., 1971). This
was going to be the slick goody in this assortment which started in the abyss
with Mr. McKuen and Mrs. Wyse. Stanley Kunitz says on the blurb that he
has been "astonished" by these wild, bloodcurdling poems. Kurt Vonnegut
contributes a preface. Miss Sexton stares from the rear jacket in her white
sun porch in Weston, Massachusetts, with alarming composure. Her honors
are legion. *Transformations* is retellings, in jokey, prosaic language of sev-
enteen tales by the Brothers Grimm. I have tried, but I cannot take any
interest in them, any more than I'd want to drive a Chrysler Imperial or live
in Weston, Massachusetts. I fear Miss Sexton and I would not be entertaining
to each other. I am so deaf and blind to her possible virtues that I surely
cannot give them to you. (And, to say it just one more time, that is one of the
dangers of one poet writing about another poet.) Anyway, I have vague
memories of Uncle Milty doing cute revisions of fairy tales on TV that seemed
better than these. We were spared such lines as:

Inside many of us
is a small old man
who wants to get out.
No bigger than a two-year old
whom you'd call lamb chop
yet this one is old and malformed
His head is okay
but the rest of him wasn't Sanforized.

He is a monster of despair.
He is all decay.
He speaks up as tiny as an earphone
with Truman's asexual voice:
        (from "Rumpelstiltskin")

Hand over hand she shinnied up
the hair like a sailor
and there is the stone-cold room,
as cold as a museum,
Mother Gothel cried:
Hold me, my young dear, hold me,
and thus they played mother-me-do.
        (from "Rapunzel")

She slept on the sooty hearth each night
and walked around looking like Al Jolson.
        (from "Cinderella")

Gretel
seeing her moment in history,
shut fast the oven,
locked fast the door,
fast as Houdini,
and turned the oven on to bake.
The witch turned as red
as the Jap flag.
Her blood began to boil up
like Coca-Cola.
Her eyes began to melt.
She was done for.
Altogether a memorable incident.
        (from "Hansel and Gretel")

I cannot agree that that is a memorable incident in the least, but before getting on to the literary meat of this inquiry, I'll stop and read a few pages of *I Was a Fugitive From an Eastern-Establishment Brain-Gang*. I can see all those academics at Tufts and Brandeis ready to savage my next book; I can feel the fury of *New Yorker* readers, their pinpoint eyes surveying the Sound behind granny-glasses, etc.

(5) *The Gambit Book of Popular Verse*, edited and introduced by Geoffrey Grigson (Gambit Inc., 1971). I have not managed yet to write the book-length essay asserting that Mr. Grigson is the most valuable man of letters on either side of the Atlantic, but it remains heavily on my mind. It

should not have to be said by an American (and a dubious one, at that, in Mr. G's style-book); however, myopia is only on the increase in Great Britain. Mr. Grigson is thorny as a gorse bush, and, what is worse, randy as a biscuit about poems. That is unseemly in a land where passion is so watered.

The criteria for this anthology are set out nicely: "Popular verse is not 'literary', it is not egoistic or private, or—except by corruption sometimes— obscure: it does not deal with the exceptional, its vocabulary is not idiosyncratic, its images are few and immediate in their appeal, its forms are uncomplicated. All of this, in any climate of the 'literary', especially today's climate, offers some rest or relief; as well as some instruction in the nature of language and poetry."

What we have is a series of poems and fragments from the thirteenth to twentieth centuries, arranged in categories from the cradle to the coffin. The material is, essentially, British, and why not? The only point here is that Americanos will have their dialect-work cut out for them. A dialect is very off-putting unless its sound has been directly in your ear. I suppose I never had too much trouble with the remarkable "Western Wind":

> Westron wind, when will thou blow,
> The small rain down can rain?
> Christ if my love were in my arms,
> And I in my bed again.

But the stanzas of "The Lyke-Wake Dirge" make much more sense to me now that I have walked the terrain and heard the North Riding accent and seen the gorse moors in the fog:

> From Whinny-moor that thou mayst pass
> Every night and awle,
> To Brig o' Dead thou comest at last
> And Christ receive thy sawle.

On another hand, I know far too many people in the USA—including several from Perineum, Oklahoma, who went off to study with Leavis— who'd only sniff at two homely dialect classics:

(1)

> he boiled my first cabbage,
> he made it awfully hot . . .
> when he put in the bacon,
> it overflowed the pot.
> (Bessie Smith: "Empty-Bed Blues")

(2)

well, Milo Venus was a beautiful lass,
she had the world in the palm of her hand;
she lost one of her arms in a wrasslin' match
over a brown-eyed handsome man.
(Bob Luman: "Brown-eyed Handsome Man")

Mr. Grigson would have poems like this, and perhaps a few Merseyside
numbers like "Eleanor Rigby," except he did the vast reading and searching
for his anthologies back in the 30s. A poet cannot be expected to distract
himself with contemporaries in his sixties as he did in his personal thirties. I
shall now ask those readers who have kept the faith and flagged not a riddle
from Grigson's indispensable anthology. It is an ancient Lincolnshire product.

Fatherless an' motherless,
    Born without a skin,
Spok' when it ca'ame into th' wo'ld
    An' niver spok' sin.

The answer to this is: a *fart!* Before this sublime sonic invention we stand in
considerable awe, as even that gent known as Le Petomane. Shall we, during
the interval, try a few choruses of "Rock of Ages"? Have you ever been in the
Cheddar Gorge, where the Rev. Toplady hid out during a storm and hummed
the initial bars of "R of A"? Pity. Culture isn't what it was.

Since so many seem concerned with the popular and the public, I am
going to become involved with the pubic and the private(s—if possible). I
shall soon edit *The Penguin Book of Poets Private Parts* (from Dame Edith
to David Bowie). The frontals are (e)*recto*; the posteriors are *verso*. Smile,
baby, your ass is on Parnassus TV.

Dentdale, Cumbria 1972

The Camera Non-Obscura

20

"I am of two minds as I take up my humble pen on this cool August morning," as diarists like to begin their job. One mind is on the cottonwool weather (the Meteorological Office promised "dry & sunny," a desperately sanguine forecast for northwest England) and on the $2^1/_2$-inch-to-the-mile Ordnance Survey Map of the Howgill Fells, where three of us want to walk this afternoon. For those of you who care about such things, let me tell you that the Howgills are England's most shapely and remote hills. When you are at the upper fastnesses of places like Langdale and Uldale and Weasdale and Bowtherdale, the only persons you are likely to meet are Frodo Baggins and Aragorn, son of Arathorn. More and more I think Professor Tolkien must have logged some miles in the Howgills and the English Lakes to their west during his young days in the English department of Leeds University. Maybe not, but his imaginative landscapes are much more fabled and strange than those evoked by the southrons: Vaughan Williams, Elgar, Holst; and even Delius, the quondam Yorkshireman.

The second mind is on how prodigal the times are; and how few of us scrutinize hard enough and pay close enough attention. To what? To our friends and loves, to what we eat and drink, to our gardens, to our manners, to the arts; i.e., name me ten jazz pianists to whet our appetite on this now-rainy day. Must I always be playing just Herbie Nichols, Adam Makowicz, Thelonious Sphere Monk, John Lewis, Art Tatum, Erroll Garner, Jelly Roll Morton, McCoy Tyner, Bill Evans, Duke Ellington, Cecil Taylor, and Red Garland? (And Three-Fingers Mamie Desdoumes, just to thicken the plot.) A true fan should be able to name twenty-five exceptional pianists from the history of jazz. And fifty photographers! The USA, particularly, is glutted with world-class talent. Pass the redeye gravy—it's all happening.

I recently drove from the North Carolina mountains to New Orleans. For the eye there was our giant interstate highway system, as balefully impressive as that created by the Romans. We have shown Nature who's boss. In a swamp off Interstate 10, framed by long-leaf pines and festooned with kudzu, a billboard declared, America Means Business. I believed it. For the mind, a certitude that one was surrounded by money-grubbers, nigger-haters, paramilitary Christers, hedonists of the Neo-Butch Right, dummies, druggies, and just plain old maniacs—many of them armed. (I do not include that gentle fiction, The Nice People, because the adversary society in the previous sentence has replaced them.) The first three people who spoke to me after I read poems in New Orleans appeared to be clinically mad. And Mae West died. John Lennon died. Colonel Harland Sanders died. (Poor Mr. Lennon. Perhaps he should have stayed home and paid the monstrous British taxes and retired to the Lancashire moorlands to read William Blake.)

What I am saying—in this roilsome, pyrotechnic language—is that there is little or no context in 1981 for poets or photographers, that their pleasures are nothing at all to the mentality of any region or the power and ordinance in industrialized capitalist states. Maybe the Old South offered *gentilesse* to the Fugitives/Agrarians way back when? Nowadays, around plantation houses like Houmas House in Louisiana, they are busy with petrochemical plants and anxious to build the largest toxic chemical waste disposal plant in the United States, courtesy of a California outfit called Industrial Tank. Selah. But, the battle seems to be a losing one, though one takes momentary comfort in Memphis ribs, the shrimp remoulade at Gala-toire's, in the fact that Walker Percy is over there across the Lake in Coving-ton, and that Miss Eudora is still there in Jackson, producing prose as savory as the recipe for southern meatloaf.

I went to Black Mountain College in 1951 to learn how to use a camera from Harry Callahan. There was a huge, myopic man named Charles Olson shambling about the place and he turned me in other directions. But, the interest in camera work and photographers never left me. That summer I bought my first print. It was by Aaron Siskind (also teaching with Callahan) and I paid ten dollars.

May I say that the idea of investing in photographs is absolutely repul-sive. Of course, this un-American sentiment comes from a hillbilly idiot whose whole life must seem shockingly inept to most of the citizens around him. He's still messing around with child's play at the age of fifty-one and doesn't even get paid very often, unlike George Blanda—if he still has a toe. He doesn't have any securities, and no insurance. (His "Personal Banker" at

Wachovia gets an extra week of paid vacation for trying to cope with him.)
He finds it impossible to kill animals and —so far—humans. Yet, this cunning snake-oil salesman from Parnassus County contrives to live with more
style than most millionaires. "Living well is the best revenge." If you are a
Luftmensch, then a little *Sitzfleisch* won't hurt you, to coin a strange, new
adage. Us rusticated goyim must definitely live by our wits and our scattered
talents. Remember, "There is hope for us all—if we only get good pitching,"
as my friend Bill Midgette liked to say.

To get back to this investment business, I was just reading an issue of
Brown's Guide to Georgia, that extremely surprising and useful journal out
of Atlanta. The writer was commenting on collectors of photography in the
state and called our attention to a young man only sixteen years old who was
already a two-year veteran. How marvellous, I first thought. And then she
quoted the young enthusiast as saying he thinks the photography market is
filling up with people interested in small, quick investment gains. "He is
selling off a group of Civil War photographs as well as original prints by
Laszlo Moholy-Nagy to define his collection more tightly." Silence, of the
stunned kind.

The Republic and the arts of the Nation are in plenty-bad-trouble if
sixteen-year-olds are as cold and calculating as adders in the employ of Dow-
Jones.

A final bit of advice. Avoid Big Names. Irving Penn, Walker Evans, Bill
Brandt—alas, we must leave them to the merchants and the art lovers. If you
are young and ungreedy and lacking in megabucks, seek out the photographers your own age and collect what moves you. (There are between one and
two hundred excellent photographers in this overloaded country.) Trade
prints for pots, or medical services, or legal advice, or words, or vegetables,
whatever. Never sell prints. Exchange them or give them away, if you've
worn them out or they've worn you out. And, always burn with St. Walter
Pater's hard, gemlike flame: ". . . to maintain this ecstacy, is success in life."

———

Poets and photographers do not necessarily believe in public audiences or
constituencies. They believe in *persons,* with affection for what they see and
hear. They believe in that despised, un-contemporary emotion: *tenderness.*

———

Before sitting down to write yet another introduction to an exhibition of
photographs, I've been reading Bernard Levin's column in today's *Times.*
Speaking of Kenneth Tynan's last book, he mentions some of the purposes
of reportorial prose: to entertain, amuse, assess, shed light, inform, pay
homage, and encourage thought. And he mentions those terrible members

of the Literary Merchants' Sodality whom he calls *les marchands d'ordure,* "who naturally sink to the occasion." Though I become increasingly reluctant to unleash my typewriter in order to fill the pages of a book before the photographic images begin to entertain, amuse, assess, shed light, inform, pay homage, and encourage thought, I shall try to be "responsive" and not palaver merely about myself.

But, being a fretful and nervous writer, I have a persistent, perhaps unfortunate need to explain why—in the name of Daguerre and Fox Talbot—I get myself into these explanatory situations. Is it a good thing to tell readers how pig-ignorant one feels about most things under the sun? I don't know.

From this desk in the library at Corn Close I regularly look out across the valley of the River Dee to a cluster of Scotch pines in a field of grass. The light in Dentdale, Cumbria, is unusually dim and the pines are inconspicuous and unremarkable. But, let the late sun shine its rays up the dale—particularly in a month like October—and the trees become transfigured, with the forms of the foliage and the trunks and those of the elongated shadows endlessly fascinating to the eye. The air is as cool and palpable as amber. Everything is seen "in a new light."

To invoke that gnomic picture-maker, Frederick Sommer: "We are talking about graphics: images about images are truly display; and *position* is truly inventiveness in display. . . . If we had to deprive ourselves of the feeling that we have the support of vision, we would really feel lost." Only a passion for words on the reader's part will reveal what the poet has contrived—and turn on the light. The real turn-on is to fathom what Herr Doktor Professor Freud had to tell us about the difficult word, *Besetzung* (cathexis). May I spare you my ignorance-masked-as-omniscience on that one?

———

Gore Vidal went to see E. M. Forster on some occasion back in the 1960s in his rooms at King's College, Cambridge. And the old man revealed the existence of his proto-gay novel, *Maurice,* which has male characters in bed, etc. "And what did they do?" asked Mr. Vidal, the ever-practical, inquisitive, politely lascivious American. "Talk," muttered the Englishman.

When it comes to "photographic talk," it can usually be guaranteed to bore the tits off a hog, to use the rustic vernacular. In fact, I am almost reduced to silence by a sentence from the venerable Ralph Steiner: "No person writing on photography has ever said anything that helped me do better on Thursday what I'd done less well on Wednesday."

———

It is an excellent thing to look at photographs in which, as Oscar Wilde must have observed, you get nothing but photography. That is, images in service to Seeing. Not in service to Sociology, The Class System, An Excess of Rationality, Cosmic Adumbrations, Self-Expression, Masculinity, Document. One constantly hears in England: "Art is not so important as People. Art is not so important as Life. Art is not so important as Nature. Art is Small Beer." Blimey. Is it as important as itself? By Bright Apollo and by Nicéphore Niepce, let us declare that it is.

There's an old saying, "You can't turn a silk purse into a sow's ear." Sure you can. We do it all the time. Most of us view the ordinary with just about enough perception to keep from being run over by a milk lorry. I think I have seen that phenomenon referred to as "the economic determinism of vision," but you will pardon me if I eschew abstract nouns and the lingo of the academy. I like prose to jump about, and dance and sing.

The North Carolinian/Cumbrian person writing these words sets up in life with the vocation of poet—the only thing more silly than being a photographer. I am neither authority nor critic. I am an appreciator of photographs. What are poems for? Equally, what are photographs for? Louis Zukofsky, who knows better than most, says their purpose is *to record and elate*.

Highlands, North Carolina
Dentdale, Cumbria 1980/1981

21

The Flâneur & Bricoleur
Get It Awl-Owl-All Together
(A Non-Review of
Susan Sontag's *On Photography*)

Enough is enough. I must have read fifteen critical observations on Susan Sontag's engaging volume. I missed the magisterial one in *Sports Illustrated* and the quasi-mendacious *omnium gatherum* in *National Geographic*, but I feel I know more about the book than I do about the three famous blasts Reggie J hit in Yankee Stadium last October. More than about D. Dawkins and the Gorilla-Slam-Dunk, as executed by the Philadelphia 76ers on the banks of the River Schuylkill; more than about the drolleries of Bert & LaBelle of Calhoun, Jawja. And certainly everybody has read it—including people who have never read a piece of writing on photography in their lives and who would not know whether to invite Beaumont Newhall, Helmut Gernsheim, John Szarkowski, Aaron Sharf, and A. D. Coleman to dinner or not. The gent who drives the bookmobile through Macon, Jackson, and Swain counties in western North Carolina has read it; the poet who runs a leather bar in the Castro District of San Francisco has read it; the retired Shakespearian scholar from Haverford has read it.

Well, why not read it? I am sure that Susan Sontag would say, with that disconcertingly serene wisdom of hers, if you are going to think about something, you might as well do it well. I am no one to argue. I'm a poet who would give up Kapellmeister Bach's Mass in B Minor (and all his other great works) for Herr Fred Delius's *Messe des Lebens* any day. Yep: any day. The Rational Mind? Sure, but you put up with it like you put up with Jacob Javits or George C. Wallace. It's *something else*.

I sat in an auditorium at the Corcoran Gallery, Washington, D.C., back in February, 1978, and observed a symposium, "Photography: Where Are We?" Sontag was there, participating. I had never seen her and had, oddly, never read her. Intelligent? And how. Attractive? Definitely. Polite and responsive to the audience and the occasion—which struck me as the most appealing aspect of all, since some of the panel members were engaged in being anything but.

Frederick Sommer (the only prominent photographer invited that weekend in Washington to fall amongst thorns, critics, and metaphysicians) "thinks" more than any veteran photographer I have known. Harry Callahan is said to "think" very little, but he and Fred Sommer take vast pleasure in each other's company. What either would have to say to Sontag still eludes me. Her book, urbane and thoughtful as it is, remains for me a book for New Yorkers to read and talk about. (New Yorkers and, apparently, the man on the bookmobile in Macon, Jackson, and Swain counties in NC.) I approach it very timidly, like the goyische dummy in the presence of Jewish-American Princes and Princesses on East Sixty-third Street. (In an essay Hannah Arendt quotes an article by Morris Goldstein that appeared in 1912: "We Jews administer the intellectual property of a people which denies us the right and the ability to do so." I do not mean to speak for anti-Semites, those who grumble about pointy-headed intellectuals, and those who wish to hickify the nation, when I raise matters relating to aesthetic and local distances.) Because Manhattan is seldom the provenance and purlieu of those of us who ramble about in the American Deadly Desert seeking the Frederick Sommers, Henry Holmes Smiths, and Clarence John Laughlins. When Susan Sontag speaks of Laughlin, that eminent Louisiana *Luftmensch,* he seems strangely "at a remove" to me. And so, one feels there *is* this gulf, the enormity of the continent in apposition to the island of Manahatta, where one perhaps makes too much of Diane Arbus, Irving Penn, and Richard Avedon and what one happens to see in the agora of galleries.

I continue to find myself and my sensibilities described year after year in a passage of Henry James's *The American Scene* (1907), which Susan Sontag quotes in *On Photography:*

> He doesn't *know,* he can't *say,* before the facts, and doesn't even want to know or say; the facts themselves loom before the understanding, in too large a mass for a mere mouthful: it is as if the syllables were too numerous to make a legible word. The *il*legible word, accordingly, the great inscrutable answer to questions, hangs in the vast American sky, to his imagination, as something fantastic and *abracadabrant,* belonging to no known language, and it is under this convenient ensign that he travels and considers and contemplates, and, to the best of his ability, enjoys.

It is clear that most people don't need to cultivate and work at dumbness as poets do, so, sure, buy *On Photography* and read at it. You'll need some time. Which, summer 1978, you can easily have by not reading the *Memoirs of Richard M. Nixon,* by using your Cuisinart, by cutting out jogging.

Dentdale, Cumbria 1978

Lea, the Place
Where Light Shines
(for Wynn Bullock 1902–1975)

22

Lea is one of the things you find if you dig into the body of the word *light*, which was Wynn's meat. Wynn's mead; Wynn's meadow—now you can see how *lea* gets close to *meadow*—"and the brightness begins."

Wynn Bullock was deeply (perhaps sorely) affected by Alfred Korzyb-ski's dictum: "the word is not the thing." Yet, there are things in the Indo-European roots of the word *bullock* that give us some light: *bhel-*, to blow, swell; with derivatives referring to various round objects and to the notion of tumescent masculinity. It comforts this man, who makes his world out of words, to recognize that Bullock was indeed the spatio-temporal continuum he insisted he was. Not just the Old Norse *boli*, from whence *bull* and *bollix*, but such wonderous connections with the world as the *bole* of a tree; with *boulder*; with *bowl*; with *bulwark*; with *bold*; even with *baleen*.

Wynn Bullock was a luminous man, with a windy, cloudy, lovely nature. I don't forget my times with him along the Big Sur Coast in the 1950s and 1960s. Very special times—it seemed that the photographers at work on those sacred places (Wild Cat Creek, Point Lobos, the Highlands, Tassajara, Carmel Valley, Monterey) whistled Sibelius's *Oceanides* as they made images.

I am one of Wynn's opposites—a poet of fact and of found objects, who is earthy, mundane, and pedestrian—and so maybe that gives me a chance to celebrate him in a way that most others would not. It allows me to be very moved by a list of plates in Wynn's forthcoming book, *The Photograph As Symbol* (The Artichoke Press, 1976):

1. Rock, 1973
2. Wood, 1972
3. Tree Trunk, 1972
4. Wood, 1973

5. Wood, 1971
6. Wood, 1973.

When I wrote about Wynn Bullock for *Aperture* in 1961 ("The Eyes of 3 Phantasts: Laughlin, Sommer, Bullock") I invoked the poetic Objectivists and that old spouting whale, Henry James. I'll do so again.

George Oppen is on my mind, because of a passage in Hugh Kenner's *A Homemade World* (Knopf, 1975). "The little words that I like so much," said Oppen, "like 'tree,' 'hill,' and so on, are I suppose, just as much a taxonomy as the more elaborate words." It is cognate to Mallarmé's famous realization that nothing is producible of which we can say *flower* is the name: "I say, 'a flower,' and musically, out of oblivion, there arises that one that has eluded all bouquets." That the word, not anything the word is tied to, is the only substantiality to be discovered in a poem gave Mallarmé ecstatic shivers; to command words' potencies was to oversee magic; to let them take the initiative was to set in motion glitterings "like a trail of fire upon precious stones." Oppen prefers to note that whatever words may be, men cannot survive without them. "They're categories, concepts, classes, things we invent for ourselves. Nevertheless, there are certain ones without which we really are unable to exist." Is the concept of humanity valid, he invites us to ask, or is it simply a "word"? "All the little nouns are the ones that I like most, the deer, the sun, and so on. You say these perfectly little words and you're asserting that the sun is ninety-three million miles away, and that there is shade because of shadows, and more, who knows?"

The word is the word; the thing is the thing. But what about that dream Charles Olson had, where Pound's shade appeared and said: "Let the song lie in the thing!" Our selves are like the famous Cloud of Unknowing, full of music and light. It's futile to try to put pins in a cloud, but here are the places—for me—where Wynn Bullock gets closest to the revealed mysteries in his prints:

To begin with I distinguish the difference between 'seeing' and 'perceiving.' 'Seeing' is a simple almost automatic act and not to be confused with perceiving.

For the photographer, things perceived are primary.

— a universe not only greater and more mysterious than I think it is, but greater and more mysterious than I *can* think it is . . .

Too much emphasis is placed on external physical qualities of objects. An object is actually a visual *or* mental concept. It has no independent physical existence. Only events exist.

When I feel a rock is as much a miracle as a man, then I feel in touch with the universe. Not the object rock, not the form rock, but the light that is the rock.

There as the frontispiece of the book on Bullock, *Photography, A Way of Life* (Morgan & Morgan, Inc., 1973), is a reproduction of a print, *Half an Apple*, 1953. In truth I relish it more than any artist's semantics. It is the veritable Apple of the Eye, the globular apple-like pupil that sees what we cherish. And surely it is Wynn Bullock's insistence as a photographer that we must learn to read what our eyes show us. For him such learning is like the scales a pianist practises: the eyes, like fingers, are subtle, are limber, because they have learned how not just to see, but to go on seeing. Wynn, the man, has left us, but the body of his photographic work is there for nourishment. We will make of the legacy what love permits us. Henry James was used to having the last word. It is a pleasure to give him his due: "It may often remind one of the wonderful soil of California, which is nothing when left to itself and the fine weather, but becomes everything conceivable under the rainfall."

the redwood
is 'dead';

the horsetails
'live on'. . .

Highlands, North Carolina 1976

Aaron Siskind at 75

I was beginning to write a few words about Aaron Siskind at seventy-five when the phone rang. On the other end was that nonpareil typographer and designer from Taloga, Oklahoma, Alvin Doyle Moore. He said: "I'll tell you something you don't know. Art Sinsabaugh tells me that Siskind had no running water in his darkroom in Chicago. . . . And I said to Art, 'That just means that if you're really good, you can do it anywhere—even on the ground with a stick.' "

I flew into Kennedy from Heathrow on last December 3, just in order to join a distinguished company in toasting Aaron with champagne at midnight: it would be his seventy-fifth birthday. I had not seen him in ten years, not since Chicago. Older, certainly, with a bit of Buddhistic paunch, but much the same man I had come to revere back in 1951 at Black Mountain College.

Then, he was simply introduced to me as a friend of Harry Callahan's from New York; an associate of the painters Kline and de Kooning and the abstract expressionists. Over the summer I had much of his counsel in the darkroom as he taught me the rudiments of what to do with a Rollei. And those of us fortunate to be in nether Buncombe County, North Carolina, then (Charles Olson, Dan Rice, Lou Harrison, Joel Oppenheimer, Fielding Dawson, Ben Shahn, Katherine Litz, Francine du Plessix Gray, to name a few) spent many a long evening down at Ma Peak's Tavern, three miles from the college, drinking beer and listening to the lore that Siskind and Callahan commanded between them. Edward Dahlberg once said: "Literature is the way we ripen ourselves by conversation." The beer joint in Hicksville, USA, should never be underestimated. You would not have done better at the Deux Magots or the Café Flore in Paris that summer. And I somehow doubt that you would have found Brassaï and Cartier-Bresson there amidst the too-many tourists. Besides, in Siskind and Callahan, we had two American

92

pioneers who were photographing Chicago, Martha's Vineyard, and Harlan County, Kentucky, in ways no one had seen before. Were they not precisely on another Black Mountain poet's wavelength?

All my favorite avuncular adjectives trot forth when I think about (i.e., have feelings about) Aaron: kindly, astute, enthusiastic, loyal, masterly. He wears his years more lightly than in the SX-70 snaps I did of him that midnight where he looks like the oldest tragedian of the Yiddish theater—"Jesus, you think I'm mellow? I'm so mellow I'm rotten!"

As for the exhibition of work from 1976 and 1977 that Light Gallery put on to mark Siskind's birthday, what is there to say except that it was one of the great, ennobling, wondrous things I have ever seen. You could spend hours, days, or years in front of any particular print getting its savor, fathoming how a man's unique feelings can be limned on walls and in stones, from Nantucket to Rome to Lima to Paris. A show so good one can hardly bear to look at it. I wrote down *Peru 349, Peru 307, Peru 210, Peru 208, Peru 465; Paris 50; Senagalia 28;* and the set of nine prints from Cusco—those are quite enough in my three days. There have been few photographers in the history of the craft with equal gifts, with such pictorial quality from one work to another over the decades. If we go to painting, there is Pierre Bonnard, conspicuously—and Vuillard. And Monet, at Giverny. In America, one thinks of Grant Wood and Richard Diebenkorn; well, *I* think of Wood and Diebenkorn—you're on your own to find the odd pairings.

I've stuck to the adjectives of old-fashioned poetical virtue to write of Aaron Siskind. Except for one or two pieces by Tom Hess, most magazine writing about Siskind has been cold and technocratic. You know the words: *anthropomorphic, animistic, typology, methodology, perceptual ambiguity*—about as welcome as a Christmas card from the IRS or another Committee to Reelect Richard Nixon. Recall that Siskind and Franz Kline spoke of "dancing" and of delight. "Is not the aesthetic optimum order with the tensions continuing?" asks Siskind, with precisely the warm linguistic savvy you'd expect.

Seventy-five and better than ever. "Why not?" he asks. "What else have I got to do?"

Highlands, North Carolina 1978

The Shadow of His Equipage

24

Writing notes for this essay, I thought: I will now command a pellucid American idiom. I will write about Clarence John Laughlin with the startling clarity of a certain ice-water spring I know on the flanks of Mt. Le Conte in the Great Smoky Mountains. But, it can't be done. Clarence is all phantasmagoria and gumbo—Archimboldo, *The Invasion of the Body Snatchers*, Grandville, Belle Grove Plantation, the Wizard of Oz, and skillet cornbread. *Bizarrerie* is what you're having for dinner. Be my guest; eat what you like and leave the rest for Genius Loci.

Item: *People to Talk About the Next Time I See Clarence*: Virgil Finlay, Ralph Eugene Meatyard, Sergei Rachmaninoff, Boosie Jackson, Abe Merritt, Henry Dorsey, Atget, Robert Barlow, Simon Cutts, Bill Brandt, Carlos Toadvine, Balthus, Jess Collins, Enid Foster, Henry Clews, Edgar Tolson, Hans Bellmer, Lord Berners, Frederick Sommer, James McGarrell, Redon, Richard Dadd, Russell Edson, Scott Joplin, Joe Tilson, Bart Parker, Beatrix Potter, Clarence Schmidt, Baron Corvo, Baron Von Gloeden, Baron Von Pluschow, Robert Barnes, John Furnival, Ivan Albright, Mervyn Peake, Gallé, Mackintosh, Robert E. Howard, Geoffrey Grigson, Barbara Jones, Guy Mendes, James Broughton, Squire Waterton, Raymond Isidore, Delius, William Hope Hodgson, Magritte, William Burges, Count Orsini, L. Frank Baum . . .

Item: *Places to Talk About the Next Time I See Clarence*: The Villa Lante; La Maison de Picassiette; Grandpa Bissett's Shell-Garden; the Park of Monsters at Bomarzo; Levens Hall; the Pleasure Ground at Stourhead; Koerner's Folly; the Watts Chapel at Compton, Surrey; the Dentist's Junkheap at Rockingham, North Carolina; the house covered with 20,000 rubber boots in Sacramento; Olana; Seizincote; the Royal Pavilion; the Garden of Eden (where was it: Tarzan, Texas?); the Henge at Roswell; Bibleland USA; the Blocher Tomb; Carnac; Castello Balduino at Montaldo di Pavia . . .

94

Clarence John Laughlin was born in Lake Charles, Louisiana, in 1905 and later lived on a plantation near New Iberia. He remains as volatile as Tabasco sauce, walks twice as fast as anyone else on earth, and looks like Frank Lloyd Wright with just enough of the ventriloquist's dummy in *Dead of Night* to make it spooky. For there is certainly something preternatural about Clarence and his ability to unearth mysteries with his camera. I feel confident that you could head CJL down that street of drab, ordinary, public housing in Chartres, and his psychic antennae, like a dowser's rod, would point to La Maison de Picassiette, whose mosaic'd wonders are hidden from plain view.

He is the Master of Ignored Ghastliness, of the Eldritch, the Psychopompous, the Metamorphic, the Mephitic, the Fearsome, and now and then of Trumpery and the Fulsome. Purists and the mean in spirit have regarded him with disdain for almost forty years and have ignored him as being in the same league as Carmen Cavallero, "The Poet of the Piano." Well, if you're going to put titles like "Starlight in Steel" and "And Tell of Time . . . Cobwebbed Time" and "The Vials of Wrath Have Opened," then you're going to have trouble. No matter.

The crux is this: Clarence John Laughlin has the right to be as "corny," as cosmic, as bumptious and excessive as he likes. A black writer commented recently that most American white folks were a bunch of nobodies trying to be somebodies. *Clarence is Clarence.* Amen. There is no one else in the history of photography who has his feeling for the animate life of architecture. No one else has given us records of "Old Milwaukee Re-Discovered," of Victorian Chicago ("Phoenix Re-Arisen"), of Salt Lake City, Lake Geneva, Eureka, Los Angeles, St. Louis, Memphis, Little Rock, Minneapolis, San Jose, San Francisco, San Antonio, Galveston, Cripple Creek, and castles in north Texas; of the Zenon Trudeau House, Ellerslie Plantation, Belle Grove, Afton Villa, Windsor Plantation; and, above all, of the buildings of New Orleans and the rural cemeteries of Louisiana. When Laughlin works on Chicago, you don't just get the Rookery Building, you get the mansion of "Bet-A-Million" Gates on South Michigan; you get Sullivan's Holy Trinity Russian Orthodox Church; you get the John G. Shedd mansion, and the Samuel Nickerson house with the great Tiffany glass dome. There have been over 200 exhibitions of his work, and there are now over 17,000 cut-film negatives.

Baudelaire, writing of Edgar Allan Poe, remarks "Nature makes a point of bestowing a special vigor of temperament upon those of whom she expects great things, just as she gives a rugged vitality to those trees whose function it is to symbolize grief and mourning." This immediately made me think of Clarence John Laughlin, amazing the inhabitants as he pushed his wheelbarrow full of view cameras and film through the streets of Paris at fifteen miles per hour, headed for the next miracle of the Art Nouveau or the Moreau Museum. And that makes me think of le Facteur Cheval and his legendary *brouette* (wheelbarrow), filled with suggestive stones, headed back up the lane in Hauterives for the next additions to his Ideal Dream Palace. Clarence could have built the *Palais Idéal* twice as fast as the Postman. A man who is All Eyes ("and two feet that couldn't be beat," as Jelly Roll Morton used to say)—if you get in the way of the Vision, the wheelbarrow runs over your foot.

Laughlin belongs to that breed of men who live in shells as resolutely as the tortoise. Who are they? Hermits, on the whole. The one at Stourhead in Wiltshire lost his job because he got caught sneaking out to the pub. Sylvester Houédard, the Benedictine monk of Prinknash Abbey, is a current anchorite. No one can imagine Sylvester making his way in the trackless world. William Blake said to someone: "I live in a hole here, but God has a beautiful mansion for me elsewhere." Edward Dahlberg lives in miserly tenement rooms, out of misanthropy, bile, and necessity. Kenneth Patchen always lived in a Walt-Disney-enchanted wood, surrounded by milkmaids and visionary emblems. He was caged by spinal injuries like a heavy cat. Ian Hamilton Finlay lives in the Pentland Hills; his agoraphobia keeps him always at home or fishing when it gets dusk in a loch of his own making near the house. Laughlin is afraid to leave his attic in the Upper Pontalba Apartment Building on Jackson Square in New Orleans—fire might destroy the negatives and his library. H. P. Lovecraft only went out at night. But, he had to be especially careful, for if it was too cold in the streets of Providence, he might faint. All these men are burrowers, scratching further and further inside themselves, for whom the world at large is a terrible menace.

In all the time I have been looking at Laughlin's photographs (I acquired *Ghosts Along the Mississippi* in 1948 and met Clarence in 1958 in New York), I have hardly ever read, or heard, or written a sentence on his work that bears notice. I still think the best statement was a very brief one written by Weeks Hall in New Iberia, Louisiana, in 1941. Weeks was an artist of the same plantation-house milieu as Clarence John Laughlin. He had for his carapace one of the great architectural masterpieces of the United States: The Shadows-on-the-Teche. To save his house from being turned into the asphalt parking lot in front of some tax-shelter shopping center, Weeks sacrificed his public life and his career. He was the last member of his family and he lived long enough to insure the preservation of The Shadows by the National Trust. You can get a glimpse of Weeks Hall in Henry Miller's *The Air-Conditioned Nightmare*, 1945.

Weeks was an aristocrat, an excessive, a man with friends like Arthur B. Carles, Sherwood Anderson, and Gertrude Stein. He called himself the Last of the Nigger-Lovers. He hated modern, oil-producing, racist Louisiana, so he retired behind his cane fence and the live oaks and stood guard in his undershorts, with his cane and his bottle of brandy. "Get out of here, you goddamn silly women," he'd yell as another busload of garden-club ladies would rattle the gate and try to violate his privacy. He cared for no one local except his two black manservants, Clement and Raymond. However, he still bore affection for Bunk Johnson, the cornetist, who had worked in the gardens at The Shadows before Bill Russell bought him the famous false teeth and lured him back to music and fame up North in his old age. Weeks would sip his drink up on the second-story balcony. Bunk would sneak his out there in the boxwoods while he cut and trimmed. "Play your horn, Bunk!" It is quite a vision to imagine—these two lonely old men reeling around to tunes like "Panama" and "That's A-Plenty" under the Spanish mosses of that dark green, sacred place. It was Weeks who got the local priest to bury Bunk secretly in the Hall family plot. Bunk had said to him: "Mr. Weeks, please don't let them bury me with them field-niggers—I couldn't stand the cane dust and mule farts."

Maybe I shouldn't go on so about Weeks Hall, but there is a story to be told and nobody seems to tell it. Somewhere in my things are many hours of tape, which unreeled as we sat in the night on the balcony at The Shadows with little silver cups of coffee, with crystal sugar, drinking brandy. He was a glorious raconteur and he had more insight into Clarence John Laughlin than anyone:

> The direction of his talent has fortunately been succored by its environment. His city wears an air, confirmed and expressed by its Carnival, of fantasy sobered always by thoughts of mortality. His New Orleans is also the Paris of Meryon, the Bermuda of *The Tempest*, and the Brussels of Ensor. His achievement consists in the fact that these prints are *not* photographs of these places and these things, but are photographed symbols of his thoughts about them. . . .
>
> The text of most essays on photographers are a waste of everybody's time. . . . There is nothing, under present conditions, that can be more easily and exactly reproduced than a technically good black-and-white photograph, and it is utter rot to burden those interested in them with irrelevant biographical trivia and pet long-winded theory. Other photographers are interested only in mechanical procedure in so far as the maker of the prints explains what creative genesis led up to the use of that procedure. Prints themselves are what count. So, enjoyment must be in seeing; and, as enjoyment must be the result of experience, it is no more possible to substitute a dozen paragraphs for that experience than it is possible to substitute the text of Brillat-Savarin for a well-roasted capon.

That is expressed with great charm, with great accuracy. Since I am now sitting on an Umbrian hillside, the best thing I can offer Weeks amongst the

Shades is a glass or two of red Torgiano. He was a man who cared about the best a place could produce. So, of course, he recognized Laughlin's visionary talent and knew what had nourished it in those bayous so far from the outside world.

Clarence has been quite frank in saying that he thinks I will misrepresent his true position in this discursive introduction of mine. He also suspects that *Aperture* will err in its selection of the photographs for its monograph on him. "I especially want it made clear that I am an *extreme romanticist*—and I don't want to be presented as some kind of goddammed up-to-the-minute version of a semi-abstract photographer." No fear, Clarence, no fear.

CJL's worry is that nobody in life *sees* what he's up to. He, being All Eyes, is surrounded by sightless, pathetic materialists and abstractionists *who do not understand.* Though I venture to think he's wrong, he's the guy who has had to work in a quagmire for forty years, with never enough space, never enough time, never enough money, and never enough serious interest. The brewery next door to his apartment shakes the building; he has to carry developing trays on a bus across New Orleans and use a borrowed darkroom; the grant he finally got after years of begging was 25 percent of what was really needed to do the work. And so he writes statements like "The Personal Eye" and "The Camera As a Third Eye," in which he talks about "the mystery of time, the magic of light, the enigma of reality"—precisely those abstractions that have nothing to tell us of the luminous, exact images that he alone gives us. Kenneth Patchen used to feel the same way. Here he was, the authentic W. Blake of Niles, Ohio, and none of the establishment lunkheads knew it. Then he'd invent terrible blurbs by people from nether Belgium with names like Pierre-Henri Charcuterie that said: "This sad and gentle hermit of the American Desert," and so on and so on.

May Zoroaster and Daguerre keep me from avuncular chiding that hardly becomes one of my years. CJL deserves to be named a national treasure, for who has done more to record and salvage and cherish an America that has almost been destroyed in one generation? I think he works harder, against more stupid obstacles, than any artist I have ever met. The blind spot of this man, who is All Eyes, is that he won't trust us. It's hard on one's vanity to be around Clarence. I'd known him more than ten years and one night after a poetry reading in London he said, blandly, "I hadn't realized you were a serious poet." There's not a malicious bone in the man, so you can't be offended, just bemused. You can invite Clarence to a particularly good dinner at a friend's who prides herself on her clarets. Clarence will say: "I hope you don't mind if I put sugar in the wine? I was brought up on a plantation in Louisiana where we drank blackberry wine and that's the way I like it." All one can do is say: "Why, of course, Clarence, have two spoonfuls if you care to." I'm not telling these tales out of spite, but to indicate that CJL has work to do and his own notions. He is the despair of cooks on an international level. Abstract photographers have been known to flee Chicago when they heard he was coming in by train.

All Eyes, devoted to the visions. Clarence has no vanity and this is what allows one to remember to surrender one's own for a while. You don't breakfast at Brennan's when you visit CJL's attic suite atop the Pontalba in the Vieux Carré. Once a week Clarence buys a box of cornflakes, a carton of milk, some sugar, and some tea bags. Tea is made by putting a tea bag in a cracked white mug under the hot-water tap. Lunch is a poorboy sandwich from the market. Dinner isn't Galatoire's. It's another poorboy sandwich, if he remembers to bother, as he prowls through his library in search of an image by Bresdin or Ernst.

A green corduroy jacket is as familiar to CJL's friends as the Postman Cheval's wheelbarrow that he worked with on the Dream Palace for twenty-seven years, and some walking shorts that allow Clarence to propel himself down the yellow brick roads of the earth at speeds previously unimagined. Clarence has things to see and work to do. Hang in with him, or give up in despair. "That poets [using the word comprehensively as including artists in general] are a *genus irritable* is well understood." Baudelaire, on Poe, again. "The poetical irritability has no reference to 'temper' in the vulgar sense, but merely to a more than usual clear-sightedness in respect to wrong, this clear-sightedness being nothing more than a corollary from a vivid perception of right—of justice—of proportion." Why spend money on food and drink when there are remaindered copies of a book on Redon you could buy up and present to many friends?

You can spend four days with CJL in the famous attic and only get to see seven prints. Each one is likely to require hours of briefing as Clarence clutches it to his bosom, smiles patiently, and explains that the mysteries are about to be revealed at long last. I once heard him go through his spiel in New York City for seven nights running. The invention of the tape recorder was unnecessary. Not a note, or a nuance, or an aside missed or misplaced. "I call this one: 'Feast of the Dead in the House of Iron Beyond the Gardens of Ultima Thule.' " I keep telling these stories both as a warning and as a request for a modicum of charity. Clarence is a shy man, over and over forced to leave his shell behind him and to sing for his supper. The public side of him can be incredibly overweening, if you insist. Us intellectuals mostly smile and roll our eyes and implore: "Clarence, *please,* may we see the photographs?" The answer is no. You are not going to change CJL one iota. You're not going to get Ivan Albright to title his pictures like Josef Albers; or get Edward Dahlberg to eat tinned ham; or CJL to drink Sancerre Sauvignon. One either learns to laugh at oneself and at one's friends, or the world is a hideous place, full of affronts, in which one is never comfortable. Laughlin's photographs—even the ones I consider the worst, with the veiled figures and the snake oil—are part of congeries—a world in which he must be allowed his head and his reach.

Debussy asked Satie after the première of *La Mer* how he liked it. The first part is titled "From Dawn to Noon on the Sea." Satie replied: "I liked the bit about quarter to eleven." Satie was another "funny" man, with his twelve velvet suits and his white celluloid collars and a pile of unopened mail under his bed of twenty years' duration. But Milhaud and Poulenc and Debussy and Ravel loved the music. A man who has done as much great work as Clarence John Laughlin deserves our respect, our love, and our indulgence. Who are we, who don't have such distinguished and memorable foibles, and hardly one-tenth of his accomplishments? Think of the odds he has fought against—a lotus-eating city with only Lafcadio Hearn and Louis Moreau Gottschalk to lend it high-culture distinctions before CJL. The name *Gottschalk* has currency today only because it is the name of a department store. Since Laughlin has been the recipient of hardly any local attention, for decades, it's not surprising that he wouldn't bother to know the difference between Al Hirt and Kid Thomas Valentine. (I first went to New Orleans in 1949 to hear George Lewis, not to seek out the mysterious CJL.) You'd need a skin as thick as a carapace to survive in that Delta miasma. Bruckner got so addled and lonely amidst the baroque backwaters of St. Florian's abbey that he began counting leaves on the linden trees. Clarence gets on the local bus named Desire and goes across town to see the latest double bill of grade-Z horror films, hoping against hope for the fifteen seconds of visual magic that only he will recognize for what it is. What lengths he goes to. Not us folks— we who know so damn much and have stopped looking for anything beyond the American dream of color television, new money, and the violence it takes to make it.

Since Charles Baudelaire was one of CJL's starting points, back in the 1920s, I thought all kinds of light might be shed if I ransacked the Frenchman for his insights into the imagination. Not particularly. True, one will find a few sentences like the following: "The whole visible universe is but a store-house of images and signs to which the imagination will give a relative place and value; it is a sort of pasture which the imagination must digest and transform. All the faculties of the human soul must be abandoned to the imagination, which puts them in requisition all at once." But then, one will encounter the critic of the *Salon of 1859* fulminating against the dread craze, Photography:

> Let it rescue from oblivion those tumbling ruins, those books, prints and manuscripts, which time is devouring, precious things whose form is dissolving and which demand a place in the archives of our memory—it

will be thanked and applauded. But if it be allowed to encroach upon the domain of the impalpable and the imaginary, upon anything whose value depends solely upon the addition of something of a man's soul, then it will be so much the worse for us. . . . Each day art further diminishes its self-respect by bowing down before external reality; each day the painter becomes more and more given to painting not what he dreams but what he sees. Nevertheless *it is a happiness to dream,* and it used to be a glory to express what one dreamt.

How odd it seems, now, for Baudelaire to be so blind to the "mechanical" similarities between a piece of wood with animal hairs clustered at one end to hold pigments, and held in the hand; and a contraption of wood, metal, and glass, held in the hand, to focus light for things without or things within the artist's imagination.

Laughlin's best statement is: "The limitations of photography are nothing more than the limitations of photographers."

Baudelaire's: "Others enough will speak the jargon of the studio and will exhibit *themselves* to the detriment of the *pictures.* In many cases erudition seems to me to be a childish thing and but little revealing of its true nature. I would find it only too easy to discourse subtly upon symmetrical or balanced composition, upon tonal equipoise, upon warmth and coldness of tones, etc. O Vanity! I choose instead to speak in the name of feeling, of morality and of pleasure. And I hope that a few people who are learned without pedantry will find my *ignorance* to their liking."

Poe, in "Ligeia," quotes Bacon: "There is no exquisite beauty without some *strangeness* in the proportion." This, at last, is the final rallying cry of the Romantics. Mae West, oracular to the end, would dare to say it a little too amusingly to suit Clarence, when she says to her dwarf: "Honey, you ain't seen nuthin' yet!" Where the Lady stops, nobody knows. Give Clarence John Laughlin an object—the chances are exactly the same. It's a brand new ball game, fans, and we're going into extra innings.

Polgeto, Umbertide, Perugia 1973

"They All Want to Go and Dress Up"

Hamlin Garland once quoted Doris Ulmann's remark (above) and went on to say: "It is not an easy task to induce a farmer's wife to have her picture taken in her kitchen gown peeling potatoes." It is precisely this ability to capture the old farmland-potato style—earthy, yet savory—that distinguishes the Ulmann photographs of Appalachia and puts them in the realist tradition—a tradition, apparently, known to almost no photographer of the present, let it be said. Ever since Mnemosyne and the Muses became a rock-group franchise and moved into a commune near Tabula Rasa, Arkansas, the profession includes multitudes of shysters. However, we will certainly learn to go to Doris Ulmann's hundreds of prints of the southern Appalachians at their date in history (the late 1920s and early 1930s) as we have learned to go to John Jacob Niles for his discoveries of mountain folk-ballad. It is an apt thing, that they were traveling companions. Miss Ulmann gives us a dated record of a particular home-place; she does so with sufficient art that Julia Cameron, Alvin Langdon Coburn, Atget, and Lartigue are some of the names with whom I would like to link her. I'd like to be at dinner with all of them one evening in Viper, Kentucky—with plenty of applejack, plenty of Maker's Mark, plenty of Johnny Niles's home-cured ham, plenty of beaten biscuits. I doubt that the talk would get very loud. Nobody but me would bring up topics from the dark side of rustication, like Marx's notion of the idiocy of rural life; or, that chilling sentence from James Dickey's novel, *Deliverance*: "There is always something wrong with people in the country."

Doris Ulmann said: "I have been more deeply moved by some of my mountaineers than by any literary person. A face that has the marks of having lived intensely, that expresses some phase of life, some dominant quality or intellectual power, constitutes for me an interesting face. For this reason the face of an older person, perhaps not beautiful in the strictest sense, is usually more appealing than the face of a younger person who has scarcely been touched by life."

It is useful to compare Miss Ulmann's straight forward portraiture and its somewhat wistful tone of reverie with what came immediately after her— the Farm Security Administration, Roy Stryker, Walker Evans, et al. She is not about to give us "the dream in the peasant's bent shoulders." A person of her alien refinement, photographing proud country people, would have considered that an invasion of privacy. One kind of vision should not obliterate another, meaning: the art of the quiet is no less than public yelling and propaganda. Most of the persons in the Ulmann photographs—for all their character and handicraft—are "sociologically redundant," but that is hardly the point. It is sad to think of them as statistics in some icy governmental report on poverty pockets. Doris Ulmann wanted the photographs to show the existence of a rural handicraft movement and to suggest that a number of mountain men and women could get by on their own with a market for their goods. She said to John Jacob Niles, "Johnny, you're a poet, you don't need much. Poets don't need much. If you overpay them they stop being poets." Underpay a craftsman and a poet, the result is the same: a vestigial occupation, a disappearing people, scorned by the middle class as hillbillies and as freaks.

Dentdale, Cumbria 1971

With George and Ashley, on the Crags

26

George and Ashley Abraham, the "Keswick Brothers," were born into an established photographic family in the English Lake District. They were there at the infancy of British rock climbing and were protégés of the great man of the 1890s, Owen Glynne Jones, an academic who taught physics at the City of London School. He was the hard man, the tiger of the sporting art. He wrote: "A line must be drawn somewhere to separate the possible from the impossible, and some try to draw it by their own experience."

A studio portrait of George and Ashley in the late 1930s when their hard climbing days were over shows George standing, so bandy-legged that the family always said he couldn't stop a pig in a blind alley. Ashley is seated, indicating his ample girth, over fifteen stone, which he moved about the crags with remarkable ease and surety.

Derek Smith, who organized an exhibition of the Keswick Brothers' photographs at the Brewery Art Centre in Kendal, Cumbria, writes effectively in a letter of the superb achievement of the Abrahams; i.e., the simple fact of taking the photographs:

> With fully loaded darkslides the Abraham wholeplate kit weighed in at 22 pounds. On the midpoint of Great Gable's Abbey Buttress it regularly turned into a monster 3000 feet up, on a path termed v. diff in climber's jargon, with a ledge two feet wide to support the tripod. The climbing camera was re-discovered recently, immaculate, and now rests at the Wastwater Hotel, the base for the Brothers' cherished Great Gable ascents. In their hands it survived forty years, rendering the quality of light that filters through patchy rain clouds into the surfaces of damp rock. It had identified, and at the same time celebrated, the activities of the men in tweeds with nothing between them and eternity but physical effort, intense calculation, and a frail, more often than not, useless rope. . . . Fine pictures and second rate pictures were swiftly identified, but in their

104

making a mere knife edge difference in decision and action on the machine conspires to separate the two. Creating the revered kind of picture is not the elusive, mysterious art many claimed it to be. Fine pictures like these evolve naturally out of a mature knowledge of what lies in front of the lens, fused with affection. For the Abrahams, this sensibility was acquired through the direct experience of climbing, and their photographs, both fine and eminently popular, relate something of their thrill at reaching high and difficult places.

Though crawling with rock climbers and fell wanderers and nature lovers for 150 years, the Lake District has not crawled with major artists with brush or camera. Turner and Cotman spent little time there. Ruskin left us his curious, introspective drawings of stones and boulders. And you would hardly suspect that Pigling Bland might have had to cross the high fells when escaping the coziness of the nursery world of Beatrix Potter at Near Sawrey. What visions we have in our heads come mostly from the Wordsworths and from S. T. Coleridge. Thus, the archive of the Abraham Brothers is doubly important. Nowhere else do we have such evocation of the quality of the crags and the exhilaration of the sport of rock climbing.

Chester, Massachusetts 1981

27

Carte de Visite Photographique Pinned Too Late on His Cottage Door, for Frank Meadow Sutcliffe Now in Heaven Eating Raspberries in the Garden at Carr Hill

"As Ruskin has written about this, I won't say any more"—except there is no Ruskin in this case. The mythical quotation would be on the back of a post card from a young English miss on first viewing San Marco, Venezia, on the Grand Tour.

Frank Meadow Sutcliffe (1853–1941), of Headingley, Leeds, the West Riding of Yorkshire, England. In the Gernsheims' *Concise History of Photography,* information about Sutcliffe is concise indeed. He is noted twice as one of the naturalistic disciples of Dr. Peter Emerson.

Why do we still know so little of Sutcliffe (or of P. H. Emerson, for that matter)? Why did the savants and/or dealers put all their money on Rodin for three generations and ignore the unique and beautiful Medardo Rosso. Only through the exhibition "Pioneers of Modern Sculpture," organized by the Arts Council of Great Britain at the Hayward Gallery, London, 1973, could we see what we had been missing; one of the two or three finest sculptors since the Renaissance.

The industrial West Riding of Yorkshire was hardly an oasis on the grand tour in the middle of the nineteenth century. Yet, these dales of the rivers Aire and Wharfe produced not only satanic energy and work from ordinary folk, but also a few artists of unique imagination: Frederick Delius, Frank Meadow Sutcliffe, and J. Atkinson Grimshaw. (There will be other names, which Ignorance will choose to ignore.)

Delius we know—some do, at least—because he became an internationalist: a German heritage, some time in Florida, some time in Norway with Grieg, years in Berlin, and many final years at Grez-sur-Loing in France. Yet, the quintessential English musician. The atmosphere of Ilkley Moor, the "soughing of the wind," is in *all* his music.

For Atkinson Grimshaw, you'd best start in the City Gallery in Leeds and look at *The Old Mill: Audby,* a picture vaguely related to the Pre-

Raphaelite Brotherhood, but as eccentric and private as those by Richard Dadd. A revelation!

For Sutcliffe, you have to go to the coastal holiday and fishing town of Whitby. "This decrepit and smelly old town," is one description of it. But, not the way Sutcliffe saw it: "England without Yorkshire would be nowhere, and the world without England might just as well give up the trouble of turning on its axis." (Which recalls, with amusement, Novalis's remark: "Not only is England an island but so is every Englishman.")

Sutcliffe was one of these homely, symbiotic creatures who stayed put—at the bottom of the Esk Valley, where it flowed into the North Sea, and where the sea blew its fury against the land to its west. He called himself "The Fixed Photographer" and "The Limpet"—a limpet being a gastropod mollusc with a tent-shaped shell, adhering tightly to rocks. Mr. Sutcliffe had to spend ruinous decades telling kiddies to smile and have their mums wipe bits of Whitby Rock off their sticky faces. Portrait photography supported him and his large family. His "real" photographs did not compete in the marketplace. Now and then they'd go off to exhibitions in distant cities and win prizes. The odd view of the backsides of twelve fisher-boys leaning over a jetty wall, called *Stern Realities*, got shown in a Parisian salon as *Triste Réalité*. (Perhaps another excellent reason for staying home and avoiding the *bizarrerie* of alien art lovers.)

The best way to go to Whitby is to walk there. First, go to Helmsley on the edge of the North York Moors National Park. Then walk "The Cleveland Way" (101 miles to Filey, down the coast below Whitby). Or, walk the Cleveland Hills, then along "The Lyke Wake Walk" about to Goathland (in order to catch a glimpse of the three spectral white radomes of the Fylingdales Early Warning Station); then backtrack and drop down into Sutcliffe's Glaisedale, and, finally, down the Esk to Whitby. The best time is early September, when the heather moors are in flower and many of the bingo-maniacs have left town. Before trekking, stay at the Feversham Arms in Helmsley; and dine very well at the Star in neighboring Harome. Then a week on your feet, minus the cumbersome apparatus and wet plates the frail Sutcliffe had to carry.

FMS: "If you wish for pictures to please yourself and three or four of your friends, you will take no notice of the weather, nor the wise people, but will stroll around, seeking your prey in fine weather and foul."

FMS: "Fog in these islands is absolutely indispensable."

If you look at the British heavens long enough, you realize that Turner, Palmer, Cotman, Constable, Coburn, and Sutcliffe were not exactly making it up. And Yorkshire, with its crypto-Texan spaciousness, is the most special case of all. It is the home of the *yorker*, that nebulous and eldritch weapon in the arsenal of the fast-bowler in cricket. Rather like the *knuckler* or the *spitter,* it floats up in your face and falls off a table. Fred Truman, a current master of the craft of the yorker, says it is made possible only because of the dark backgrounds of the vicinity and the passing clouds. N. B.: Frank Meadow Sutcliffe was born at Headingly, the home of the Yorkshire Cricket Club!

So, Sutcliffe bided his time: "If we can only get what anyone can get at any time, our labour is wasted."

People used to complain that all he took pictures of were fisher-folk and remote, unspectacular dales. Perhaps they would complain even more now. Konrad Lorenz makes the point in a new little essay, "Civilized Man's Eight Deadly Sins": "One of the worst effects of haste, or of the fear engendered by it, is the apparent inability of modern man to spend even the shortest time alone. He anxiously avoids every possibility of self-communication or meditation, as though he feared that reflection might present him with a ghastly self-portrait, such as that of Dorian Gray."

Naturally, I have a mind that wanders as my steps do, so I like to think on peregrinating feet. I am, thus, reminded of some of the kinsmen of an artist like Frank Sutcliffe. For instance: Cézanne, and a lifetime devoted to painting those blessed and/or cursed apples. D. H. Lawrence was remarkably acute to say somewhere that it took Cézanne thirty years to roll the apple away from the mouth of the tomb and give it afterlife.

And what about old Steichen and that shadbush tree of his he devoted those years to in all weathers, lights, and seasons? Or the photographer in Japan—whose name is not at hand—who only makes images of Fujiyama? I have a friend in North Carolina, the Reverend Rufus Morgan, who has climbed Mount Le Conte in the Great Smokies over 150 times. Now eighty-eight years young and almost blind, he continues climbing, realizing that he still does not "know" the mountain except on 150 of its different instances under the sun.

"Be in the world—but not *of* it," said Melville.

And two more keys to the Sutcliffe vision. I continually *quote,* because Goethe knew what he was talking about when he said: "The Truth was known already, long ago." It is up to us to remember it; and for me to do the responsive patchwork in order to make you keen to see Sutcliffe's world at Whitby—as you might wish to visit Point Lobos after the Westons or Canyon de Chelly after Timothy O'Sullivan and William Current; or, Walden Pond.

So, one key: Thoreau. I use a journal entry of his, June 6, 1857, in a poem of mine:

  a year is made up of a certain series
  and number of sensations and thoughts
  which have their language in nature . . .

now I am ice, now
I am sorrel.

Second key: John Ruskin (who knew Sutcliffe's work, admired it, and invited FMS to Brantwood in the Lakes), writing on July 30, 1847, in Warwickshire: "I was struck, as I walked back, by the starry groups of plantain with a little mixed clover, edging the footpath, covered with dust so as to take off its green. The plantain seeds standing up, gave it relief; it might have been turned into bronze on the instant, and put Ghiberti to shame."

Sutcliffe did as much with the ruins of Whitby Abbey as Claude Monet with the façade of the Cathedral at Rouen. So, please permit Key Quote Three, as Gaston Bachelard (in *The Right to Dream*) is so beautiful on Monet:

> One day Monet wanted the cathedral to be a truly airy thing—airy in its substance, airy to the very core of the masonry. . . . Feel how the two towers are trembling with every shade of blue in the vastness of the air. . . . It has wings, blue wings, undulating wings. . . . On another occasion a different elemental dream took hold of the will to paint. This time the cathedral is a mellow, buff-coloured heavenly body, resembling some creature that has fallen asleep in the heat of the day. . . . Here the two towers are closer to the ground, more earthbound, burning only with a little blaze, like a well-tended fire in its hearth.

Sutcliffe could even turn a gaggle of thirteen naked fisher-boys into a monumental composition (with almost Venetian lighting) called *The Water Rats*. One would like to think it is his most famous photograph because of its craft, not because local ecclesiasts excommunicated the whimsical image-maker "for showing such an indecent print to the corruption of the other sex." Now, if Baron Corvo had brought his Uranian cameras into Whitby in 1886—perhaps in the company of his painter friend from Falmouth, Henry Tuke—that might have caused a ripple amongst water rats. But, alas, they have a saying up North: "You can always tell a Yorkshireman, but you can't tell him much."

Sutcliffe said he never had a really good lens all his life and he delivered warnings on photographing in storms, at low tide, at dusk, etc. "There are other dangers besides pig meat to be met with at the seaside."

Dentdale, Cumbria 1974

Some Speak of a Return to Nature— I Wonder Where They Could Have Been

28

Roy Strong of the Victoria and Albert Museum, London, sent a letter into the depths of the Blue Ridge, requesting one of my peregrinations (at about the tempo Anton Bruckner liked to walk) addressed to the relationship between Photography & Poetry. I can imagine some wit solving the mystery in one provocative sentence: "They both share five letters of the alphabet in common; they are both generally best when in black and white; and both occur most often on paper." *Merde alors,* would that I could turn myself into a nonexistent gentleman by the name of John Geoffrey Szarkowski-Grigson—then I would probably know the truth of Bill Brandt's assertion that the ancient track between Lewes and Newhaven is the most beautiful road in the world. (My eyes tell me, *sans* being J.G. S-G's, that Mr. Brandt's *image* is one of the most beautiful. But, since each of us operates out of such a partial view of "the sights," we each remain partial to our own encounters with landscape. I would want to ask Bill Brandt if he's walked sections of the Lyke Wake Walk on the Cleveland Hills during the heather season, or the green tracks around Upper Wharfedale: the one from Cray over to Stalling Busk in Wensleydale. Beauty is in the feet of the beholder.)

Well, a ramble then, and I only hope that the reader and I stumble over the odd insight along the way.

Photography & Poetry. It was Walter Pater's contention that "all arts aspire to the condition of music." Ezra Pound agreed and insisted that poetry atrophies when it gets too far from music. Goethe declared that architecture was just frozen music. And Arthur Dove gives us a clarification (and alarming complication) in notes to his exhibition at Stieglitz's the Intimate Gallery (1929):

> There is no such thing as abstraction.
> It is extraction, gravitation toward a certain direction, and minding your own
> business.

If the exact be clear enough its value will exist.
It is nearer to music, not the music of the ears . . . the music of the eyes.

Which gets us to a good place to stop—how about a picnic in the
Dordogne with J. H. Lartigue as host, responsible for the pâté and the
champagne?—and ruminate on Alfred Stieglitz, himself, and the uses to
which he put clouds. These excerpts from "How I Came to Photograph
Clouds" (1923):

> I, poor, but at work: the world in a great mess: the human being a queer
> animal—not as dignified as our great chestnut tree on the hill.
>
> I'd finally do something I had in mind for years. . . . I wanted to photo-
> graph clouds to find out what I had learned in forty years about photog-
> raphy. Through clouds to put down my philosophy of life—to show that
> my photographs were not due to subject matter—not to special trees, or
> faces, or interiors, to special privileges—clouds were there for everyone
> —no tax on them—free.
>
> I had told Miss O'Keeffe I wanted a series of photographs which seen by
> Ernest Bloch (the great composer) he would exclaim: "Music! Music!
> Man, why that is music! How did you ever do that?"
>
> And when finally I had my series of ten photographs printed, and Bloch
> saw them—what I said I wanted to happen happened *verbatim*.
>
> Some "Pictorial photographers" when they came to the exhibition
> seemed totally blind to the cloud pictures. My photographs look like
> photographs—and in their eyes they therefore can't be art. As if they had
> the slightest idea of art or photography—or any idea of life. My aim is
> increasingly to make my photographs look as much like photographs
> that unless one has *eyes* and *sees*, they won't be seen—and still everyone
> will never forget them having once looked at them. I wonder if that is clear.

Yes, Mr. Stieglitz, very clear—though perhaps no clearer than the Hudson
River painter, John Kensett, writing in 1842 from Paris. It might be wise to
"air out" Kensett's prose *à la manière de* Buckminster Fuller. That is, remea-
sure the words and give them musical "point," enough to stick in the memory:

> it is by mixing up
> intellectual and spiritual associations
> with *things*,
> and only so
> that they have any importance
> to our minds,

things
are nothing
but what the mind
constitutes them,
nothing

thus,
this humble habitation
becomes a shrine
of continued worship . . .

be it but
the fragment of a rock, a
decayed branch, a
simple leaf—

by an *infusion*:
an object of intense interest,
a relic,
priceless
as memory
itself

The poet as *compositor*. Literature is simply "highborn stealth" (Robert Burton), and I don't like to hide my tracks. On my shelves, in my mind, I keep stored the gooseberry preserves I need for the given occasion. I was taught this early—by Mrs. Tiggy-Winkle in the Catbells, by Mole in his den next to the Thames, by Mr. Bilbo Baggins in Hobbiton under the Hill. Shore up the fragments against thy ruin. Mr. Baggins remarked one day to his cousin: "It's a dangerous thing, Frodo, going out of your door." Yet, circumstances took him all the way to the mountains of Mordor. This exhibition of photographs (the occasion for this essay, *The Land*, held at the Victoria and Albert Museum in the winter of 1975–1976) takes you all the way to the moon and out into the galaxies. Celebrate the departure with a bottle or two of Daguerre & Niepce 1839.

Leave clouds for now to Stieglitz, with a bow also to Alvin Langdon Coburn, who was photographing clouds in the Sierra Madre in 1911, and who noted: "It has been my privilege to present my camera to very many things which have caused me to experience true wonder. . . . If we make the most of our opportunities we shall be granted further visions." Coburn read his Plotinus.

Trees next, and first two triggers that inevitably set me off a-wondering while wandering: (1) John Szarkowski in his absolutely indispensable book,

Looking At Photographs. He is commenting on Frederick H. Evan's print, "A Glade in the New Forest." "Evan's forest is not the forest of a botanist or a hunter, but of a literary man. It is a sublime forest, free of stinging nettles and poisonous insects, in the depths of which a man of books might meet all the ancient ghosts of Hampshire." (2) Samuel Palmer, one day in Kent: "Milton, by one epithet draws an oak of the largest girth I ever saw, 'Pine and *monumental* oak': I have just been trying to draw a large one in Lullingstone; but the poet's tree is huger than any in the park." (I don't deprecate Palmer's oaks, but of course it is his horse chestnuts he delivers to the world as they were never seen before. If the light from one moon isn't enough to get his vision across, he'll add one or two more moons. Why not? TOO MUCH IS NEVER ENOUGH! I forget whether I made that up, or was just messing about with Palmer's mentor, W. Blake).

Quickly: name the trees that stick in your head or your craw or your left breast. Well, this is a game like naming the five most notable structures east of the Mississippi river. (My choice there, since we are peregrinating—and too much *andante* and not enough *adagio* for Herr Bruckner's taste: the Round Stone Barn built by the Shakers in Hancock Village, Massachusetts; Roebling's Brooklyn Bridge; Thomas Jefferson's Rotunda and the ensemble of buildings on the lawn at the University of Virginia at Charlottesville; Louis Sullivan's department store for Carson Pirie Scott and Company in Chicago; Frank Lloyd Wright's residence for E. J. Kauffmann, Falling Water, at Bear Run, Pennsylvania. A mite grandiose, that quintet. Could be the destroyed, nondescript cabin in which Thoreau composed *Walden* is really more notable to those with less worldly insight?) But, *Trees.* Interesting how many of them, for me, are photographic: aspens by Ansel Adams, and that orchard of peach trees in the Portola Valley of California seen by Adams with as much refinement as a screen by Ogata Korin; the Monterey cypresses by Edward Weston; the black silhouettes of elms near Lake Michigan by Harry Callahan; oaks (or maybe cottonwoods?) by William Current in Canyon de Chelly; swamp cypresses by Lyle Bongé in Scotland County, North Carolina; Steichen's shadbush; Bullock's redwoods and horsetail ferns; Art Sinsabaugh's "Midwest Landscape 97," where the scale is so condensed and delicate as to suggest Webern's musical calligraphy and sound as well; and a tree, with chicken, by a French photographer, Edouard Boubat, presented in Szarkowski's book. What a tree!

Painted trees? Courbet's, Albert Pinkham Ryder's, Constable's, Cotman's, Pavel Tchelitchew's "Hide and Seek," Soutine's, Van Gogh's, Bresdin's, Klimt's, Monet's; a "Blazing Tree" from a Shaker community, a Mondrian tree, a Cézanne tree, an Atkinson Grimshaw tree, a Marin tree, a tree in a recent painting by Jess Collins of San Francisco, magic as George Mac-donald. Apologies to a thousand years of painters and ink-masters prior to 1775—their adumbrations are hardly lost on any of the above listed.

Worded trees? Joyce Kilmer? "I think that I shall never see / A poem lovely as a tree." Nope—not even in Al Hibbler's death-defying rendition.

Trees in literature—one could spend a lazy afternoon in Joyce Kilmer Memorial Forest just filling in the gaps: a line in Thornton Wilder's *Our Town* about a butternut tree that reduces me to tears no matter how often I hear it; the hallucinatory dead tree on the Cyclopean walls of Gormenghast Castle as revealed by Mervyn Peake; a sunflower a hundred feet tall (qualifying it as *tree* in this instance) in a visionary poem by a forgotten Baltimore poet named William Force Stead. Yeats liked it, too, and put it in his anthology. Ah, but for interior verdure, how are you going to compete with our beloved Andrew Marvell?

> The Mind, that Ocean where each kind
> Does streight its own resemblance find;
> Yet it creates, trancending these,
> Far other Worlds, and other Seas;
> Annihilating all that's made
> To a green Thought in a green Shade.

That final image is so much "in me" that it set my feet moving to the original site: Nun Appleton House, on the banks of the River Wharfe. I wanted to see "The Garden" that so in-formed the music of Marvell's mind—even if the inquiry were 325 years after the fact. It was obviously a very different place, with little but a naturalistic park left. But, an enormous rosemary and a few conifers survived to take contemplation back to the middle of the seventeenth century. I took some slides of branches reflecting in the water below; but no photograph can give us what those six key words do. Not *precisely*. However, poems may be looked at too, just as pictures. I have a little celebration of the Marvell original that looks like this

G R E E N T H O U G H T
G R E E N S H A D E

The title is *Andrew Marvell Wanders in the Grassy Deeps Along the Wharfe at Nun Appleton House and Attains a Small At-One-Ment*. It looks very good in 128-point Garmond italic lower-case decorative letters, cut by Déberny & Peignot. The two greens should be transparent enough to produce a third green. Another version has been etched into two sides of a piece of heavy glass, the glass then set against a background of trees. The new pleasure is that the shade in the poem is "in" the thought, for the first time.

I'm not even sure that "real" trees exert their power over most of us as, perhaps, they once did—I mean in comparison with the six Marvell syllables, which resonate to the ending of the world. I think Ian Hamilton Finlay is right when he says that ninety-nine per cent of the people no longer go to the country—they go to the "strange." As for going to the wilderness, few if any will go armed only with a hunting knife and a loincloth. No, even Ansel Adams will want his Sierra Club cup and about $350 worth of the latest camping equipment, not to mention some means of transporting his camera equipment. Still, if you are on your own feet often enough, you will some-times find what you are looking for. (And who knows what you are looking for until you have found it? Who knows, and Who isn't talking?) Having hiked the Appalachian Trail from Georgia to Connecticut (1,407 miles, give or take a few); the Pennine Way from Gargrave to the Borders; the length of the River Wye; the north coasts of Cornwall, Devon, and Somerset; the Cleveland Way; the Lakes for two months; all over Wiltshire; and bits of the Rockies, I have found a few sacred groves and they remain in my head. I have paid my respects to particular trees, just as Bashō did on his famous pilgrim-age to the far north. Nothing has ever been more inspiriting than the stand of tulip poplars as you hike from Cades Cove up the flanks of the Great Smokies to Gregory's Bald, to see the top of the mountain covered in hybrid-ized native azaleas: lemon yellow to darkest crimson. *Liriodendron tulipi-fera*—a magnolia in fact, not a poplar—the largest specimens known; ob-served in that unique summer forest light of the Smokies—unbelievably blazing green, like Chartres and Bourges blaze red and blue.

Mountain! Herr Bruckner always liked to climb one in the last move-ment, open up the heavens, and bring down the house. "There is nothing in nature that is not in us"—Naum Gabo. And that goes for *mountains,* plus the Little Dells, and Nooks, and Corners of Paradise. One would therefore assume that a few peaks, northern hardwood forests, and assorted waterfalls were necessary for any of us to get the Fifth Symphony of Sibelius, or his *Tapiola,* otherwise those noises vibrating at their certain intervals might just stay noises. Or, how to hear Delius without knowing the wind soughing in the heathers and the rowans of the Airedale moors? A lot of people never get Bruckner, Sibelius, or Delius, to my continuing bemusement. They need aeration, even to know that Half Dome in Yosemite, by Ansel Adams, is not the same thing as a cauliflower, just because it is the same *size* when repro-duced on a piece of paper by lithography.

William Blake, writing at the beginning of what we would now call the Emergence of the Ecological Consciousness, declared:

> Great things are done when men and mountains meet;
> this is not done by Jostling in the Street.

I'm not really sure that Blake ever saw anything more mountainous than the Sussex Downs, except with the third eye, but that didn't stop him from clanging away in Fountain Court, a busy part of the City of London. He also said (and I have to guess the wording since my Blake books are 3,850 miles away in Cumbria this stormy Appalachian afternoon):

> Nature & Art in this together suit;
> what is most Grand is always most Minute.

There is a Buddhist technique: to imagine oneself as small as an insect, and to view things from this perspective; and then immediately to become in imagination as large as a mountain and survey insect and man from this perspective. The photographs in *The Land* reenforce the point. No longer are we merely dealing with pictures of "things," but with records of the *processes* of things. Difficult to tell whether we are looking at "Stagnant Lake at Edge of Columbia Glacier Beside Ruff and Tuff Island" by Bradford Washburn, or "Vascular System of Yolk Sac of Shark Embryo," courtesy Harvard Medical School. Gyorgy Kepes, on this ambiguity, from another indispensable book, *The New Landscape of Art & Science* (1956): "Seen together, aerial maps of river estuaries and road systems, feathers, fern leaves, branching blood vessels, nerve ganglia, electron micrographs of crystals and the tree-like patterns of electrical discharge-figures are connected, although they are vastly different in place, origin, and scale. *Their similarity of form is by no means accidental.* As patterns of energy-gathering and energy-distribution, they are similar graphs generated by similar processes."

I have been preaching—without quite saying so—that photography shares with poetry not only a bond in musicality, but often a basis in *geography*. I know few photographers, or poets, who would agree with Edward Dahlberg's baleful remark: "The only reason we travel is because there's no place to go." There are places! Witness the Wonder Book in front of your eyes in this exhibition. Maybe poets do more mental traveling than their colleagues with view cameras? Still, their purposes are the same: *to record and elate.* Good old William Wordsworth—a pedestrian if there ever was one. He could walk most of us to death, and talk the ears off; but, his attentions were nourished by the earth. Now and then, he delivers lines we have been waiting for always. (He was fortunate to have sister Dorothy around the house to suggest it was better to say *cloud* than *cow* when recollecting wandering lonely.) John Clare was another man nourished by earth. He was in Epping Forest in 1840 when he confessed:

> I found the poems in the fields
> And only wrote them down

At nearly the same time a reclusive Yankee was sitting by a pond outside Concord, Massachusetts. Thoreau said these things:

You sat on the earth as on a raft, listening to music that was not of the earth, but which ruled and arranged it. Man *should be* the harp articulate. When your cords were tense . . . Our thoughts and sentiments answer to the revolution of the seasons, as two cog-wheels fit into each other. . . . I long for wildness, a nature which I cannot put my foot through, woods where the wood thrush forever sings, where the hours are early morning ones, and there is dew on the grass, and the day is forever unproved, where I might have a fertile unknown for a soil about me. . . : All that was ripest and fairest in the wildness and the wild man is preserved and transmitted to us in the strain of the wood thrush. It is the mediator between barbarism and civilization. It is unrepentant as Greece.

Unrepentant it remains—every day about 5 A.M. this time of year it succeeds in waking me up from too little sleep and too much exposure to the artificial birds in the Schubert, Mahler, Dvořak, and Messiaen I play.

Now, please check back to the title of this peripatetic exercise. The question is a question posed, and poised by Frederick Sommer. I don't know whether Bill Brandt includes any of the Arizona landscapes by Sommer in the current exhibition. If so, we will see austere, masterful evidence that "photography is an acceptance of the landscape, which exists for itself." If not, we might be jarred into going all the way to Prescott, Arizona, to face Sommer's world for what it is, i.e., to realize that a photographer, like any maker, faces his own nature first, then works out from there, clicking the shutter at what he alone sees. No exhibition or book is excuse enough for thinking we may stay home indefinitely. The hobbits among us will now lead us in a few choruses of the old hymn, "We Shall Gather by the River."

Highlands, North Carolina 1975

Distances

"American, eh? Then what are you doing here?" These were the opening words of a Welsh nationalist, supremely insular and insolent, despite his drinking Scotch whisky, wearing Ulster tweed, and standing in an Englishman's pub in Llanrwst, Denbighshire.

"Well," I said, "I'm walking for a month to enjoy your famous hospitality and your bloody weather. My father's ancestors left Radnorshire about 1730, so I thought I'd come see why. Williams is the name."

Not to be fazed in the slightest, he replied: "Radnorshire, eh? English-speaking county—the worst county in Wales!"

So I said: "How can you tell?"

He let that one pass, and after another double whisky came back with: "I suppose being an American you're interested in antiques?"

"Certainly," I would like to have said, "a little Regency and, particularly, the Late Stone-Age productions of the Bleeding, Blue-Bottomed Welsh." But one is never *that* quick, and one *is* uncomfortable in xenophobe country.

A recent month afoot in Wales raised a variety of questions. "I go where I love and am loved." I think that is Laura Riding, but I am writing this in the English Lake Country, one day after quitting Wales in a final thunderstorm on Snowdon, and there are no reference books. For anyone who would like to find himself on his feet in a region of poets and sheep, hopeless weather, icy hotels, severe ancient mountains, and sinuous rivers, this is a brief report.

I began in Great Malvern, Worcestershire, two hours forty-three minutes west of London's Paddington Station, with a visit to Michael Shayer—poet.

The hills above the town are where William Langland had the vision of Piers Plowman. We drove north near Credenhill in Herefordshire, the birthplace of Thomas Traherne, of the "orient and immortal wheat which never should be reaped, nor ever was sown." We stopped by Great Witley Court, that extraordinary baroque ruin that Sacheverell Sitwell so amusingly refers to as Victorian Italianate Angkor Wat. Next, to Church Stretton, Shropshire, where I got my Kelty pack out of the car and began hiking the broad moorlands atop the Long Mynd. Housman country, with Wenlock Edge running parallel to the east:

> On tarnish late on Wenlock Edge,
>   Gold that I never see;
> Lie long, high snowdrifts in the hedge
>   That will not shower on me

Poor Housman. I visited the churchyard in Ludlow to see the plaque in his honor. Poor Housman—all the signs said ALL FLESH IS GRASS, KEEP OFF THE GRASS, lest the Shropshire Lass Society run you out of the county.

> Clunton and Clunbury
>   Clungunford and Clun
> Are the quietest places
>   Under the sun.

No so quiet anymore—and, besides, the local version has always been "drunkest" for "quietest." The Mersey Sound is big in Knighton ("a quieter place than Clun"). Most of the lads are in mod clothes, with transistors tuned to The Rolling Stones.

Knighton's the Welsh Border. From there, up across the Radnor Forest in a snowstorm, and down past the waterfall with the lovely name, Water-Break-Its-Neck. And then a night thawing at the amiable Forest Inn comparing notes with Mr. Lander, the publican. And then down to the Wye Valley at Builth Wells. And from Builth to Rhayader to Llangurig—the Wye too beautiful to believe, yet never has it had its Samuel Palmer, John Cotman, or John Constable to celebrate it properly. The Black Lion in Llangurig, by the way, is one of the few hostelries in mid-Wales to which the sybaritic notations of palatable food, comfort, service, and atmosphere seem ever to have occurred—all thanks to Mr. and Mrs. St. Johnston.

From the Youth Hostel in Nant-y-Dernol, then, up over the hills to the headwaters of the Ystwyth Valley. This in order to see the bleak remains of the legendary Domain of Hafod, Thomas Johnes's killing effort to turn this part of Wales into Eden (starting 1785). The horrific story you may read in Elizabeth Inglis-Jones's book, *Peacocks in Paradise*. The house, rebuilt in 1811 with John Nash's *chinoiserie* wing (original of Coleridge's "stately pleasure dome"), was finally dynamited by the Forestry Commission in 1958 as a menace to the public. The rubble is now surrounded by a trailer camp.

Johnes's six million trees, half of them larch, have been cut down, the lead mines exhausted—it must look very much like it did when he arrived. Even the great Chantrey monument to his only daughter, Marianne, is a relic, the marble exploded by firemen's hoses in the church fire of 1932. Johnes's head now lies there at the base of the family group, streaked with ochre and black, staring with absolute obsession. *Vanitas vanitatum.*

The Valley of Hafod remains full of a vacant savagery. George Borrow walked through in 1854: "There was much mire in the street, immense swine lay in the mire, who turned their snouts at me as I passed. Women in Welsh hats stood in the mire, along with men without any hats at all. . . . They held their tongues, the women leering contemptuously at me, the men glaring sullenly."

Borrow's *Wild Wales* is still worth reading for such prose, despite a mire of ridiculous posturing, anti-popery, and general tiresome omniscience. He was one hell of a walker if he can be believed at all; viz., the assertion that he once walked from Norwich to London (112 miles) in twenty-seven hours flat. After some 4,000 miles on foot these past five years I can seldom go more than 20 miles in six hours without snarling. There were giants in the earth in the days of Before, yes yes.

I went on north to Ponterwyd and to sanctuary from the rain in the inn named for Borrow. It too may be recommended for its simple decency. While sitting in the corner of the pub by the fire talking with some local shepherds, I heard a cultivated voice at the bar remark: "You know that scene there, it reminds me of early Magritte." I swung round and said, "If you can tell early from late Magritte in weather like this, I'd better buy you a drink." So I got into a conversation with a gent who turned out to be the medical officer of a neighboring county. He not only knew his George Borrow, he knew his Allen Ginsberg, the Orange Bowl, the Antarctic, and the latest probings of the Cambrian Archeological Society. In other words, a man at ease wherever he was—which is the measure of real cultivation. He had dug his own roots. And a few days later on he was kind enough to show me such places as Montgomery Castle, birthplace of George Herbert, and Shrewbury, the town of Charles Darwin and Mary Webb. Also Robert Owen's birthplace, Newtown.

Easter Sunday found me trudging over the hills from Talybont with sore ankles from the cold, past a place called (spuriously) Taliesin's Grave. No more authentic, I am assured, than Homer, Ga. But, poetically, each place is endowed with the remains of a few derelict automobiles, abandoned by country folk in the hope they would go to seed. I came down past the waterfalls at Furnace and walked on to the vicarage of the Rev. R. S. Thomas at Eglwysfach (New Church), no relative at all of that other recent bard, the Rimbaud of Cwmdonkin Drive in Swansea.

Their separate solutions of how to live in Wales as poets are remarkably different. The one, boozing and gregarious in London, the enemy capital, but only productive during the quiet respites in Wales. The other, a vicar of the Church of Wales, and very much the shepherd of a simple flock, reluctant ever to cross the Cambrian mountains because so much English is spoken on the other side, and because there are so many English there, all poisoning the hill shepherds and men of their own tongues with their television and automobiles. Just like their descendants in the Appalachians, these Welsh Lambs have a taste now for the English Calf of Gold. Father Thomas laments all this, he is austere to a degree that few literary men could imagine.

Here are some lines from one of his poems about a shepherd, Iago Prytherch, entitled "A Peasant":

> There is something frightening in the vacancy of his mind.
> His clothes, sour with years of sweat
> And animal contact, shock the refined,
> But affected, sense with their stark naturalness.
> Yet this is your prototype, who, season by season,
> Against siege of rain and the wind's attrition
> Preserves his stock, an impregnable fortress
> Not to be stormed even in death's confusion.
> Remember him, then, for he, too, is a winner of wars.
> Enduring like a tree under the curious stars.

I hope I *half* understand such a man and such a poem. If I do it is because I am not just an urbanite. Yet, I like the Appalachians better if I can see them from the Cambrians now and then.

But, back in Wales and Portmeirion, the Portofino of Merionethshire. Clough Williams-Ellis, architect, planner, and specialist in the pleasures of buildings, has devoted thirty-five years to creating this fantastic folly village and hotel. This sparkling octogenarian cuts a regal figure in his tweed knickers and bright yellow wool socks.

"I knew it should be possible to develop and exploit even a very beautiful place without thereby spoiling," he said. "Indeed, given loving care and sympathy, it could be made yet more lovely by manipulation. I wanted, too—and this was basic—to prove, as I firmly believe, that architectural good manners are also, ultimately, good business." Nestling on its headland full of hydrangeas, rhododendrons, and azaleas, Portmeirion is an eye-catching pleasure in the grand style. Cape Cod beds down with hill-town baroque; a colonnade from Bristol with Buddha in a grotto.

Portmeirion is a "Home for Fallen Buildings," its maker affirms, and one of his treasures is a seventeenth-century sculptured, vaulted ceiling, depicting the Labors of Hercules. Frank Lloyd Wright once paid a visit and seemed genuinely approving—very polite at any rate. He told Clough Williams-Ellis a favorite anecdote of two clerics: "There is no need to quarrel. We are both doing the Lord's work—you in your way and I in His."

Noel Coward wrote *Blithe Spirit* in a single week's sojourn at Portmeirion. It is the Oz of Wales, making the rest possible. Bertrand Russell is one neighbor, in Penrhyndeudraeth. Directly across Traeth Bach (the "great shore") is the white house of Richard Hughes. I took advantage of the amenities to visit the writer and economist, Rupert Crawshay-Williams, whose radio was offering Bernstein's performance of the Mahler Eighth from the Royal Albert Hall. Edible food in stomach, Mahler in head—next day it was a damn sight easier to walk on in the rain.

Actually, I got a ride to Caernarvon, and a bus from there to Bangor, overlooking the isle of Anglesey. Then on to Llandudno, the Victorian watering place hopefully known as the Naples of the North. The bay is, in fact, extraordinarily and deeply curved, flanked by two promontories, the Great and the Little Orme. Lewis Carroll used to walk with "Alice" along the sand dunes, and there is a statue of the White Rabbit consulting his watch—now being mended after mod-and-rocker vandalism.

Shortly, there was one of the month's three sunny days, whetting the appetite for what is probably the best cooking to be found in Wales: at Pen-y-Bont Inn, Llanrwst, Denbighshire. Commander and Mrs. Hindley-Smith. One rings them up some days in advance, tells them what one would like to eat, and they comply in the style of a fine French country place. I had been suffering indifferent food for too long to remember anything else, so I just asked for a few of the house specialties: prawns in a pastry shell filled with a whipped cream deliciously seasoned as a starter; the main course, Pen-y-Bont Chicken, tender breasts in a wine sauce with pears and obviously many ineffable mysteries; peas for once the size they should be, cheese properly aged; coffee just ground. Personal cooking—it is what one asks of life now and then. And a decent ambiance, simple atmosphere, with none of the pomposity and "ambiance" of such places as the Bell House in Wiltshire, where to eat high off the hog you are treated with insufferable hauteur if *sans* proper tweed and school tie.

At the head of the valley I went by way of Capel Garmon (the "Roof of Wales") and visited the Chambered Long Cairn, a megalithic cromlech in the fields looking across to Moel Siabod and Snowdon itself, both covered in snow. This is the real stronghold of the Welsh nationalists. Dynamite had just been discovered in the fields of one farmer, linking him to the recent blasting of the Clywedog reservoir. Question: Why drown Welsh valleys in order for the bloody English to drink? It is a good question, in its way, and is apparently too hot for anyone to answer satisfactorily.

Adrian Mitchell, the poet, has a cottage near there at Capel Siloam, in which he is able to work at present on a translation of the *Magic Flute*—thanks to the royalties for his job on *Marat-Sade*. We took advantage of the next two days of rain and blather to check all pubs within a twenty-mile radius. Finally, my schedule called for Snowdon itself, the Realm of Eagles. So the Mitchells let me out at the Pen-y-Gwryd Hotel, a haunt of climbers near the flank of the mountain, to wait for an engineer friend from Newcastle to join me for the ascent.

We suffered from an evening of ho-ho jollity at the hands of eighteen members of an organization with a name like the Derbyshire Pennine Hiking Club, featuring more in-conversation than Beat or Concrete poets ever dreamed of; dinner accompanied by really vile Russian red wines brought back by some idiotic expedition to somewhere; and next dawn we awoke to a further heavy torrent of rain and thunder.

To hell with it. We packed up and drove as fast as possible to the English Lakes. Today we made it up Great Gable, the clouds suddenly broke, and the whole panorama opened up: Wastwater sparkling, the Isle of Man, Scotland, Windermere, the Pennines—one of the great vistas in the British Isles. As H. H. Symonds, most devotional of Lakeland guides, has said: "No man should die without having seen this sight."

So, get yourself some Maine guide shoes from L. L. Bean and get with it! "Great things are done when Men & Mountains meet. . . ." William Blake could assert this, walking only the mountains in his broad forehead. The rest of us seldom have it that good.

Hawkshead, Lancashire 1966

Every time I undergo a poetry reading, some particularly baleful lines from the letters of Parson Mason Locke Weems, the redoubtable pamphleteer and bookseller of Colonial America, come to my mind: "My prospects, as to comfort, Health, Life &c are gloomy & uncompromising. Even the Natives are afraid to travel through the Sultry, infected air of this fenny, loggy dreadful Country. Shou'd anything happen to me, I cherish a hope that you will do Justice to my Poor Widow & children—You owe me money!" The Parson spoke like a poet. I was thinking those thoughts one evening last December, at the lectern in the theatre of the American Embassy, Grosvenor Square, London, as the fogs began to obscure the handful of lost souls who'd come to a poetry reading on a night like this. Having survived over 200 readings in America, I had begun to think of myself as an authority. However, a season of London readings, often on the listening end, has bemused me indeed. Unfortunately, I have not had Stevie Smith's experience of reading to a group of nudists, tea cups poised on their bony knees, but hath been many an orb of dulcet light to crown the Muse's diadem, so let me tell you about the wildest, one evening in Kensington.

The mimeographed announcement came to me via Peter Russell. Peter runs a helter-skelter bookshop in Soho (the only one in the district, I believe, not just devoted to pseudo-sexy magazines and poor editions of the *Kama Sutra*). It's around the corner from Poland Street, where Will Blake used to see his tygers. There is a parking garage on the site now. Peter writes a clutch of sonnets a day, fraught with couplets like:

Marmoreal sunrise with a roseate spa
Outshines the diamonds of the night's last star

Well, that's England, unquote—everybody's got at least one thumb up the arse of the seventeenth century. Anyway, he has been asked to read some of his discreet sonnets, *Images of Desire*, to the Moderne Muse & Music Circle, and wants company along on the outing. So we hop a bus in Shaftesbury Avenue—out Piccadilly to Hyde Park Corner; past Harrod's and Knightsbridge; past the Albert Hall and Kensington Gore; and we get off near Prince of Wales Terrace. We walk to Stanton Coit House, Number 13. This proves to be genteel, somewhat decayed, Georgian, now taken over by various societies. The only thing I noticed upstairs was a unique teakwood commode which flushed by one's pulling a rod straight up three feet from a marble fitting, but I'm sure that if one explored the building one would find the Acupuncture Circle and the Pro-Vivisection Group.

First there is the Book Table (let us pray) "to which everyone is invited to bring slim volumes [the slimmer the better] and little magazines [the smallest] for sale." Behind the table is Bernard Stone, the bibliographer of Durrell, C. P. Snow, and Muriel Spark. He's looking like he wonders why he's there. But, so far we've not penetrated the Sanctum. It's only later that Mr. Stone confides he hasn't been in the other room to listen for over two years. Ah well. So, everybody stands around eying the dread, slim volumes when a small, nearsighted mole emerges from yon icy chamber across the hall and announces the hour has arrived.

The Sanctum is occupied by a hamstrung Bechstein and about fifty iced leather chairs on which the audience of eleven is huddled. The mole is a gentleman by name of Aston Upbull-Dickey, Music Organizer, and he opens the evening by introducing Peter Russell, who regales us with a few *indiscreete sonets*. The minutes pass, the sonnets flow, a little man begins to squirm and look at his watch menacingly. "Finally," says Peter, "a poem about culture." This builds to a powerful couplet rhyming *fart* and *art*. Somebody blushes, somebody moans, somebody yawns.

A quote smattering of applause unquote. Aston Upbull-Dickey says: "And now, ladies and gentlemen, Madame Salome Saskatch-Trapper will present a short *lieder* recital. He stumbles into the side of the Bechstein, finds a chair, and knocks all the accompanist's music to the floor. (He's doubling in brass.) Meantime, Madame Saskatch-Trapper is taking off her furs, assisted by the previously squirming poetry lover. It is now Their Moment. Madame keeps reaching endlessly into her beaded rucksack to find the key— which she doesn't—but she is a trouper in the great tradition. She is helped by the fact that Ashton Upbull-Dickey only plays three notes and those with full pedal. Kind of a cosmic drone back of it all—very unusual that, jolly strange.

Finally, that much is over. Back in her furs goes Our Soprano. Back to the lectern shambles Our Congenial Host. Now, ladies and gentlemen, we are going to hear poems by a young lady unfamiliar to us all. I have not had the pleasure of hearing her poems either, so let us all welcome Mrs. Samantha

Cowwe. Hear! Hear! Mrs. Cowwe looks like she ran all the way from Golders Green—or, make it Yonkers. She smiles demurely, of course, and announces: "My poems are all about love. Please do not expect anything else. . . ." She's telling us the bloody truth, straight from the (gasp) heart. The fact that love is to be conveyed in words never seems to have clouded her homely visions:

> Darling, know that I will be standing by the door
> of our flat upon your return from the office, tired,
> at close of day from the office, yes, tired, yes,
> I will be there smiling, smiling, smiling,
> Darling. . .

Ten more minutes of glazed eyes, tight jaws, and upturned toes.

Now it's the interval, ladies and gentlemen. I want you all to read the announcement about coffee and biscuits in the programme and then do what you can. One reads: "The revenue from collections and the sale of refreshments has tended to fall. All supporters are asked to attend regularly and to introduce their friends; also, to contribute more generously to the collections. It is particularly hoped that these requests will not go unheeded." So, back to the Book Table, and to coffee and biscuits and ninepence per person. "Black or white?" Black, please. Lady begins to pour boiling milk in the coffee. Please, I asked for it black, "Oh, I thought you said white." No speaka da Inglesa. Meantime, the Book Table is doing a thriving business. Mr. Stone's take is eight shillings sixpence: $1.19.

All right, ladies and gentlemen, more poetry, more song. Back we go! And back it is. We are going to hear from Mr. James Hole-Hogg from Brighton, Sussex, who will read from *The Pindaric Ode (sent to General de Gaulle) in Honor of Cromwell and Milton.* Dame Flora Robson has recited the poem for charities and writes: "What beautiful lines! What a joy it is to read such glorious words, and understand them, without a battle." The poet's aunt, Lady Sally Hole-Hogg, remarks: "Thank goodness for some poetry *I* can understand." Mr. Hole-Hogg's volume of verse is distributed in America, by the way, by Soccer Associates, New York.

The Poet, Himself, has risen and stalks slowly toward the lectern— black suit, grizzled hair, the wild look in the eyes often seen in the minions of Sir Oswald Mosley. Fixing the audience with enkindled gaze, he begins to intone:

> Like Cincinnatus from the plough
> Haled by the people's voice, his country's need
> Compelling, he with watchful heed
> Observed the royal usurpations flow

From power's corrupted fountain: Liberty
Sank in those poisoned waters, soon to die—
[etc., for fifteen minutes.]

Mr. James Hole-Hogg looked 'bout with wild surmise and walk'd he in silence from th' empurpled lectern of the Pierian Nine. Peter Russell was having a quiet convulsion; my pulse was nearly gone.

Later, we repaired to a public house called The Goat and drank pint after pint of Watney's dire Red Barrel and wept for poor Mnemosyne. The prognosis for poetry didn't seem too good.

London, 1963

From St. Bees Head to Robin Hood's Bay (A Bison-Tenniel Walk across Northern England by the Pseudo-jubilation T. Cornpone)

31

> To see what remains led our walking sticks to Unganji. . .
> —Bashō, in the *Oku-No-Hosomichi*

I meant to begin a journal on Independence Day with a displaced, Cumbrian paean to the Republic. Alas, whether as the result of six months' ingestion of Aldomet and Lasic to soothe the high blood, or of the miseries of a listless prostate, I was feeling genuinely pisspoor and was typing less and paying less attention to the postal authorities than for years. Fourth of July, however, got celebrated in our own idiosyncratic, Dentdale fashion. Oliver Turnbull arrived early in the morning with a magnum of Louis Roederer Brut (1966). The *élan* that ensued found some raspberries with which we could conclude lunch in company with Oliver's second offering: a delicious bottle of Sauternes, Chateau Lafaurie-Peyraguey (1961).

Rather than the obvious music-for-the-day-appointed by Charlie Ives, I chose that depressive-cum-glorious score by Fred Delius, *Eine Messe des Lebens.* Mr. Delius, our premier proxy-Florida composer-feller—yet always a Yorkshire Dalesman in the Seine-et-Oise or in the mountains of Norway. Our Fred probably came over the the moors from Langstrothdale Chase once upon a time and wandered down Dentdale past our cottage along the River Dee. "Ich furchte dich Nach, ich liebe dich Ferne" (I fear you near me, I love you far off), he has Zarathustra singing to the peckerwoods along the St. John's River, back in 1884. And, indeed, the country is still fearsome. But, as Jonathan Winters suggests: "You can only stay in your motel room for so long with your Gideon Bible—then you got to go outside." *They* are out there in them bushes—yessireebob.

September 9:
Even in a Bison-Tenniel year, it doesn't pay to indulge in much palaver on the national character. I have been in forty-eight of these states; I know some

thousands of fellow citizens I have liked and a few hundred I have loved. I have walked and driven to more Sacred Places than I can keep track of. Anyone who knows me knows that my diet is the isolated, cathectic, extraordinary, and hypertensive, and my America is not the venal and banal miasma owned by the Franchise People From Beyond Space. I like to scold and I believe in non-righteous indignation. The Pejorocracy I learned on Charles Olson's knee keeps me in vigorous gadfly-training. (No gadflies without a horse's-ass society.) So it is not surprising to find me in the summer of 1976 living on the margins of the Modern World, reading Bashō, listening to Mompou and Charles Tomlinson Griffes, leaving the North Carolina hills for Corn Close, the stone cottage in the Yorkshire Dales.

It is a relief of sorts to live there. No one is going to shoot you to death there, though terminal boredom is a common fate for Americans opting out in an old world. Many critics contend that Imagination fled the British Isles by the seventeenth century, and there is little since Victorian times, surely, to make you doubt it. Kenneth Grahame and Beatrix Potter and Tolkien caught the secret identities of the middle classes. Most of the folk you meet are merely personifications of Ratty, Mole, Badger, and Toad. A lot of bunnies and little people wander about as well. It is all homey and snug, with nursery tea arriving every few minutes. It is as gray as the heavens. *Stodge* is a word that works overtime in England. (Now and then one meets a vestigial specimen of the genus *Gentry*. Gentry have sangfroid, stiffupperlip, and a metal pole in the neck that inclines the nose at the precise angle to produce the famous fluted tones once heard never forgotten. Gentry also have one hell of a case of *meilikhoposthoi*—"vagueness of mind & cock" in the ancient Greek. Gentry can be dreadfully amusing.)

So, in order to get away from both English and American visitors in the late summer of 1976, and to get away from over two months of drought in Dentdale and the business of toting ten-gallon milk-kits back and forth from Sedbergh, the nearest town with water, Tom Meyer and I—poets in their pride—decided to walk "The Coast To Coast Walk," a ramble of up to 190 miles devised by that redoubtable, implacable old mole, A. Wainwright, of Kendal, Cumbria. Mr. Wainwright makes some of the best pictorial guides for hikers available in any country (they are published by the *Westmorland Gazette*, the local newspaper-weekly in Kendal), but Wainwright is a man with dour, tireless feet, a taste for little but "beauty," having an occasional cuppa and a packet of crisps in a cheerless inn, and then heading out for twenty-five more miles. Thus, you will find us using Wainwright, but in a revisionist way. You can't make a *grande route gastronomique* out of crossing England from St. Bees Head on the Irish Sea to Robin Hood's Bay on the North Sea. But you can try—and you can try not to be captured by Calvinist misery.

In *English Landscapes,* W. G. Hoskins asks: "How could one bear to live in a country with only a hundred or two hundred years underfoot, above all bear to die in it?" Well, *Ginkgo biloba* can be found in petrified state on the bluffs of the Columbia River in central Washington State; also, in the cliffs at Scarborough on the east coast of Yorkshire.

Living trees of the genus arrived at Kew Gardens only in 1754 and in Philadelphia thirty years later. Despite a history of 200 million years, the ginkgo seems no more ancient or alien to me than the rowan. I know the rowan first from the flanks of such mountains as Le Conte in the Great Smokies, and then in the limestone gills of Yorkshire. This mountain ash tree seems to have been guardian of the shrines of Malponus ever since the Celtic Brigantians lived there. "Knowst thou Pan?" asks the poet, as the red rowan berries fall into white snow at the end of Delius's extraordinary song, "An Arabesque."

September 10:
Sixteen eighty-nine and Bashō left his house by the Sumida River—"There were places I had heard of but had not yet seen." He made a cautery of *Artemisia moxa* and applied it to his shins to strengthen them. In 1976, standing on the foreshores of St. Bees, there was no use in applying western artemisias—nothing in *The Englishman's Flora* by Mr. Grigson implies powers to the wormwood or sagebrush or southernwood. And neither was there a bottle of Moxie to consume in front of the local sweetshop. Nothing to do but bid farewell to our friend, Bill Milburn, who would drive the VW back to Dentdale, and make a start.

The thing to see in the town is the Priory Church of St. Mary and St. Bega, whose red sandstone west doorway (three orders of columns, zigzags, and grotesques, c. 1160) is the richest in Cumbria, according to Professor Pevsner. Inside, the wrought-iron screen by Butterfield (1886) between nave and the present chancel is to my taste. Incidentally, to venture from one's door without the appropriate volume of Sir Nicholas Pevsner's *Buildings of England* (Penguin) is a folly.

Wainwright takes you from the seawall and, curiously, the path heads *west* along the top of the cliff. Soon, it heads north through fields full of handsome cheviot sheep to Fleswick (pronounced Flezzick) Bay. A secret place. You have to drop down a cleft in the red sandstone to the beach, asking the cows to move and stop munching the watercress and the herbs in the crannies. When the tide is right the beach is knee-deep in pebbles, all endlessly rounded and polished by the Irish Sea. It is easy to pick up jasper, green slate, and many yellow and black stones. Ikebana People, prepare to die of *shibui*. On around St. Bees Head, past the lighthouse, along the cliffs, with views of the town of Whitehaven in the distance and, beyond, the hills of Galloway in Scotland across the Solway Firth. At a disused quarry, you go by sunken lanes eastward at last into the village of Sandwich (pronounced Sanith), where a retired and stately policeman, Tom Bell, may be found dispensing beer at the Lowther Arms. I recommend the White Shield, by Worthington, which must be poured carefully to keep from roiling the sediment in the bottle. Two beers and I am plotting a visual poem in my head called "Seven Sheep Pretending to Be a Lesser Cumbrian Stone Circle."

Back outside to the walk, and the rain that was promised from Ulster now begins to fall. (It will fall in one form or another the entire rest of the walk, and I later surmise that The Breaking of the Famous Drought of 1976 is a pure Bicentennial gift from Thomas Meyer and Jonathan Williams to the British people.) On with the anoraks, made in poet Thomas A. Clark's hometown of Greenock in Scotland, and on through a series of farms with very mucky tracks. The Whitehaven Chemical Works isn't much of a vista, but ahead you can make out a hill called Dent. By the time we slide into the village of Cleator and sit in the dry porch of St. Leonard's, it is already five o'clock and the wetness has worked its predictable woes on my miserable feet—much too bony, narrow, and archless to support a poet of amplitude. Blisters the size of silver dollars on each heel, to move 125 miles across land to the North Sea. The practical advice is: apply all the Dr. Scholl's and junk to the feet *before* hiking, not after the first or second day when everything is already breaking down. I never learn. Anyway, no time to climb the green hill of Dent, see the bogus stone circle at Kinniside by way of a ravine called Nannycatch. Rain now pelting down. Phone for a taxi, for the night's destination: The Shepherd's Arms at Ennerdale Bridge. Old Wainwright has a perceptive remark about the exhausted industrialization that has pitted the villages of West Cumbria: "Travellers through these places in search for four-star rest and refreshment can abandon hope: they make no claim to be holiday resorts or tourist centers. The primary concern of the inhabitants is to earn a living for themselves, not to cater for the leisure of others." Yet, four miles away the hostelry is a pleasant surprise, and not just because the rain is becoming torrential, the wind is up, and the night's closing in. A young couple has revived a grotty, abandoned pub and turned it into an agreeable, small private hotel. It will be one of the few places recommended, should this journal make you drop everything, buy transportation to St. Bees, and take to shank's mare. Nicely cooked food; genuine hospitality. And there was an English couple also staying who knew more about walking the countryside than any English people I've ever met. They, too, thought this remote inn an excellent place to use as a base for outings. Happily, this couple were not the usual English guests, grunting quietly to themselves in the corner. They enjoyed a drink; they had been to the Himalayas twice and were going soon to the Atlas Mountains. They lived in the Pennines, near Snake Pass, east of

Manchester. I imagine he might have been a solicitor. (It would have been asking too much for even these semi-ebullient islanders to reveal profession or name to a stranger.)

September 11:
Awoke very early, hearing the storm. More wind and more heavy rain. I'd had a vivid dream in which I was asleep in a veritable Samuel Palmer landscape. The color was that of the ink and sepia drawings in the Ashmolean Museum. I was sleeping on a hill with haystack shapes about. When you begin long walks you often dream you are sleeping in spaces neither indoors nor outdoors—the blowing curtain is a waterfall, etc. Anyway, vintage Palmer: entranced shepherds and light from several moons. Some rocks in the distance were like draperies framing the scene, hung down from the sky. F. L. Griggs, that recent graphic artist and disciple of Palmer, was the artist in that quarter of the dream.

We took the easier footpath around the end of Ennerdale Water, along the north shore. The track begins to go through a forestry plantation. Many complain that this is out of character with the fells of Lakeland—in some respects they are right. It is all conifers, planted too closely and neatly. Hard to imagine the look of Ennerdale as paleo-climatologists tell us it was once: trees up to 2,000 feet, a sparse collection of oaks, ash, larch, rowan, beech, and birch. On a day like today, very helpful to be going through a miniature *Schwarzwald*—the gales are up to ninety miles per hour on the coast behind us. Everything inside the Kelty packs is already soaked for the second day, including Wainwright's dreaded guidebook. There are glimpses of Pillar Rock high on the right and the roar of the River Liza in spate. An hour or two brings us out of the forest to the ancient shepherd's bothy that now serves as Black Sail Hut, the loneliest youth hostel in England, in its cup filled with drumlins and becks. We are surrounded by Great Gable, Pillar, Kirk Fell, Haystacks, and High Crag. Water is bubbling and rushing everywhere.

Wainwright sends us steeply up the right side of Loft Beck, which isn't all that easy in such a wind. Plus it is beginning to hail. Visions of hypothermia take shape, because once you hit the Brandreth Fence and take your bearings from Blackbeck Tarn for Honister Pass, you have a good mile-and-a-half to traverse in very exposed conditions. So, it's a relief to stagger down the path of the old tramway through the slate quarries and arrive at the automobile road leading down into Borrowdale—shelter within range at last. This is a very hard day, fourteen-plus miles, under such conditions (not to mention one's own parlous condition). Hause Gill has fine waterfalls on a wet day like this, no use following Wainwright onto the old toll road and have trouble finding the way into Seatoller. Borrowdale I remember from my first Lake District rambles, back in 1962. It is relatively unchanged for all its popularity.

Bicentennial suggestion: let a delegation from Buncombe and Henderson counties in North Carolina go to Borrowdale and see how it's done. The first answer is: stop every rednecked, greedy idiot in the country from working his own particular vision of schlock on the enraptured, doting public.

Outside, the Langstrath Hotel in the village of Stonethwaite was appropriate. Inside, we knew we'd hit Mole Central. Not a place for walkers or poetic soreheads. A place for the Tory middle class. No pub; a "lounge." Never stay in an English hotel without a proper bar. In the lounge before dinner were clusters of aging badgers, hiding behind editions of the *Daily Telegraph*, each whispering to his or her companion, and occasionally daring a glass of dry sherry, which you had to extract with difficulty by ringing a buzzer and disturbing a gloomy girl from the kitchen. The pub was two miles away in the rain and dark at Rosthwaite. Nothing to do but drink what one could, eat quickly, and retire at nine P.M. to read a few minutes' J. G. Ballard. Gales shook the old building. Downstairs, the denizens groaned into the night at the thought of a multi-racial Britain and the numinous wickedness of Sir Harold Wilson.

September 12:
More of the storm. (Six feet of water pouring through Stokesley-in-Cleveland, a week ahead on our route, during the night.) The quick getaway from the Langstrath. (Stay at farmhouses and bed-and-breakfast places if you can. They were all booked up in Borrowdale, which is why the hotel. And I only wangled that because I know a member of the English Tourist Board. They leaned on the management, telling them I was American travel-writer.) The walk up Stonethwaite Beck and Greenup Gill is one of my favorites, with Langstrath Beck's pouring waters coming down from the valley to the right, just below Eagle Crag. It's an arduous walk, but there's time. As we'd nearly climbed to Lining Crag, here came Joss Naylor, the hill farmer from Wasdale, plunging down the path on some Sunday-competition fell-race. Naylor is one of the great natural athletes in the world. Even at forty-one he must be in a class with the Kenyan marathon runners. He has accomplished all the peaks in the Lake District over 2,000 feet (a number like forty-eight), about 20,000 feet of climbing, and ninety-six miles of running in less than twenty-four hours! A yell to Joss as he zips by: "Mind how ye go, lad!" His performance is really nothing to think about as one struggles to do a mere twelve to twenty miles a day without even going right over the high tops.

Lunch up at Greenup Edge, at 2,000 feet, a looking out over ranges and ranges of glacial drumlins and down the valley of Wythburn. The direct route to Grasmere is down Far Easedale. Rowans and waterfalls and huge black boulders. Instead of racing to get over the next line of hills to Patterdale, we devote the afternoon to the Wordsworths and to Sara Nelson's excellent gingerbread, which you buy from a little shop at the edge of the parish churchyard. More a kind of biscuit than what most of us know as gingerbread. Lovely. The customary coachloads of tourists wandering the village. Many photographing William's grave. (I once collected Allen Ginsberg there, as he was chanting from the sacred texts, to the amusement of some and the bemusement of others.) Today, we walked over to the museum next to Dove Cottage, where I was caught by a letter from Benjamin Haydon, dated 13 June 1815. Haydon was engaged in making a life mask of WW. He writes: "He came into breakfast with his usual cheerfulness, and delighted & awed us by his illustrations and outbursts of inspiration, and one time he shook us both in explaining the principles of his system, his views of man, & his objects in writing." Yep, those were the days when breakfast was breakfast. "Dorothy!—more Kedgeree, more Comfrey Leaf Fritters, more Anglesey Eggs, more Mushrooms with Braised Guineafowl, more Giblet Pie, more Stout and more Claret." Old Bill—eating like a horse, looking like a horse, and talking occasionally like one too.

September 13:
Stephen Gorton had rescued us from the rains and poetry lovers of Grasmere and taken us to his cottage at Hartsop, above Patterdale. A good respite. This morning, early, we drove with him into Kendal, where Bill Milburn met us and drove us back to Corn Close to get some dry clothes. With unsettled weather like this, the best solution is for us to take the VW, plant it here and there, walk as we can, then hitch rides or take taxis back to the car. So, goodbye to Bill a second time and up the M-6 motorway to Carlisle. To Brampton for a further look at St. Martin's, by Philip Webb. The east window, by Morris & Co., designed by Burne-Jones, is one of their very best, particularly the panel of the Pelican In Its Piety. A look at the pretty village of Wetheral on the Eden River. Then Armanthwaite, the Chapel of Christ and Mary, for a late window by Morris & Co. And then, courtesy of the omnivorous Professor Pevsner, a terrific find: St. Mary's Church, Wreay, Cumbria. "The west doorway and west window have surrounds with vine, corn ears, waterlilies, roses, pine, monkey-puzzle, and also beetles, birds, and butterflies, all naturalistically but flatly carved, of a stylization which would be expected of 1900 but is unique in the 1840s. The gargoyles (needless to say not Romanesque at all) represent snakes, a tortoise, an alligator, etc." The architect of all this splendiferous stuff was a local lady, Miss Sara Losh, who built the church as a memorial to her sister Katherine. Wreay is not easy to find—a hamlet nearly run over by the motorway, with no access

for many miles. But do visit St. Mary's. What it suggests more than anything else is the world of the Rev. Charles Dodgson. "The carving of the inside of the west door was done by Miss Losh's gardener, and represents a gourd plant with a caterpillar at the base of the stem which is eating it off."

The rest of the afternoon is spent meandering through the quiet country to the southwest of Penrith: Yanwath, where friends keep a pub called The Yat, Tirril, Askham, the Park at Lowther Castle, Bampton, and a drive along the east shore of Haweswater. The night at Shap.

September 14:
Two walks in the rain, with the rain a little more spotty at last. There is a rewarding path from the ruins of Shap Abbey down Rosgill to the hamlet of the same name. Two medieval bridges to be seen. And then a circular walk around Haweswater, about ten miles. With the reservoir so low from the summer's drought it was easy to see the walls of the sunken village of Mardale near the head of the Lake.

Then back into the VW and east across the limestone plateau of Crosby Ravensworth Fell towards Kirkby Stephen. No one would guess it driving this empty territory that we are back on *la grande route gastronomique,* for the night's destination is the Bay Horse Inn, Winton (a village just north of Kirkby). You must book weeks in advance at the inn, and, in fact, you should locate bed-and-breakfast in the vicinity because the Bay Horse only provides rooms now to old friends of the management. There, Giles and Sylvia Gilson inevitably provide good beer, good wine, and food cooked to personal taste—as good as we are accustomed to having at home, especially if guests are coming. There is only one table catered to in the Gilson's own dining room, with a maximum of seven, so this explains why it is difficult to get a reservation. Sylvia's reputation has passed succulently and quietly from mouth to mouth. She has a star in both the *Good Food Guide* and the *Egon Ronay.* Though these guides indicate more the taste of twits, colonels, and bloated commercial travellers, they are still indispensable in a land where people are as bored with cooking as with everything else. Giles can be counted on to have Younger's or Theakston's bitter from the wood, ample stocks of claret and burgundy, and a good supply of disgusting Irish jokes. A dinner of Sylvia's might consist of an onion soup made with Devonshire cream and laced with sherry; *Gigot au miel* (which is a leg of lamb stuffed with *foie gras,* coated in honey, and roasted); fresh vegetables from the inn's garden; home-made breads; strawberry Pavlova, and a cheeseboard, usually including Soft Ayrshire, Sage Lancashire, Stilton, or Blue Wensleydale. Mr. Gilson's vintage port and cigars make walking across England almost the act of reasonable people.

September 15:

By car up the eastern side of the Eden Valley. In rain this terrain is a bleak morass of peat and what the locals call glishy slutch. Now if that isn't glishy slutch caking your boots, what the hell else would you call it? Over the crest of the Pennines and down the headwaters of the River Swale to the village of Keld. Back on foot: upstream to the Wain Wath Force; then up the side valley, West Stonedale, to the inn at Tan Hill. It purports to be England's highest. It is certainly one of England's dreariest, now that the lead miners and locals have disappeared into history. Just a way station for the poor fools slogging the Pennine Way and few day-trippers out in the car from the industrial parts at the bottom of Teesdale. The publican was new to his surroundings, in fact, and could advise no travellers of the location of the strange places in that part: Kaber, Barras, Muker, Thwaite, Arkengarthdale. One positive note: the Webster's Pennine Bitter is tasty and well kept. We went back to Keld down the opposite side of the valley. Abandoned farms, just a few Swaledale sheep, nothing much to comment on until back at the river, where there are three fine waterfalls: Catrake Force, East Gill Force, and Kisdon Force.

There is a deep limestone gorge below Keld with many rowans, but the light was going. We took the car down Swalesdale to Reeth and put up at a hotel we'd been advised to use by the *Good Food Guide*. Rather a mistake: jokey, mildly hysterical, disorganized, and much too expensive. If you can get in at the Kearton Guesthouse in Thwaite, you'll probably do better. The rule in England (particularly when on foot) is to stick closely to farmhouses and rural inns, I repeat. Otherwise, unless you are forewarned, you will get bogged in the gloomy pretensions of the muddled-classes. Of course, some people long for the nostalgia of comfort in the style of the American tourist home of 1937 and of food in the *echt*-Holiday Inn manner.

September 16:

Back to Keld and the long walk down the Swale to Reeth. The Farmer's Arms in Muker has Theakston's beer, and you can buy bread, cheese, and fruit in the village for lunch. Take lunch by the Ivelet Bridge, a mile further downstream. The most beautiful, single-arched medieval bridge in the Dales. On to the Gunnerside through the fields above the north bank. About a mile beyond the village, back across a bridge to the quieter south side of the dale. At the junction pointing to Crackpot and Low Houses, you go left to Low Houses. This is the most handsome Georgian house we encountered in Swaledale, with a forecourt paved in flagstones and fine old gardens. Several mucky miles along a green track. Stopped to chat with an amiable farmer who was dry-walling. He was full of precise information about the local sheep, cows, and places of interest. Don't ask shopkeepers—they will barely know the way to the bank and will not have walked even there if it is more than 200 yards up a hill. Grinton possesses a good Perpendicular church surrounded by old yews and a tangle of giant headstones. Another night in somewhat grotty Reeth. You can get a decent pint in the Black Bull, but the people on the whole continue to be out of sorts in this year of the drought or the flood and the ever-sinking pound sterling. There was a bit of bizarre dinner conversation in the hotel dining room. A prune-faced person was saying to his gloomier sister: "I used to put the *Guardian* down for my bathmat. I found it excellent."

September 17:
Another longish walk in ye rain. By Marrick Priory, up through the woods on a stone path to the hamlet of Marrick, and through the high fields to Marske, a posh village with a good eighteenth-century bridge, the grounds of an ancient hall, and the Church of St. Edmund. Then on to Richmond. Egon Ronay misled us again. The King's Head (pretty Georgian façade) has been turned into a boring commercial hotel. And the town, somehow, is not nearly so attractive and charming as the books keep saying it is. There is, to be sure, the Norman Castle Keep, and the restored Georgian Theatre; but, the town square is jumbled and dirty like a very provincial place in Normandy. The shops are poor. However, we've arranged to be joined by our friend Nevart Smith for dinner and we are lucky enough to discover (by walking about) the French-Gate Hotel. This is clearly the place to stay, should you go to Richmond. It is being revived and run by a retired airline pilot in very precise, personal style. Excellent menu and very decent cooking. The hotel is not in the guides. The proprietor shrugs at such standardizations.

September 18:
Barbara Jones's *Follies & Grottoes* alerts us to two notable follies in the vicinity. One is Culloden Tower, in an estate at the top of Newbiggin Street (the one street in the town with trees and much sense of Georgian style). Sadly, the tower is being relentlessly vandalized by boys from a reform school, much to the disgust of the ancient, patrician lady who owns it: "They ought to keep people like that where they belong." Alas, it was people like this lady's ancestors who built not only follies to mark the Jacobite defeat in 1746, but also the famous dark, satanic mills for wicked boys to work in. The folly's delightful chimneypiece, in the manner of William Kent, has nearly been dismantled by abuse since Pevsner noted and photographed it for his *North Riding of Yorkshire* volume. The other eccentricity is The Temple, at Ashe Hall, four miles in the countryside. The butler of the Marquis of Zetland led us through the Capability Brown park to this bit of Richmond Castle rebuilt into a Gothic eye-catcher. Strange double-faces on the corbels

of the interior main room—a place now for the gentry to gulp champagne during some annual chase after unfortunate animals.

The rest of the day we spent driving madly, looking at churches, bridges, trying to find a decent pub, and, finally, locating the Druid's Temple, a half-sized copy of Stonehenge on a forestry commission hilltop near Swinton Part, west of Masham (home of Theakston's Old Peculier Strong Yorkshire Ale). This is a truly grotesque folly by William Danby. I suppose it's only its remoteness that keeps it from being wrecked. We end up at the Cleveland Tontine Inn (yet another of our many mistakes) for the night. The atmosphere makes us drive twenty miles across the Vale of York to Moulton (the Black Bull) for an indifferent, noisy, overpriced meal in their seafood restaurant. A day of too much of a muchness. But they can easily get like that, if you get to feeling desperate and want England to yield more invention and panache than it will. The English really want to be left alone, with roses and pipe, and not forced to cope with demanding outsiders.

September 19:
Starting at Mount Grace Priory, one of the best Carthusian remains in the country, this is a taxing, exhilarating walk—one of the ones that keeps you from flinging Mr. Wainwright's little red guide off a cliff. Beacon Hill, Coalmire, Scugdale, up onto Live Moor, and then along the edge of the Cleveland escarpment. Here you follow the Lyke Wake Walk and the Cleveland Way. The way is celebrated in the ancient dirge as the route along which corpses were carried to the eastern seacoast. Carlton Moor is next, below which are abandoned alum and jet mines. Then Cringle Moor, then Cold Moor, and Wainstones (a jumble of huge boulders), and steeply down to Hasty Bank. Much up and much down but all just the kind of walking that one appreciates most—even in the rain. And then, down the automobile road to the village of Broughton. There you encounter a strange little hotel called the Wainstones. Georgian/Swiss/Spanish style. Some maniacal industrially successful yodeler has spent a fortune tarting up a country inn and turning it into a mecca for expense-account cretins. One of those places with a menu (90 percent frozen) presented on a carte three by four feet. The executives from the ICI complex on Teeside apparently love it. (The Golden Lion, at Stokesley, under French management is a possibility, but it's three miles further if you're on foot from Hasty Bank. It had been damaged by floods and was closed when we wanted to use it.

September 20:
From Hasty Bank there is a steady climb back to the 1,400-foot level along the spacious, heather-covered Urra Moor. Incised stones (from as far back as Saxon times) line the way at intervals, including the famous Hand

Stone. At Bloworth Crossing, Wainwright follows the bed of the disused Rosedale Ironstone Railway. We depart from Wainwright after traversing the head of Farnsdale—southeast from the Lion at Blakey—another primordially grotty pub for bikers and hard lads, up on the moors like Tan Hill. We drop down into Rosedale and walk down towards Rosedale Abbey. The name's better than what you find. All Genuine Pastoral, etc., but not much after the Pennine Dales and the Lakes—best to stick to the tops of the North York Moors. The remains of the iron mines high on the side of the dale are the only thing notable. Our destination, the Abbey View Guesthouse, is yet another exercise in totalitarian moledom on the attack. However, we are able to escape the "evening meal" with the VW and drive to Helmsley. The Feversham Arms is a comforting place. The owner is Spanish. Better accommodation than cooking, perhaps, but it's ok and a useful place if you are wanting to walk in the vicinity of Rievaulx Abbey. We were too tired after dinner to phone up Piers Paul Read and ask him to have a drink with us. Back to Rosedale Nether.

September 21:
Rain, yet again, so into the VW and off to see the finds: the High Victorian Christ Church at Appleton-le-Moors by J. L. Pearson. Not so fanciful as Miss Losh at Wreay, or William Burges at Studley Royal, or Newby Hall, but very impressive. Then two Norman churches (Wintringham and Weaverthorpe) en route to the monolith at All Saints, Rudston—a generous, ithyphallic hunk of gritstone nearly twenty-eight feet tall in the churchyard. The Saxons may have tried putting a cross-head on the menhir to Christianize the profane stone. But, it rears on, in this quiet Wolds village in the valley of Gypsey Race.

On to Wharram Percy: "Deserted Medieval Village," it says on a green sign from the Ministry of Works. Pleasant stroll to the site and little to be fathomed from going there, except that two workmen were puttering about on the ruins of the church. Into the town of New Malton for a pub lunch. A good one may be had at the Green Man in the square. John Smith's ale from Tadcaster. And next, on to our destination: Goathland, on the moors. Three miles southeast you suddenly see looming to the right the Fylingdales Early Warning Station: "three perfect white globes of great size on three perfect black plinths in the grandiose undulating silence of the moor," says Professor Pevsner. It's René Magritte come to life, especially when you can barely see the radomes in the thick fogs of the area. Having checked into the Mallyan Spout Hotel, we are encouraged—for once. It was recommended by a friend in Leeds and he's not failed us. Just right for impossible Americans: private bath, color television in the room(!), radio in the room, comfortable beds, heat—all those things you learn to expect in Missoula, Montana. Off to view a stretch of the Roman Road on Wheeldale Moor, and then to walk down the beck below the waterfall of Mallyan Spout to the hamlet of Beckhole. Which is the veritable picturesque, where even the pub has a sign painted by a member of the Royal Academy in the Corot manner. How I enjoyed being able to watch a football match in the room after dinner and not to have to sit in the tiny bar with the whispers and mutterings of *la bourgeoisie anglaise* darkening one's life. Except for the Swaledale farmer, we had not encountered a single native with any lead in his or her pencil since the couple back at Ennerdale Bridge. Perhaps you might do better to tour all the Trappist monasteries in the United States than go looking for good chat coast-to-coast from St. Bees Head to Robin Hood's Bay.

September 22:
A tough walk, but the culmination. And a break in the rain bringing the prospect of decent light for photographs. I had one hundred slides in hand which surely look as though taken at eight in the evening with the help of a forty-watt bulb.

Northeast over the moors. Just before reaching a district called Eskdaleside Cum Ugglebarnby, we headed east along the flank of a hill above Parsley Beck. Just past a tumulus, rewarded with our first sight ever of an adder retreating slowly into the heather. A lot of rough going through trackless fields (and visions of adders biting at every squishy step). Eventually one gives up on the maps and heads for the waterfall of Falling Force in a wooded ravine further east. Good place for lunch. The way then climbs back up on the moors and follows back roads to the village of Hawsker. Another rarity: the slow worm moving quite quickly to get out of our path. There are only three different snakes in England and we'd seen two of them in the course of an hour (though the slow worm is, in fact, a lizard, it's snake enough for the folk). We made the pub in Hawsker with one minute to spare, just time to sink a pint of cold, pallid Newcastle Exhibition ale. It used to be good, but not from the icy, pressurized keg.

And then it is past the Northcliffe Caravan Site, down the hill to Maw Wyke Hole, and you are standing on greater cliffs than at the beginning at St. Bees Head. The North Sea disappears in the mists in three directions below our feet. Four miles south and west to Robin Hood's Bay, with cattle, barley fields and brambles to keep company.

Ian Gardner, the wee man himself, was waiting for us at the Victoria Hotel, waiting less patiently for a pint than us. Handsome doors with brass fittings, but another establishment run by people so dour and incompetent that you wonder that they ever wanted the slightest commerce with the Great Vile Public. Poor food and a poor attitude. Ah well, it's still Robin Hood's Bay. The village plunges crazily down to the beach and at the bottom are several pubs worth stopping in. We spent the evening so engaged, and left the hotelier and his toadish guests grumbling about poets and artists—"They should find work and get to it like decent people!" The biggest tides of the year had exposed a curious coastline. Many folk were out on the shingle, looking for bits of jet and for fossils washed out of the sandstone cliffs.

September 23:
    Ian drove us back to the Mallyan Spout to pick up the VW and then we all head for Corn Close. Bashō's words seemed just right: "More might be said, but feeling hesitant at such a place, I put aside my brush." He also said: "Who with brush or speech can hope to describe the work of heaven and earth's divinity?" Time to put anglophiliaphobia on the shelf to hibernate for awhile. Time to pack for America, to get back to the Blue Ridge and see its effulgence. Sumac and sourwood, dogwood and sweet gum were beginning to smolder. The Nation would have plenty of sap in it. And if nobody forced one to listen to AM-radio for twenty-four hours or to ABC-TV for a weekend, the chances of staying sane were fairly bright.

Epilogue at the Winter Solstice
    Today's the day. For eleven weeks I have watched the geriatric forces of George Allen play football. Can Old Whiskey master The Scrambler in Bloomington, Minnesota, this afternoon? My addiction to the Washington Redskins is venerable and hard earned. It goes back to the days when Slingin' Sammy Baugh and Andy Farkas and Charlie Malone did their thing in Griffith Stadium thirty-five years ago. Here, ten miles out in the woods from Highlands, I can watch not only the NFL but, by changing focus, look beyond the Sony and see the whole of the Nantahala Mountain Range stretched out along the western horizon. The leaf color was not good this fall but the sunsets have been up to snuff and the weather's been usually clear and cold. Otherwise: life at the desk. Or, life on the hard road. Out of one ear I keep exploring Schumann and Mompou, Granados, and Dutilleux. I have promised Robert Kelly to check the *Funeral Cantata for Gustave III of Sweden* by Joseph Martin Kraus. Another "K" is Charles Koechlin. Will I ever get to Wlodzimierz Kotonski?
    A trip at Thanksgiving reminded me that a man of my persuasions has more business in Lexington, Kentucky, than he does in London town. To drive down that back road on the Frankfurt side of Lexington and encounter, again, that sign

O'NAN'S AUTO SERVICE

is a cosmic infusion indeed. It's not that English English is entirely void of such zany color. Take Ian Gardner's poem:

BLUE
VEIN
SOLO

—which is not about a wheel of Stilton cheese but is Lancastrian euphemism for a bit of body English. In England my eyes and ears receive an epiphany of that order about twice a year. Not enough.

There are so many adumbrations in the Kentucky landscape. And more poets and photographers and characters than the law allows. "Gentlemen abed in England shall think themselves accursed they were not here!" Of course, the road to Lexington is fraught with digestive danger. Driving from there to Duke University we dared four franchise joints in a row: Bonanza Steak House, International House of Pancakes, Pizza Hut, Red Lobster. Bletch. (I never seem to get sick from a Big Mac, large fries, and a medium Coke.) And so we continue to live on the margins of this great greedy, lusty continent. January? After Super Bowl XI, a little trip to visit the three Southern photographers I have business with. And since I go to Bainbridge, Georgia, to talk with Paul Kwilecki, there's no point in missing a minute or two at Flannery O'Connor's grave, or photographing the temple complex of St. EOM in Buena Vista. Or, maybe, even stopping in Plains to buy some of those "Jimmythings" Miss Lillian talks about. No matter how far poetry gets dug in between a rock and a hard place, "Fish or cut bait" is still the first and the great commandment.

The next walk across England will be from Lancaster to Filey.

Highlands, North Carolina 1976

Further Adventures While
Preaching the Gospel of Beauty

32

Like the goliards of old, poets now ply the routes of civilizing culture on the grid between campus and campus. (For instance, take away Austin, Baton Rouge, Oxford, Tuscaloosa, Athens, Columbia, Chapel Hill, and Charlottesville, and see what a dark geographical night of the soul you are left with.) It is sobering work. You begin to think crazy things like: It's really a gas being An Established Younger Poet—instead of having *three* readers in Kentucky, I now know of *eight,* after three readings in Lexington, and Berea, but nothing yet at Pippa Passes. And: Gosh, I seem to have two readers in North Dakota I haven't even spent a single day cajoling in person.

Such curious thoughts help remove that lingering doubt that poetry has a place in the United States at all. Oh, it has a place, but involves less people than belong to the Cast-Iron Lawn-Deer Society of America, or who make Impeach Earl Warren samplers in petit point. If you want a jolt, I suggest you drive, say, from Penland School of Crafts in the North Carolina mountains up to Berea College in Kentucky, Cumberlands. Go by way of Kingsport, Tenn., then on U.S. 421 into Kentucky. William Blake never saw anything to touch it, dark satanic mills or not.

The town of Chevrolet, Ky. Dead as a doornail; dead, junked cars lining the highways for miles, sometimes with dogwood and flowering Judas growing out through the shells; and people who look like you imagine the poor of the Middle Ages, standing around and sitting around in this absolutely despoiled, stripped landscape. Thrown-away cars, thrown-away people. As Harry Caudill's *Night Comes to the Cumberlands* points out, there must be few places even on mainland Asia to rival this region for squalor. Chevrolet seemed the worst—the metaphor of the name helps of course—but it is town after town. You felt that each empty, silent town square should have a John Chamberlain sculpture in it—some memorial to the juicy smash-up in August, 1961, when eight locals got it on a slick road with a coal truck with its brakes gone. But, to build Chamberlains from the debris would be too much. It would come as a suggestion from Outside, and that is when triggers begin to get cocked. Like the gent who shot down one of Francis Thompson's cameramen last summer for photographing his house somewhere around Harlan.

You drive these roads turned corridors of junk, listening to Billy James Hargis and the Rev. Carl C. McIntire and "Life Lines" out of Dallas, and you come up against the basic American temper, the real heart of darkness. Caudill pegs it exactly: "A passionate lover of a freedom that was licentious, he was resolved to avoid even the mildest limitations on his liberty required by any kind of organized society."

Of course, the truth of the matter is that the poet or any worker on what *is* with his own hands is equally "licentious" to the in-groups of this society as those cast-out mountain folk. So poets and writers often duck into rat holes at academic institutions and hang about until their credentials are found wanting, or their morals. See there, I told you—you can't expect decent behavior from people like that. I'm afraid Mr. Keats gave the game away to the Philistines when he said that he had come only to trust the holiness of the heart's affections. That will only get you to heaven more quickly than you might care to go. Poets don't get silicosis working in the mines of eastern Kentucky, but the mortality rate in the profession is remarkably high. And for somewhat similar reasons. They get what's coming to them because they are shiftless, proud, and won't behave.

It was 8,000 miles around the Friendly Agora this past autumn by car. It amuses me to read members of the Urban Wolf Pack rejoicing on the liberality of the American character. If people in Macon County, N. C., read any number of my poems, my house would mysteriously burn down. But in New York or San Francisco the court poeticules can go downtown and see McClure's *The Beard* or read about Warhol in *Woman's Day,* and that's where it is, baby. Out beyond the flare of neon campfires, it is still indeed something else. Capote in Garden City, Kan.—the thought is very droll. I've put in some time in the Earp Country and it don't do like it say it do in that there nonfiction-type novel book. I forget which Russian novelist said that nice people were people with depraved morals, but he had it by the neck.

I recall an evening sponsored by the Illinois Arts Council, reading to an adult audience in Quincy, a remarkable river town, sensitive to its Victorian origins, not slavering to destroy them all, and managed by citizens with unusual enthusiasm for the arts. That the reading was held in the auditorium of an old bank with a Richardson flavor made it particularly pleasant for the reader. One gentleman told me afterward he had never been to a poetry reading before, but he hadn't slept at all. Also, he had done some research, and he could find no record of a literary evening in Quincy since Mr. Herman

Melville was there in 1848 to tell about the cannibals and curiosities of the South Seas. I wonder.

At any rate, it was dismaying to realize (again) how little currency the poem has for even citizens with the best will in the world. They have no time for it. My friend, Harold Cohen, who trains "untrainable" youths, tells me the ultimate human question is, What's in it for me? And, he says, you'd better damn well answer it—the organism is not wrong.

To address and try to elate 800 high-school students in Quincy at eight o'clock in the morning in an icy auditorium is another sobering adventure. You can see in the snake-eyed regard, the wise-guy angle in the collective shoulder, that "What's in it for me?" has been answered long ago, and tossed off with gum wrappers. Poetry is made by emotional cripples, guys who couldn't ride bicycles or anything else, left prone to the emotions, who can do nothing but what the words and the heart's affections and Orpheus tell them to do. All the poems in the world about Stan Musial, George Wallace, the sexual sweat, non-polluted language will cut no ice in 99 percent of these hearts where ice forms early. No wonder Orpheus found it easier to melt rocks and move trees than thaw the human heart. The Beatles get in there and begin poking about in the emotions—the kids drop them for the Monkees, who are like the nineteen-cent milkshake made of fish oil and plastic, guaranteed to contain no milk or ice cream at all.

Is it really true in the land of Whitman, Pound, Williams, Stevens, cummings, and infinite others that more people are interested in needlepoint than poetry? Of course. Which is more vestigial, the coelacanth or the hendecasyllabic line? Who can name the 500 leading American poets over six feet two inches, 240 pounds, born south of Homer, Ga., totally unknown to the *New Yorker*? Is it true that Marshall McLuhan was caught in a weekend raid at Miss Mnemosyne's Camp for Fallen Writers? Why did no one protest when the power company built a dam across Helicon and flooded the Elysian Fields?

There is this creep named Orpheus, an undesirable alien, running this here radio station in Antissa, Tex., and the sounds go into the ground and, O Gentle Readers, they are likely to stay there. This has been Freedom Talk No. 57, send twenty-five cents and your unheated heart to the Sidewinder-Central, care of this station. You never had it so cold, old buddy, although the song keeps saying things are getting better all the time.

Aspen, Colorado 1967

"We Take the Golden Road, to Samar, Kansas . . ."

33

The title means there has been a roadblock put between Occupied America and the sunset land of Frederick Delius. You have to go to the last chorus of his opera *Hassan* to get the music. If you go to Jacksonville, Florida, these days, the joke is on us.

I missed the dedication of "Delius House," adjacent to Swisher Gymnasium, Jacksonville University, 8:00 P.M., March 3, 1961.

> The Delius House has stood for three-quarters of a century at Solano Grove, thirty-five miles south of Jacksonville. Discussion of moving this historic homestead from its beautiful but isolated location on the St. Johns to the Jacksonville University campus first took place between Mrs. Henry L. Richmond and President Franklyn A. Johnson in 1957. However, the University felt unable to administer such an undertaking until this year. Now, thanks to the gift from Mrs. Richmond of the house and funds towards its re-erection, as well as the support of other friends of music, the Delius House will soon be visible to all. Its four rooms and four fireplaces, its two verandas and ornate woodwork, will be completely reconstructed.

I drove to Jacksonville the night of April 14th from Huntsville, Alabama, "Space Capital of the Universe," according to a billboard on the outskirts of town, donated by Governor Patterson or the local White Citizens Council. (I'm guessing.) I telephoned an old, tired socialist/humanist friend, recently arrived in the city to teach high school physics and chemistry. The school is named after Nathan Bedford Forrest. Remember him? Fustest with the mostest, and after de Wa he started the KKK. Ah well, it's a terribly modern looking school. So, we agreed to try to find out where poor Delius's house used to live: Picolata, a nineteenth-century English colony on the St. Johns, also notable for its early Spanish fort and for its mention in the journals of

William Bartram. Driving south next morning in the face of weather warnings of squalls and probable tornados, we crossed the river at Green Cove, now the home of the mothball fleet, straining at anchor to get to go to Cuba. At that point the St. Johns is, incredibly, four miles wide. Across the bridge, on the east bank, you turn south down a county road and head for Picolata, nine miles. It proved to be a matter of four private homes, one fish camp, an abandoned company store, and a workers' retreat owned by some large trucking firm. The proprietress at the fish camp was Typical Southren Waitress #1—fat, peroxided, rednecked, and blank. Nothing exuded from her except suspicion, particularly of two strangers who wanted to know about old houses being moved into Jacksonville. So, I knocked on the front door of the local gentry. All four mailboxes on the highway bore the same family name. An elderly woman came to the door, blowzy as the last but "substantial" in terms of Picolata. Back in the darkened living room an ancient woman was rocking. I again explained our mission. Solano Grove meant nothing, Frederick Delius meant nothing. Her attitude: well, we own most of the land around here and we'd know about anything like that that went on. I insisted, the house had been moved within two months and all authorities spoke of Picolata, including Delius. No, she said—impossible. If they moved some shack around here all they got was some darky cabin. Chuckle, chuckle, thank you, ma'am. We went back up the road towards Jacksonville about three miles to a gas station, thinking some working men might be inside who'd had to do with the transplantation. Again, no luck. The proprietor knew nothing. He said telephone the forest ranger. The forest ranger said, oh yes, I've heard there was some foreign music fellow around here a long time back, but his name was Vernon. I asked if he recognized the name Delius? No, Vernon was the name of the man you want. Amen, back to the car.

   Determined not to succumb to the collective unconscious quite so simply, we drove back to Picolata and on south into the oaks and mosses, which were behaving like a Cocteau wind tunnel in the turbulence before the storm. Couple of miles down the road I spied a turpentine camp and some of the hands sitting out in the yard—a Negro settlement. The crackers had so benumbed us that I came on very cautiously. Hello, we're looking for a cabin that got moved into town sometime lately, that used to belong to a man from England who wrote music. One of the men looked at me coolly and said, you mean Frederick Delius's plantation, Solano Grove, it's been moved to the campus of Jacksonville University. I said, gulp, yes. An older man then said, with equal clarity and poise, it's a shame, the people that used to come out here from Europe and New York would be terribly disappointed at what's happened. You know it's only been moved so they can make some money out of the tourists. Gulp, again. This man was an autocrat. His features and color suggested a Seminole strain. The younger man showed what Jelly Roll Morton called the Spanish tinge. Two other men sitting there were very dark, very simple country people who said nothing. We talked on for fifteen minutes or twenty minutes about a variety of things and each of the men employed a rich, exact vocabulary with a sophistication simply a world apart and ahead of what I had encountered earlier from three resident crackers. Yet the senior of the two spoke of lacking formal education after the third grade. I have no purpose to turn the search for Delius's plantation into a brief on Crow-Jimism—yet, how to deny it is a *constant* temptation as one lives more and more in the South. It is no secret where quality lies, and don't think that certain people don't know this, inside. At any rate, I must suggest that as the grove workers of 1884–85 were Delius's companions, whose songs he used in *Appalachia,* the *Florida* suite, it is only the Negro tenants south of Picolata who reverence his memory and spot the exploitation of his locale for just what it is. The older man said, as we left, one of the things wrong with this country nowadays is that all the neighborhoods are being destroyed. They got people on the move, nobody respects his neighbors anymore. They don't live anywhere steady so they don't work except for quick money and they'd do anything to get it, they'd do anything to land or to people. Which is a very cultivated remark—not culture-mongering.

Meantime, Jacksonville University has Delius's Solano Grove. In its setting next to the gymnasium, at the bottom of a hill beside an area like a football field, it faces southeast towards no water. At Picolata it gave upon the four-mile-wide St. Johns in the midst of orange trees and sheltered by a giant live oak some seven feet thick. "This property was practically inaccessible as a Shrine," claims the University. By which it means there isn't a Howard Johnson's within forty-five minutes. Well, let's get with it. The final chorale of *Appalachia* should now read: "O Honey, we are going down the drain pipe in the morning." Like the sign says, You Are Now Entering Fabulous Florida.

Highlands, North Carolina 1961

It is impossible to know this country. Keats's expression "wild surmise" still works. I can imagine the wild surmise on the faces of Navajo Indians confronted by models from *Harper's Bazaar*, recently plunked down in the lava beds near Kayenta, Arizona, to have their images snapped by a Japanese photographer. Or, the wild surmise if those models had no Hertz cars to flee in and had to spend a day or two in Kayenta, a sociological beauty spot rivalling even peerless Harlan County, Kentucky. So, I was about to begin my thirty-seventh journey in eighteen years across this continent back in November when, at dinner in Winston-Salem one night, I suddenly knew it was *very* crazy to keep running. Edward Dahlberg had been telling me so for years, but good advice is the last thing one wants. He wrote me: "I have come to the conclusion that a man who can be seated for several hours a day is a genius. Now, please, don't imagine you can fling off a book in three months. You can, but it won't be any good."

I'd been thinking that one benison of my hapless careening about might be a little essay on the last remaining restaurants in the United States where poets—not unionized truck drivers, for once—liked to eat. I had a few places firmly in mind. Not the urban places like the Red Star Inn in Chicago, Galatoire's in New Orleans, Tadich's in San Francisco, or Obrycki's in Baltimore, but if you were in nether Kansas. Wright Morris had once told me about the hotel dining room in Osborne on US 24; I'd also been to the Brookville Hotel for a good chicken dinner, and to a nameless sparerib joint in the black section of Lawrence. I'd been to the only culinary oasis in Utah: Parry's Motor Lodge, in Kanab, where you could escape the severe indignities of Bryce, Zion, and the North Rim of the Grand Canyon. And I'd been to the Red Barn on Sea Island, Georgia; and in North Carolina to the Pollirosa in Tobaccoville, the Tavern in Old Salem, and the Nu-Wray Inn in Burnsville. Yet, I have not had a truly memorable public meal in this country in years and begin to fear it is now impossible, as we enter the era of Shirley Temple, Billy Graham, Art Linkletter, Guy Lombardo, and the other arbiters of elegance in the Nixonian Age.

I wrote for help from a number of poets and writers. Russell Edson wrote back, poignantly: "Food joints? Are you kidding? Food is just something I put in my head." Mary Ellen Johansen said: "Please do nothing to abet the poisoners! I once had catfish and hushpuppies in Missouri before the Second War—the rest is silence." Oddly, every time I read or see Mr. Craig Claiborne, he seems enormously genial and pleased with the state of nature. Maybe it is because he grew up in Mississippi and ate well at home? Or, because he lives on Manhattan Island and doesn't have to drive 573 miles for a lousy meal?

I want to talk about other aspects of the Agora Road. Last spring in Aspen, Colorado, where I was endeavoring to convince business executives that poets should not be slaughtered wholesale for the improvement of public morals—this I accomplished mainly by playing better volleyball than executives do—I read a book of travels of the seventeenth-century Japanese haiku-master, Bashō: *The Narrow Road to the Deep North* (this Penguin Classic is an excellent translation). Trying to use my eyes and his sensibility, I began a spring drive of my own from Colorado to North Carolina. Some of the notes, as I glance at them now, seem apposite to the gustatory gloom I announced earlier.

The Valley of the Roaring Fork River is very bright under the blue sky and six inches of fresh snow. The *Blau Reiter,* my faithful VW-1600 companion, also carries a six-inch mantle of snow as it leaves Aspen. Bashō: "The thought of the 3000 miles before me suddenly fills my heart, and neither the houses of the town nor the faces of my friends could be seen by my tearful eyes except as a vision." The drive to Denver—up the Glenwood Canyon, over Vail, over Goodland—is muted and hardly observed. I "come to" coming out of the mountains near Golden and the Coors brewery, where the traffic picks up. I chew three No-Doz tablets, put "The Magical Mystery Tour" very loud on the tape stereo, and head for Denver, that recent City of the Plains. Driving across Denver on freeways, it seems ridiculous and aggresively sterile. But, 4:30 on a Friday afternoon like that: the poet/executive Thomas Hornsby Ferril is in his office at the Great Western Sugar Company writing non-saccharine poems; the sisters out at Loretto Heights College are reading Dorn and Ginsberg; Fred Rosenstock is selling good, honest books in a genuine bookshop; Harry Hoffman is selling vast quantities of good liquor; and the light in the central well of the Brown Palace Hotel is probably extraordinary. To know even this *little* about one of America's vacant cities has taken me years and years. We have no guidebooks. We have no men like Geoffrey Grigson or Professor Pevsner to take us through a region and inform

us of geology, food, history, buildings, plants, birds, writers, lodging. (Mobil
Guides? AAA?—try them and see.)

On into Kansas. Beatles, Getz/Gilberto, Dvořak, Ives, Stones, Doors,
Aretha, Kurt Weill—and more No-Doz. It all works until Goodland. How
fat and black the earth in Kansas is, to quote a Kansas poet (Ronald Johnson).
But, no poet has ever yet stuck it out long enough there, like the cottonwoods
or the soil over the limestone—you would have to grow inwardly, then be a
green fist out of the ground with corn leaves and with wheat sheaves worn at
the wrist. Bashō: "Your poetry issues of its own accord when you and the
object have become one." I guess it is not surprising that John Cage and Virgil
Thompson rolled up their windows and headed for *anywhere* after being
served peanut-butter pie in Kansas. Or that Frieda left Lawrence's ashes on
a lunch counter there on the way to Taos and had to turn around fifty miles
up the road.

Bill Stafford is visiting in Lawrence, Paris of the Plains, also on the
Orphic Trail. But mostly by plane: Minnesota one day, Tucson the next.
Funny, how conversation between poets on the road is: Did you find out
about the great Mexican restaurant with the sour cream enchiladas? Boy,
did you ever see more cadaverous, hostile graduate students than at Urbana?
What do you think—will the Twins flub it again this season? Stafford is a
bright, endlessly amiable, homely, virtuous man, sort of like those prairie
dogs he evokes better than anyone else. It is good to meet him. The weather
is blustery, with a touch of rain now and then. It is good to look south across
the low hills, amid books and pleasant, quiet conversation at the home of a
Whitman scholar. Later, I type letters, read on into the Bashō text, and take
a nap while 19,000 people go to see Robert Kennedy in the fieldhouse of the
university.

In Missouri the idea is: drive on the interstate to Columbia, then head
south past Jefferson City for the Ozarks, a new run for me. Country settled
by Germans: Schubert, Westphalia (where, if you look in your borrowed
Missouri WPA Guide, you find that Father Ferdinand Benoit Marie Guislain
Helias d'Huddeghem celebrated Mass in 1838), Freeburg, and Vienna. The
Guide here informs us that the Irish in the neighborhood wanted to name
the town after a lady late of the presiding judge's family, a Miss Vie Anna.
The Germans, on the other hand, munched their kraut and said: Vienna!
After that the culture changes, you come to Vichy (a spa in its day), and then
the Gasconade River, which is still a blue green and undisturbed and handsome. But somehow I have picked the wrong roads, they are the ones with
the truck traffic and newer filling stations. But, I have been through, or near,
towns with the names: Licking, Safe, Boss, Turtle, Minimum, Braggadocio,
Huzza, and Shook, and that is *something*. On US 60 west of Ellsinore I see
one lone pine tree in the rain with as beautiful a silhouette as I have ever seen.
Bashō would have slammed on the brakes, got out, got out the inkstone, had

an amorous seizure, and written a poem. All I did was tip my cap and then thank the castrator-crew from the local telephone company. The rain begins to pour down, I duck into "The Beautiful Avalon Motel" in Poplar Bluff and do not dream of the Western Isles of Delight at all.

Up at 4:30 and off into the eastern dawn. How depressing it is to be stared at beadily by chewing-gum salesmen in the Holiday Inn breakfast counter at Sikeston. *Nothing* about their interchangeable Sears square-box worsted or their crew cuts makes me want to stare at them in the slightest. I feel precisely like something they'd like to have in their sights come Saturday's hunt down the river.

Cairo, yclept *Karo*: the junction of the Mississippi and the Ohio. It is very very vast, very sombre, the actual spot is not mucked up. Paducah: Irwin S. Cobb's home and (I learn too late, though another informant insists Mayfield, Kentucky) a cemetery with a gentleman surrounded by marble replicas of his friends, his family, his pets, his horses. At the entrance to the Western Kentucky Parkway I telephone ahead to the Abbey of Gethsemani at Trappist and tell the Brother who answers I'd like to get a message to Thomas Merton, an old friend. Oh, he says, but don't you know it's Lent! Father Lewis does not see people during Lent! Well, it would not do to crawl under the fence and track him to the hermitage without announcement, so, I have to forego the pleasure of a final hour with Monk Tom by the Monk's Pond. My Lexington host, Fesser Davenport in local parlance, is on spring vacation and in even more misanthropic mood than I. Why not? He is racing deadlines for the *National Review*. I therefore take up four-day residence at the Lexington Motor-Inn, only because it is across a beltway from the local VW place. It is run by vile types, featuring a Baptist concierge who mistrusts everything you do and sees SIN everywhere. I sip my bourbon in silence, write letters, and visit John Jacob Niles, Mrs. Victor Hammer, Ralph Eugene Meatyard, and Jonathan Greene, who tend the Orphic Fires in that particular horsey desert. (Lexington is very much like Charleston, S. C.—it is *assumed* that *genteel people* do *not* eat in *public*. Arrangements have been made.) Returning to the motel the final night I see its marquee proclaiming: WELCOME IBM COSMICOAT MULTIGRAPHS. Yes, folks, "Invaders" have landed and may be looking like Uncle George at this very dire instant. In a daze I drive on past Colonel Sanders's natal place in Corbin, Ky., and head for the North Carolina mountains. Which means you have to survive the roads of ADULTS ONLY: HAWAIIYAN THIGHS . . . LILY HIGH ONE MILE . . . MINCEY MINE . . . NELLIE TAVERN . . . 4-PAW HOTEL ERECTED '30. "Dark is Life, Dark is Death," to quote not one of them Japs but a real white-blooded southern T'ang poet, Edgar Li-Po.

The next time I write anything down is a week later, in San Juan, Puerto Rico, where a conglutination of businessmen needs to look at a poet, find it wanting, and jostle it about a little in the resort-type sunshine. The hotel is in the latest Israeli-Regency Plastic-Mishmosh style. Marshall McLuhan, the Joe Namath of Electronic Circuitry, is the keynote Knockout, chunking some very heavy ideas into mentalities as deep, blank, and receptive as ravines. Zonk! And again zonk! "There is no such thing as Time; there is no such thing as Space; there is no such thing as Place; there is no such thing as Children!!!" Some of this rapping takes place in the "Hunca-Munca Room," very psychedelic, very commercial. The electricity, of course, fails and the acoustics are hopeless. After dinner one Thursday night in a ballroom where 1,500 American executives and spouses are dressed to look like Latinos (olé!) in funny hats and plastic lace, someone comes by the table and says, Did you hear?—somebody got Martin Luther King in Memphis. The only thing to do is to sober up immediately, drink a lot more, and go out to sleep on the beach.

A week later: the day after Dr. King's funeral. Driving down Interstate 85 between Salisbury and Charlotte, North Carolina, six fifteen in the morning, sixty-five miles per hour on the dial, Mr. Ives's First Symphony blaring out the assumed virtues of the Republic on the stereo. I suddenly look to my left and see a car pacing me. Inside are three soul-brothers looking very non-soulful and downright mean. The one in the back has a rifle, not pointed, but raised carefully where I can see it. Well, *there* you might say, *it is*, it's that existential dilemma you read about in them French novels. There's no place to go on an interstate except straight ahead until the next exit. Do you say: hey, baby, wait a minute, let's pull over and talk this thing over? Here's my CORE card and my receipt from the SCLC. I was just that minute thinking about Thelonious and John Coltrane, born up the road a piece; and of what to say at my poetry reading at the university about Dr. King. No—you don't say one word, you just look back at the road, notice the absence of cars on the road, feel the sweat turn cold, try to assume that you and Mr. Ives are no more to blame than any "innocent" bourgeois, etc. After three or four minutes the car speeds up and disappears ahead out of sight. Quickly, the United States is a lonelier and sadder country than we knew. O, friend Bashō: "I wavered ceaselessly like a bat that passes for a bird at one time and for a mouse at another . . . a hundred bones & 9 orifices . . . priest I am not, for the dust of the world still clings to me."

Walter Kaufman was in Puerto Rico and said it another way: "It takes so much daring to keep one's decency." I would *love* to feel that America was more than a few sacred places and the 5,000 people I befriend or am tolerated by. ("Society is merely everybody else, and it is impossible to owe everybody anything"—Thomas Berger, in *Killing Time*.) I would love to feel like walking on this continent the 175,000 or 180,000 miles De Quincey attributed to William Wordsworth in Britain, before his sixtieth birthday. It is gloomy, very gloomy to suspect that the people all come out of cans like the food does, that the Plastic Hydrangea People are winning the battle, that Ty Cobb would no longer even try to catch the ball. Would that nationalized hope were as simple as making up picture post cards for motels: clouds added to deep blue sky ($5.00); new blue sky with or without clouds, sunsets, etc. ($10.00); substitute green grass ($15.00). Ah, Bashō: "It was a great pleasure to see the marvellous beauties of nature, rare scenes in the mountains, or along the coast, or to visit the sites of temporary abodes of ancient sages where they had spent their secluded lives, or better still, to meet people who had entirely devoted themselves to the search for artistic truth . . . to find a genius hidden among weeds and bushes."

Instead, from all these years along the Orphic Trail, the din from Pejor-ocracy is getting alarmingly loud. Maybe this is just turning forty and still being a poet? It gets harder being a man and doing child's work, poetry. So much for Youth, which becomes more and more and knows less and less. Flow softly, Shirley Temple, till I end my song. To end on a sanguine note, I quote those comforting, apocryphal words of Dorothy's at a rainbow-moment in *The Wizard of Oz*: "Oh, Toto, this doesn't look like Kansas at all!" You bet your sweet ass it doesn't!

Penland, North Carolina 1969

A la Recherche
du Sud Perdu

35

I spent an evening this Christmas in the home of maternal cousins in Atlanta. There wasn't a "real" object in the house. Every object was imitation English Gentry/Louis XV, Rich's-Department-Store crapioca pudding—strictly hideous, totally useless, and unused at all except when the Randall J. Androids from next door would drop in to compare notes on how many people had cancer, how many friends (heh! heh!) would have strokes in the next month, and how many new neighbors had queer, Commie, and/or nigger-lovin' uncles. Better conversation you get in the DeKalb County Columbarium & Garden of Precious Memories. Anyway, in the midst of this deracinated, despirited, veneered universe, I suddenly caught sight of an old plastic card-table top—which the hostess apologized for and said she would replace when she had enough green stamps. It was a magic object, aging honestly into a picture of a world with adumbrations of Ryder, Moreau, and Berman. So, of course, it was on its way to the dump.

———

Riding the New York/Asheville run of the Southern RR ever since I was a child, the memory of it is a potent one. Once I got old enough to read Thomas Wolfe I enjoyed travelling the Asheville Special even more. If you started *Of Time and the River* where it started, the platform at Biltmore, N. C., you could read Wolfe's elephant-gun prose (Bring It All Back Alive) in time to the landscape—out across Buncombe Country to Black Mountain, down the Swannanoa Gap past Andrews Geyser into Old Fort, with its six-foot cement arrowhead looming in the plaza next to the station. And by the time dinner was called, down around Hickory, and the sun was down, you'd have heard all about Tom's wild drinking bout en route to New York. One trip I was reading this and smoking in the men's room. A Thantis lozenge salesman walked in, said boy I admire that man Wolfe, produced a bottle, and said let's have a little drink.

So, Watchman, what of the South? What of this bizarre, repressive piece of geography whose doyens and docents and scions and worthies will brook no criticism without the loudest screaming and yelling? Let me explain right away that I regard the place with lifelong foreboding, yet I am currently in the midst of a twenty-six-part book on the territory, *An ABC to the Naturally Bodacious Southland*. It requires *stealth*, for, being a timid soul underneath the bulk and the energy, I live down South in a hole I have contrived, dug in the mountains, where Delius's *Eine Messe des Lebens* or the Bruckner Eighth at full volume will disturb neither the evangelists nor the vigilantes.

Highlands, North Carolina 1964, 1961, 1978

The Arts—a (Finger-Lickin') Southern Experience

36

Before I tell you anything else, let me tell one story that seems as mythical to me as anything that ever happened to the gods clothed as men.

I was camped out in the Sunset Orchard above Elk Park, North Carolina, on the Appalachian Trail. Early July, 1961. About seven thirty in the cool of the evening a man and his wife walked near, looking at the condition of the trees, and nearly stumbled over my companion and me. Later the man came back and invited us for Sunday breakfast. "I'm a poor man but you're sure welcome to anything we got." I thanked him kindly but said we have to leave right early to get on to the next shelter along the trail before dark. He said, Well, boys, I'm generally up by four o'clock. I said well, thank you, six thirty is fine by us if it's ok by you. Fine. The man's name was James Greene. He and his wife were remarkably handsome people. His hair was still black. He was sixty and had fathered fourteen children. "I've always been a farmer, but times aren't good for land around here, so I work regular for the highway department over in Tennessee." Next morning at dawn we walked down the hollow west of the orchards and came up to Mr. Greene's cabin. "Boys, come in! The woman, the girl children will serve us." The breakfast was buttermilk biscuits, wild strawberry preserves, chicken gravy, cornpone, redeye gravy, country ham, rice, sliced tomatoes, streak-o-lean, cold fried chicken, churned butter, heavy cream, fried eggs, homemade apple butter, comb honey, fresh milk, and good coffee. "Now boys, take all you want. It's simple but it's a fair start on the day. We don't often get a chance to visit with folks from away from here and it sure is nice for us. You'unses come back, please, any time, and sit a spell with us. I mean it, boys."

Mr. Greene's kindness still brings tears to the eyes. The episode comes from an America that is almost gone. Henry James in the *American Scene* remarked that the saddest thing about America, even then, was that so few people really cared for the land. It suffered, and then we suffered accordingly.

But here was Mr. Greene, of Elk Park, and "the woman" moving in that orchard in the twilight as truly as the couple in *Appalachian Spring*. Oh, that we had more such sacred folk, in such sacred places. On top of Walnut Mountain, a few days south in Pisgah Forest, I had wanted to make a particular beech grove and spring a "sacred grove." But sacred to whom? It is what we yearn for—what the wood thrush's song seizes in the mind and turns to liquid. The throat is parched.

> he is close to them,
> but he sees them not. . .
>
> he touches them,
> but he feels them not. . .
>
> he may be said
> to have lost his country—
>
> confine him entirely within the
> solitude of his own heart. . .

The words are, oddly enough, Tocqueville's. I make a poem out of them to make them even more lucid and memorable. The title of the poem might be "A Threnody on Mr. America, Privateer." It is hardly news that Tocqueville was an extraordinary observer. When I think about the "South," or think "larger" of this somewhat foolish attempt to build a civilization on a continent vaster than the body of a Titan, Tocqueville keeps coming on strong: "Everyone shuts himself up in his own breast and affects from that point to judge the world."

My father's people have been in the North Carolina hill country since before the Battle of King's Mountain (1780), which makes for no sense of tradition in me in the least. Many of the names are already forgotten. Families are the most arcane of institutions—who learns anything from them? The skeletons stay in the closets; the young never get the facts. Who is really interested in the uncle who is a judge, or the cousins who practice law or run the barber shop or the newsstand? We make our own ancestors, and mine are William Bartram and his "Franklin Tree," André Michaux and his shortia; I know that Vachel Lindsay must have walked the old road through the family orchard in 1906 from Dillard to Highlands, and that Béla Bartók and Charles Ives both visited Asheville and stayed at the Grove Park Inn to recover their health. That I was born in Asheville twenty-nine years after Thomas Wolfe is important to me. Wolfe and I both suffer from the same Buncombe County virus. There is *something* in the water of the French Broad River—demanding that one go everywhere, eat everything, read everything, drink everything, know everything and everybody. Hopeless, hopeless, but it runs in our systems and we are all much more automatic than we imagine.

What kind of "place" is the South? That's no kind of question, because it's as steep as a horse's face *and* flat as a baptist's tit. In Robert Creeley's words, there is no such thing as "place" except as it exists within a given man. But, surely, down South it takes a *lot* of digging to come up with anything but texasophiles, senatoreastlands, reptile gardens, Bombingham, and motel operators looking as poisonous as the greasy barbecue. My mother's people were Georgians. The largest ceremonial mounds in the East were on my great-grandmother's farms near Cartersville—the Etowah Mounds, whose artifacts have surprising connections with the Toltecs of Mexico. Playing in those fields as a child, I managed to avoid most (but not all) of the viruses spawned by the likes of Red-Gallus-Gene Talmadge. It took me four years in an Episcopal school in Washington, D. C., and the help of a Quaker friend to learn that all Negroes weren't named Bessie, came to work at the back door, loved to work for white folks, were actually shiftless, but could be trusted at twenty-five cents an hour if they were fat, very black, and smiled a lot. That is one "place" where I and 90 percent of the genteel people I know in the South part company. W. J. Cash pointed out definitively in *The Mind of the South* that Southerners have no minds, just tempers and passions. That most people are more concerned with the color of skin than with character as expressed in and around the eyes is something that strikes me as incredible. An utterly tragic error for which all pay dearly every day of their lives.

I was also fortunate in my grandmother's place. She lived only two blocks from Joel Chandler Harris's home, Wren's Nest, in the West End of Atlanta. So, *Uncle Remus* was an early companion. From my father I acquired readings of *Lyrics from Cotton Land* by John Charles McNeil, and of *Ol' Man Adam* and *Ol' King David and the Philistine Boys,* by Roark Bradford. Also, a few Gullah tales. My friend LeRoi Jones would consign me to Ofay Ellhay if he knew all this, but the language of these dialect writers is one thing, their social conscience something else. I don't think such books make bigots—paternalists, probably, but not bigots.

All that is way back in early childhood. Except for Thomas Wolfe, Eudora Welty, and the early Capote, I have read almost nothing "literary" from the South. Reading Faulkner, like paying attention to who was who's grandfather or reading about the Civil War, is something I have never been able to do. I read Allen Tate on Poe, Donald Davidson on the Tennessee River, but neither on aristocracy or the integration of schools. This is the distrust of agrarians and gentry one would expect from one bred in the North Carolina hills. In North Carolina I distrust anything that happens at an elevation lower than 3,000 feet. I shall *never* forget what happened in 1957 just after I had been awarded a Guggenheim fellowship. I had been making a tour of colleges all over the state, reading gratis in behalf of my press, and the poets of New Directions, Grove Press, City Lights Books, and other smaller writers' presses. It was suggested to the librarian of the Asheville Public Library that I appear in its auditorium. The reaction was: "No, if you let one of these local people in, you have to let them all in." I made a vow never to read in the town of my birth under any circumstances—easy to keep since I have still not been asked.

North Carolina is a haven of journalists, whether inbred like Jonathan Daniels or yankeefied like Harry Golden. Neither has much use for poetry since Tennyson. I went to one North Carolina writers conference in the Piedmont to find this out ten years ago, and I learned the lesson. So it strikes me as very odd to think of myself as a North Carolina writer, coming from Macon County, etc. Nothing at all stirs me, as it apparently stirred Mr. Faulkner, to consider manning the barricades of the Old North State against the federal government, or to defend Macon County against Cherokee County, for that matter. It has a lot to do with the ultimate clannishness of the Welsh and Scots, whose blood I carry. You can read all about this in Harry Caudill's *Night Comes to the Cumberlands,* or in Horace Kephart's *Our Southern Highlanders.*

My country neighbor, Uncle Iv Owens, thinks I'm in the "poultry" business. No chickens and no eggs, but, also, no questions asked, for which I thank him. *Poetry* is not a word in Mr. Owens's vocabulary—and why should it be? The old gentleman only knows a few verses of Scripture by heart and how to order off for a few things in the Sears catalog.

I can sit and listen to Uncle Iv pronouncing on God and the price of towelling for hours on end. As he says, the Feller who made time, I reckon he made lots of it. Occasionally, he apologizes for "hesitatin' " you, but, *Laus Deo,* what could be better than this speech, solid, simple as a rock wall? It is like picking up amethyst crystals in the path. The ear can find them perfectly formed. An example:

Uncle Iv Surveys His Domain
from His Rocker of a Sunday Afternoon
As Aunt Dory Starts to Chop Kindling

Mister Williams
lets youn me move
tother side the house

the woman
choppin woods

mite nigh the awkerdist thing
I seen

In this linguistic sense I will declare I too am a mountain poet. I have some symbiotic relation with a man like that, as I do with plants with amazing names like punktatum, ginseng, vipers bugloss, pipsissewa, and bloodroot. There are certain things I must see, or I lose track of time, of what I am doing, of where I am. The April day when the bloodroot appears in its delicate white blur by the trail; the September day in the high mountains when the viburnum is in color (yellow/green/brown) too rare and too translucent to describe; the shade and quality of galax and dog hobble on crisp blue days in January along the icy creeks; the wood thrush at dusk in June; the mare's-tail clouds in late afternoon in November; the meadow time of joe-pye weed, oxeye daisy, and ironweed; the migration of the hawks over Wesser Bald at that same season. These are the things that bring oneself to oneself.

Each man saves himself, in the given place, as best he can; that figures. I do it as, and when, I can. North Carolina, that large abstraction with some 4,000,000 Baptists I shall try never to meet, hardly matters—except that it seems on the whole a superior abstraction to some place called South Carolina. Paul Goodman once tried to teach me: "The society I live in is mine, or I did not live in it at all." Actually, however, the society I live in is a non-Quaker society of friends. Out of the continental conglomeration, I have selected some several thousand persons and some few landscapes: the Appalachian Ridge from Springer Mountain to Katahdin, the Big Sur coast, the Roaring Folk Valley in Colorado. The rest of it is Australia for the automobile and most of the characters think big and mean and come out of a can. The South "exists" for me because I can go to Biloxi, Mississippi, and find Lyle Bongé, the photographer, there. Or Eudora Welty up in Jackson. Or Clarence John Laughlin or Bill Russell on the job in New Orleans; or Tom Merton in his hermitage at Trappist, Kentucky; or Guy Davenport, Ralph Eugene Meatyard, and John Jacob Niles, surviving botulism and bluegrass blather in shoddy Lexington. Beware the lower elevations! If I do travel the Piedmont, I do not forget the particular spots on my underground railway: Penland School of Crafts, the Architecture School at the University of Virginia, the young editors of Lillabulero magazine at Chapel Hill, the new blood at Berea College, Jim Fitzgibbon and Dick Walser at N. C. State at Raleigh, and the receptive people in Winston-Salem, probably the best town for artists of all kinds in the South or anywhere else. They all help keep the Volkswagen moving and the bile ducts in low gear.

A bit earlier I said that I was an autochthonous mindless recording mechanism established ecologically within a mountain region. Of course, the contrary is just as true. I am as laconic as a pebble or Anton Webern *and*

garrulous as the montane lengths in Bruckner. So, life is not the eyrie I would
choose it to be, the poet living quietly, invisibly, making his poems as a peony
bush makes peonies. There are demons about to chop through poets and
peonies, and other people too. One is *engaged*.

Do I write "Southern" poems? I rather hope not, whether the material
starts in the tater patch or not. I forget where Martial came from. Roman
Empire! Ok. American Empire—who can forget it? But, perhaps this is the
most Southern poem I've written. It grew out of a remark by D. H. Lawrence
about a book by Edward Dahlberg *(Bottom Dogs)*, neither having anything
directly to do with the South. But Lawrence said of the American character
(generally) in 1929: "The spirit and will survived, but something in soul had
perished." It set me off.

Cobwebbery

the best spiders for soup
are the ones under
stones—

ask the man who is one:
plain white american

(not blue gentian red indian
yellow sun black caribbean)

hard heart, cold
mind's found

a home
in the ground

"a rolling stone, nolens volens,
ladles no soup"

maw, rip them boards off
the side the house

and put the soup pot on

and plant us some petunias
in the carcass of the Chevrolet

and let's stay here
and rot in the fields

and sit still . . .

About now is when the cultured folks are going to start climbing into the woodwork. They will ask questions like, "But why must he write about disgusting things?" Mercy me, who are the poets writing for today? The answer to that one, O Gentle Reader, is *you*, you devious bastard. For once stand there and listen and don't fink out that it's for the other guy, or for other poets, or for posterity. You and me, O Gentle Reader, let's go round and round and round.

I like to get my ear right to the ground and listen to this Nation talk its trash. In certain styles the South is impossible to beat: the billboard and the graffito; e.g., like from nature. Blush if you like, but don't duck me the way we've mostly ducked this poor polluted country.

INPEACH EARL WARRIN!
—Highway 29, near Opelika, Alabama

BY ALL MEANS
BUY AL MEANS
—Goshen, Alabama

THE LAST WOMAN ON EARTH &
I WAS HITLER'S BRIDE
—double bill, drive-in, Bay Minette, Alabama

JESUS SAVES!
BURMA SHAVES!
—200 yards of Highway 29 near Greenville, South Carolina

POLICEMEN WILL PLEASE REFRAIN FROM EATING
THE CAMPHOR BALLS FROM OUT OF THE UNRINALS
— Biloxi, Mississippi

I PASSED FOR WHITE &
SNOW WHITE AND THE SEVEN DWARFS
—drive-in, Iuka, Mississippi

THE GOVERNOR OF ALABAMA IS A MOTHER
—bumper sticker, California T-bird, east of Athens, Georgia

ON THE STROKE OF MIDNITE HER TAMPAX TURNS
INTO A WATERMELON
—Varsity Hamburger Grill, white-men-only john, Auburn, Alabama

It's finger-lickin' good, Colonels & Ladies, finger-lickin' good. Alabama is clearly more than we thought it was. Gentility is beyond the question. Much beyond.

Poems are made out of words and the construction of and between words. They are not made by the Daughters of the Confederacy, memories of Sidney Lanier and the Lost Lenore, bathos, gentility, moist underwear, Gideon Bibles, vestments of the Confederate Dead or the Grateful Dead, stuffed larks, singing in the rain. Educated ladies & gentlemen, who usually have as much to learn about life as they do about words, must not let their quondam courses in philosophy, religion, needlepoint, Texas history, stenography, how to cross and uncross the legs, and contraception blind them to this simple truth: *poems are made out of words.* You thump a poem with your ear and your eye—if it doesn't sound and look like this thing called a poem-watermelon, then you toss it aside. One has an abiding taste for good watermelons and a tradition stemming from Eden. Thump it! hump it! *abi gezunt!*

A few final severities about chauvinists, loyalists, localists. If somebody tells me, "Buddy I reckon there aint nuthin bettern the world than cornpone," I expect that citizen to know also the taste of brioche, pumpernickel, scones, sour dough, and tortillas, just to name five of a hundred breads in the world. The South has a few things, like gumbo and spoon bread and George Lewis's clarinet and houses on the order of The Shadows-on-the-Teche. Let us honor them but realize we're suckin' quite a lot of hind-titty. In a society as violent and Neanderthal as ours, I write for "cultivated" people, more or less out of self-defense. Kenneth Rexroth has put it very well: "There is no place for a poet in American society. No place at all for any kind of poet at all. . . . The majority of American poets have acquiesced in the judgement of the predatory society. They do not exist so far as it is concerned. They make their living in a land of make-believe, as servants of a hoax for children. They are employees of the fog-factories—the universities. They help make fog. . . . They turn out bureaucrats, perpetuate the juridical lie, embroider the costumes of the delusion of participation, and of late, in departments never penetrated by the humanities staff, turn out atom, hydrogen, and cobalt bombers—genocidists is the word. . . ."

An advertisement in the *New York Times* (Sunday) for the Liberty Music Shop promotes James Dickey: "a former football player, war hero, advertising executive. His poems are easy to follow, but impossible to forget." The copy writer is all but bleeding to take the curse off poetry. Will arts councils effect a viable change? Art being the act of a single intelligence, the likelihood is debatable. Cyril Connolly put the central proposition: Everything for the milk bar and nothing for the cow.

Aspen, Colorado 1967

A White Cloud in the Eye
of a White Horse:
Crafts of the
Southern Appalachians

37

> Philosophers and theologians have yet to learn that a physical fact is as
> sacred as a moral principle. Our own nature demands from us this
> double allegiance.
>
> —Louis Agassiz, *The Natural History of the United States*

The editor of *Craft Horizons* will have inadvertently stuck her hand in the
hornets' nest by asking a poet to report on the crafts situation in the southern
mountains. Nothing is madder than a wet hornet, and some will buzz, "What
would *he* know about handweaving, saddening the color of a vegetable dye,
firing a kiln, or turning a piece of walnut?" The answer to each is nothing.
However, I take it that the poet's business is to know the difference between
kitsch and wild honey. We are back in the country now, and I have the
countryman's tongue.

In his book *Handicrafts of the Southern Highlands,* Allen Eaton
pointed out the connection between the mountain ballad and handicraft.
On several occasions, readers of these pages have been reminded—to get
down to the roots of things—that the Teutonic *craft* meant *power.* Charles
Olson also reminds us of this by the oracular observation: "*He who controls
rhythm controls. . . .*" And a new statement by Robert Kelly, poet, yields
greatest clarity: "The true craft, then, of the poet is total response to the
powers of his source energy—memory or imagination or inspiration. *Mnemosyne* or *Mousa,* we shall not argue that here—arising in him. In that sense,
craft is now exactly what it has always deeply been: perfected attention." So,
let one participant in a craft process try to come to grips with others so
involved in making a marriage of themselves and their materials. Harold
Rosenberg spoke to this problem during the First World Congress of Craftsmen (1964) when he said: "What defines art as craft is placing the emphasis

on the object to the exclusion of the personality of the artist, his uniqueness, his dilemmas." My business, then, in this essay will be to see, to hear, and to make some sense of my findings.

The poet is always apologizing lest his word potency seem to affect culture less than that of the roadside maker of pink plaster flamingos. I live in Highlands, North Carolina, "Highest Incorporated Town in Eastern America," and one of the chief reasons I do is that I know *where* I am there. If someone asks, "How far is Highlands from New York," I reply, "Oh, about a hundred days." That is how long it took me to hike from Springer Mountain, Georgia, to Bear Mountain on the Hudson along the Appalachian Trail. I hear the hornets buzzing, get on with it, get on with it! But, you do not hurry here in Appalachia. It is considered uncultivated. I have stood many an hour while my neighbor, Uncle Iv Owens, prognosticated tomorrow's weather. Why not? Old Walt told us: "Loaf, and invite the Soul." So this essay is going to be done *adagio*, like afternoon clouds, like Bruckner, with a few passages reorchestrated by Erik Satie.

"A white cloud in the eye of a white horse," my title, is an image from my poem "The Flower-Hunter in the Fields," a celebration of William Bartram, eighteenth-century Quaker botanist from Philadelphia, who discovered the Appalachians in 1775 and wrote of them as Eden in his miraculous book of *Travels*. Before one talks of crafts and the present, one should have a ground sense of what the land was. Bartram gives us this, and the way to read him is in Francis Harper's "Naturalist's Edition," with commentary and annotations, published by Yale University Press in 1958. Bartram is at Rose Creek at its confluence with the Little Tennessee River in Cowee Valley below the Nantahala Mountains—near what is today called Franklin, Macon County, North Carolina. He writes:

A vast expanse of green meadows and strawberry fields; a meandering river gliding through, saluting in its various turnings the swelling, green, turfy knolls, embellished with parterres of flowers and fruitful strawberry beds; flocks of turkeys strolling about them; herds of deer prancing in the meads or bounding over the hills; companies of young, innocent Cherokee virgins, some busily gathering the rich fragrant fruit, others having already filled their baskets, lay reclined under the shade of floriferous and fragrant bowers of Magnolia, Azalea, Philadelphus, perfumed Calycanthus, sweet Yellow Jessamine and cerulean Glycine frutescens, disclosing their beauties to the fluttering breeze, and bathing their limbs in the cool fleeting streams; whilst other parties more gay and libertine, were yet collecting strawberries or wantonly chasing their companions, tantalising them, staining their lips and cheeks with the rich fruit. . . . This sylvan scene of primitive innocence was enchanting, and perhaps too enticing for hearty young men long to continue idle spectators. In fine, nature

prevailing over reason, we wished at least to have a more active part in
their delicious sports. . . .

Aye, those lusty Quakers.

It is not surprising that this source book, so important to Coleridge,
Wordsworth, and other Romantics, was much in the English mind. Carlyle
wrote to Emerson in 1851: "Do you know *Bartram's Travels?* . . . it has a
wondrous kind of floundering eloquence in it; and has also grown immeasur-
ably *old*. All American libraries ought to provide themselves with that kind
of book; and keep them as a kind of *biblical* article." Very wise, very wise
indeed. Perhaps if Americans had kept Bartram's words and spirit in mind,
when we go to the banks of the Oconaluftee River today (some miles east of
Rose Creek), we would not see the young, innocent Cherokee virgins working in a new factory that manufactures pink plastic hair curlers.

The town of Cherokee in the Qualla Indian Reservation is one of the
outstanding abominations in the U.S.—a horrendous conglutination of
bears in cages, junque shoppes, genuine Indians jogging about in pseudo-
Navajo headdresses made in Hong Kong out of plastic, reptile gardens, and
millions of decorticated modern American white folks (only) in duckbilled
caps and air-conditioned automobiles looking (as far as the ends of their
bony, blue noses) for the Lost America. In between Cherokee and Gatlinburg, Tennessee, lie the Great Smoky Mountains, some 687 square miles of
the wildest highland country east of the Rockies. Ninety-nine percent of
these faceless millions simply drive timorously over the ridge on U.S. 441
and stop only to point their Polaroids at small black bears swilling garbage
from litter barrels provided by the U.S. Department of the Interior. Then
they go to Gatlinburg, a former village which is now 160 motels, and places
with more of the same. One is of many minds about these enclaves called
National Parks. Marvellous that the lumber companies were chased out and
prevented from cutting down tulip trees ten feet thick, but dispiriting when
made motorized instant scenery for ant colonies. Even the lovely, once
remote Cades Cove on the Tennessee side of the Park below Gregory Bald
and Thunderhead is now overrun with camping sites, where mom and pop
move the entire backyard from Akron in giant caravans, and the steady hum
of transistors, Herman's Hermits, and electric shavers is heard. In Cades
Cove there is even a fallout shelter. Perhaps it is for the bears. However, all is
not (quite) lost. The best antidote is to hike the Appalachian Trail for a week
in the Smokies—from Fontana Dam to Davenport Gap, circa seventy miles.
The book you need is the *Guide to the Appalachian Trail in the Great
Smokies, the Nantahalas, and Georgia,* a publication of the Appalachian
Trail Conference. Also, I cannot imagine anyone seriously interested in the
beauties of the southern mountains not bringing along at least: Arthur

Stupka's book on the *Trees, Shrubs, and Woody Vines of the Great Smoky Mountain National Park* (University of Tennessee Press); Roger Tory Peterson's *Field Guide to the Birds* (Houghton Mifflin Co., Boston); and F. Schuyler Mathews's *Field Book of American Wild Flowers* (G. P. Putnam's Sons, New York). Since your pack for a week's trip will weigh about forty pounds, you may wish to forsake guides to the mushrooms, minerals, ferns, and small mammals for Henry David Thoreau and James Bond. Along the ridge of the Great Smokies you can still see the fields of bluets that moved below William Bartram's black suit and white horse; you can see the Catawba rhododendron, flame azelea, Turk's-cap lilies, the green flowers of American white hellebore, balsam fir and red spruce, and carpets of wood sorrel beneath them; drink from Ice Water Springs; see black snakes, salamanders, veeries, winter wrens, and wood thrushes. No man has deserved or earned a mountain until he has climbed it and been hosted there. And, by the way, to restore a sense of what the Cherokee once were when they had a culture and were not a zoo attraction, read James Mooney's *Myths of the Cherokee* (Bureau of American Ethnology, Washington, D. C., 1900).

The Southern Highlands, as John C. Campbell (*The Southern Highlander and his Home,* Russell Sage Foundation, New York, 1921) calls them, comprise an area betweeen 80,000 and 112,000 square miles, depending on your limits. Nine states: Maryland, Virginia, West Virginia, Kentucky, Tennessee, North Carolina, Georgia, and Alabama. This is a region about the size of Great Britain. I drove almost 4,000 miles in May and June of 1965 to apprise myself of a few of the facts among some of the craftsmen. What I have to report, then, will be based on instances, hunches, errors, likes and dislikes. For a survey you may go to a large volume of computerized English and exhaustive statistics: namely, *The Southern Appalachian Region,* edited by Thomas R. Ford (University of Kentucky Press, 1962), based on a $250,000 grant from the Ford Foundation. But, the only real answer is to come to the mountains yourself and talk to lots of people—what they call these days heuristic information, full of ambience, holistic intra-surfaces and encapsulations, etc., etc.

There, several thousand words and all you know is a very little about the place. We still have to look at the people before we dare examine what they make. The nature of the mountain man and woman (wife is usually known as "the woman") is nothing to seize quickly either. "We be modesty persons," as an old broommaker's woman told me. No matter how long you live in the mountains, if you are from out of the particular county by birth and brought your money from elsewhere, or earn it elsewhere, you are an outlander. These folk are the vestige of an Anglo-Saxon, Gaelic, and Celtic tradition, and hence about the most narrow people in the Western world, and among the most interesting. All the business about the remains of British balladry and Elizabethan language is true, though it is increasingly less so as the younger generations go off to factories and cities and through the military. The best book on the folkways of the Appalachians was written in 1913 by Horace Kephart: *Our Southern Highlanders* (reprinted in paperback by the Macmillan Co., New York, 1963). It was so good the government named one of the Smokies in Kephart's honor. He warns vigorously against measuring these highlanders by the usual apparatus. These are isolated, almost eighteenth-century people, despite their 65.6 percent television sets and 48.3 percent flush toilets against the national average. When I worked in psychiatric wards for the Army Medical Corps in the early 1950s, the highest incidence of catatonia and personality trauma was among boys from the West Virginia Mountains. "Buddy, ah jist can't stand such as that there. I want to go back to my own people." Here's a happier anecdote: my neighbor is an old Welshman, Iven Owens. Uncle Iv hasn't been out of Macon County more than a few times in his seventy-odd years. Once he went to Antlanter, Georgie, on a cabbage truck and the stories he told echoed through the community for years afterwards. Uncle Iv walked where he went—or he didn't go. So, one day I took Stefan Wolpe, the composer, over to the Owens house on the way to the waterfalls for a swim. I was perversely interested to see if Stefan, born in Berlin, could talk to Uncle Iv, born in Clear Creek. After much confusion and hemming and hawing, it was finally established via my intercession that Stefan came from Germany, in Europe. Uncle Iv's eyes lighted up: "Well now, I reckon that's somers yan side o' Asheville, ain't it boys?" Ja wohl, yes it is—but, then where are we? Uncle Iv don't do much book-readin', as he says, except a little Gospel. But he is perhaps the finest natural conversationalist I ever met. (Marshall McLuhan has much to say about this phenomenon in *The Gutenberg Galaxy*, etc.) He sprouts poems like a dahlia bush puts out blooms—and he calls it a "dally" bush, not being concerned with the Germanic botanist Professor Dahl. I am constantly humbled and delighted by this vernal, verbal gift of his. He is, in the root sense, a cultivated man—he is at home in his world, meagre though it may be by modern, televised standards. God knows what a government can do with a citizen like Uncle Iv. He is long surplus. Nobody needs his little sharecropper's farm and his handful of cabbage. But the Appalachian mountains need him and others like him. He has husbanded his acres, respected his land and his neighbors. Few can say as much. It is difficult to visualize what will happen to these indigenous, superfluous, wholesome citizens. The Appalachia Bill plans to devote, initially, about what it costs to kill Vietnamese in one day ($15,000,000) to retraining and educating some of the mountain people. I suppose this is comforting, but the problem is, as Paul Goodman notably keeps pointing out, that there is an increasing dearth of manly, meaningful, prideful jobs to do. What *can* these people do when less than one in twenty-five ever gets to college, though 90 percent of the old folks now think they should go? Obviously, as with the Negro and the Cherokee (or the heterosexual in the hairdressing, fashion, or ballet business), there is damned little incentive. It is very ironic that the mountain people, "reputed to be the most individualistic of all the regions," to quote Howard Odum, ". . . cooperate most fully with New Deal techniques." The federal government pours about $41,000,000 a month into Appalachian relief programs in a desperate action to ward off malnutrition, etc., until the states get serious and begin to think in terms of a viable economic and ecological plan for the region. One more remark about "work" before we finally, if we ever do, get to crafts. I heard Secretary of Labor W. Willard Wirtz tell of an incident on a plane. He remarked on what a lovely, modulated voice his stewardess had. She replied that she had been trained for the theatre but that there was simply no way for her to live from that profession. Mr. Wirtz was perceptive and humane enough to realize that the young lady was not really "employed"— she was thrown into the mechanistic, affluent service system, but she had no *vocation*. One is called to a vocation, where one exercises one's desire and talent. We need more men who know this, as citizens and as administrators. And, thus, we need crafts, which are forms of work. *Authentic,* meaning in its Greek root: what is made by a man's own hands.

Here is something else never to forget about these transplanted Scots and Ulstermen, poor folk who often perpetuate poor ways through no fault of their own. W. J. Cash speaks of it in his remarkable book, *The Mind of the South* (Alfred Knopf, New York, 1941):

> Add the poorness of the houses to which his world condemns him, his ignorance of the simplest rules of sanitation, the blistering sun of the country, and apply them to the familiar physical character of that Gaelic (maybe a little Iberian) strain which dominated in so large a part of the original Southern stocks—to this physical character as it had already been modified by the backwoods into the common Southern type—and there is no more mystery about even the peculiar appearance of the cracker. A little exaggerating here, a little blurring there, a little sagging in one place, a little upthrusting in another—and *voilà!* . . . Catch Calhoun or Jeff Davis or Abe Lincoln (whose blood stemmed from the Carolina foothill country, remember) young enough, nurse him on "busthaid", feed him hog and pone, give him twenty years of lolling—expose him to all the conditions to which the cracker was exposed—and you have it exactly.

It would take an indomitable people like the Scotch to do anything creative in a land as hard as Appalachia—as, on the Hebrides, they took wool, human urine, and black lichens and fashioned Harris tweed.

Colonial handicrafts have survived in North Carolina despite the flood of machine-made products from the factories. Isolation, poverty, the influences of tradition, and some steady local markets have served to keep alive these native skills.

—WPA *Guide to North Carolina* (1939)

The choice way to come to Appalachia is down the Blue Ridge Parkway. Get on it at Rock Fish Gap, west of Charlottesville, Virginia, and ease down to Asheville in two days. I suggest you stop at a delicatessen in Charlottesville and load up for picnics. The lack of culinary and alcoholic delights is quite as conspicuous in Appalachia as it is in Wales and Scotland. And the distances longer. Up on the parkway you get a real sense of the eastern verge of the region, and you look down into the broad central valleys to the west, where most of the large towns and rivers are: Charleston, Roanoke, Kingsport, Knoxville, Asheville, Chattanooga. To their west the Alleghenies and the plateau of the Cumberlands. So, the Blue Ridge approach is the best, the least spoiled. Or, if you must have freeways, take I-85 and I-40 into Winston-Salem enroute to Asheville and see the restoration of Old Salem, the "town museum" of the Moravians, now about to celebrate its two hundredth year. The craft sense of the Moravians was intact as a community requirement and establishes a measure for us to think about today, who live in towns and cities with blighted hearts and cancerous arteries, and who die accordingly—by precise poetic metaphor.

The Southern Highland Handicraft Guild

This is the key organization in the mountains, now in its thirty-fifth year. Every year the guild sponsors two Craftsman's Fairs: at Asheville in July and at Gatlinburg, Tennessee, in October. The 1965 Asheville Fair attracted 14,790 persons during its six days. There were forty-two exhibitors, most of them demonstrating techniques, and dancers from the John C. Campbell Folk School of Brasstown, North Carolina. You may watch Bea Hensley hammer out an iron chinquapin leaf on his anvil to tunes of his own devising; watch Persis Grayson and Golda Porter work a double-handed, two-thread flax spinning wheel that once belonged to Walt Whitman's mother. Corn-stalk pigs with rhododendron legs, okra seed eyes, and grape tendril tails sit quietly by Margaret Bolton as she fashions necklaces from seeds of the Kentucky coffee tree. Rude Osolnik's handsome walnut bowls vie with dulcimers by Edd Presnell, Edsel Martin, and Homer Ledford. The fairs are nationally known after their eighteen years of existence, and they should be. Eric Picker finds that his ceramics do better at Gatlinburg. The consensus is: "Money travels in the fall."

Crafts in the southern Appalachians are beset, of course, by the usual vast continental demons: insularity, randomness, xenophobia, know-nothingness, and know-it-allness. Observers from Tocqueville on have rued our lack of tradition. He remarked: "Everyone shuts himself up in his own breast and affects from that point to judge the world. . . . Not only does democracy make every man forget his ancestors, but it hides his descendants and separates his contemporaries from him; it throws him back forever upon himself alone and threatens in the end to confine him within the solitude of his own heart." We are peculiarly afflicted with the dictum formulated by Charles Olson in one of the most famous lines in recent poetry, from "The Kingfishers": "What does not change/is the will to change." And so craft (read *art*) tends to fade, or degenerate, into fad. I am impressed by recent remarks of the poet Paris Leary: "American poetry [read *craft*] seems rather like New York achitecture: it is constructed, admired, attacked or praised, used—and soon destroyed, its site swept clean and then occupied by a form of building that has nothing in common with it. There seems to be little or no sense of continuity. . . . We build an Edward Arlington Robinson and tear him down for a William Carlos Williams. That the best features of both might be united in an 'architecture' (genuinely new but integrally continuous with both) seems rarely to occur to the American mind."

Tocqueville, on target back in the 1830s, came up with this: "I accost an American sailor and inquire why the ships of his country are built so as to last but for a short time; he answers without hesitation that the art of navigation is every day making such rapid progress that the finest vessel would become almost useless if it lasted beyond a few years." That is from the angle of accelerated time. It now affects even the Appalachians, for, as Buckminster Fuller points out, we are now living in a Universal Village, albeit it is a pretty shoddy, venal place. You go into a remote cabin near a laurel thicket and a rushing branch in the mountains. The interiors will be spotless and austere: linoleum floors, "fotched-on" overstuffed furniture, a Bible, and a Sears catalog (it is known as the wish book), a Crisco can in the window with some petunias, a wedding portrait (hand-tinted), photographs of the sons off in the army or in a plant near Detroit, a chromolithograph of Jesus, and a few exotic souvenirs—a gilt Buddha and a piece of pottery shaped like the Leaning Tower of Pisa. The sad thing is there is almost never anything from the Appalachians. The loom in the back room may have some fine weaving in progress on it, but the people seldom see what's around them. I commented to Mrs. Ward on what a lovely view of Beech Mountain she had. She replied, "Reckon so, reckon it takes outsiders to see it."

We have in the Appalachians now (1) the indigenous mountain man and (2) the outlander who has newly arrived with his head all full of names like Hamada, Grotell, Wildenhain, Leach, and Voulkos ("which just downright aint fittin!"), so it is difficult to manage coexistence. At the recent Craftsman's Fair at Asheville I was talking with the famous Shadrack Mace, maker of settin' chairs from Mars Hill, North Carolina. He makes a sound, useful, simple product of maple, hickory, and white oak splints that his neighbors can buy for about eight dollars a chair. He had been talking to Mr. Kwumalo, an educator from Swaziland in southeast Africa brought here by the State Department to observe American craft techniques. Mr. Mace, who's been no further from home than Asheville (less than fifty miles), was amazed by this African. "Why he sure talks good," he remarked on Mr. Kwumalo's elegant Oxonian English. This is not to denigrate Mr. Mace, who is a good-hearted man, but to indicate (again) the gulf between these highlanders and the modern world. His chairmaker's tools—an ancient form of drawing horse and a knife—are quite as primitive as anything in tribal Swaziland. So, this is a basic problem. A glassblower from New York is just as foreign to his mind.

A second problem is age. When you observe a meeting of the Southern Highland Handicraft Guild, as I did at Berea College last May, or when you visit the Campbell Folk School or even Penland School, one is struck by the uncomfortable preponderance of those a mite long in the tooth—the lols and loms; i.e., the little old ladies and the little old men. One is not calling for immediate mass euthanasia, but one is crying for some continuity—from these fine citizens, many of whom began the revival in crafts fifty years ago, to new generations. This, too, is difficult to achieve in America, where everyone's middle name is Adam or Eve. However, depressing as the thought may be, 50 percent of all Americans now living are twenty-five or younger. Of these 95,000,000 citizens I have located perhaps two that write well-crafted poems. We must recall what Confucius had writ in very large calligraphy on the side of his outdoor bathtub: ALL THINGS MUST BE MADE ANEW!

Beech Creek, North Carolina
This little community west of Boone on the road to Tennessee is a good instance of local initiative. Jack Guy is the one-man impresario and entrepreneur of Guy's Folk-Toy Home Industries. He has organized twenty-five families for the making of simple, traditional toys—gee-haw whimmy-diddles, flipper-dingers, fly-killers, and bull-roarers—and this effort contributes some $400 to $800 to each family, which otherwise subsists on a burley tobacco allotment of perhaps $1,200 a year. Another authentic talent in Beech Creek is its singing, particularly its sacred music. Their most remarkable performer, even in his eighties, was the late Lee Monroe Presnell, whose ballads are very sweet, very plaintive, and moving. Little of the Beech Creek music is "pretty." It is severe and unrelieved, like the life that nurtures it. I played one side of a recording made at Beech Creek for a sociologically inclined lady friend. She gasped, "My word, I knew it was going to be folk,

but I didn't know it was going to be *ethnic!*" All is not dour, however, and anyone would enjoy Preacher Monroe's rendition of:

Oh, boys, stay away from the girls, I say,
Oh, give them lots of room.
They'll find you and you'll wed and they'll bang you till you're dead
With the baldheaded end of the broom.

Penland School of Crafts, Penland, North Carolina
A lichen is a symbiotic relationship, says the ecologist. It is a coupling—the divine couple against the world, says the poet. It is a thallophyte with some green algae, a proliferating process, growing from a center. Penland is such a process, making it up as it goes along, out of some inner necessity. It is beholden only to itself and its community and has the courage to make fine mistakes in the course of its learning/teaching existence. Miss Lucy Morgan founded Penland in 1929 "on a shoestring and it frayed," and created a unique institution until her retirement in 1962. Her choice of a successor was William J. Brown, sculptor, with training at Cranbrook, teaching at Haystack and at Worcester Craft Center; under him Penland is flourishing.

I would say that vital community begins to replace much that Black Mountain College stood for in its last phase, when there were such craftsmen there as Anni Albers, M. C. Richards, Karen Karnes, David Weinrib, John Chamberlain, Lou Harrison, Harry Callahan, Dan Rice, and Charles Olson. Penland in its valley near Spruce Pine sits easy, as the mountain people say. The beard on the young potter from Hickory is not so disquieting to the local folk as it would have been twenty-five years ago. Maybe this is television's one good subliminal influence. Anyway, a little more tolerance of "the outside" begins to occur. As I keep reminding you, we are confronted by mountain men whose ancestors could not bear the English east of Wales across Offa's Dike, or south of Scotland beyond Emperor Hadrian's Wall. What do you think of potters, poets, and lichen? Would you want your sister to marry a lichen? Penland is serious and exuberant, producing persons and works worthy of great respect.

The Pottery Shop, Rising Fawn, Georgia
On Lookout Mountain in extreme northwestern Georgia, Charles and Rubynelle Counts have established a very active center for crafts—"for the dignity of work and a love for doing a thing right." You go west from Trenton on highway 143, up onto the plateau in the direction of La Fayette. Near the settlement of New Salem turn off the pavement left onto Highway 189. The studios are on the edge of an escarpment looking into Alabama.

Charles Counts is a Kentuckian by birth and a product of the Harlan County coal fields. It is not surprising that he is "sociologically involved" and concerned with rehabilitation. Besides that, he is a very able potter. Troubled by the ugliness of the human spirit in a region once blessed by great natural beauty, but now stripped and exploited, he and his wife are busily fighting poverty of spirit and mediocrity, trying to keep their neighbors *people* instead of technological *personnel*. "Should we refuse to take up this admittedly thin thread of hope, then the possibility would be that these people would have been cast out into the human junkyard—unemployment, uneducation—more poverty and more ignorance." Besides the pottery shop, an abandoned dwelling has been fixed up for the making of quilts and appliqué work. These are new designs by the Countses ("Summertime" and "Love Me Love Me Not" are two handsome examples), executed by ladies in the community in whom the tradition is still viable. Hooked rugs are also being made, using a new tufting process developed by Ronald Everett, a local machinist. The Rising Fawn operation is small but, to my mind, very important and very moving. It confronts the precise, local situation and is effecting a clear improvement in its place. The Countses believe in their own private responsibilities, in apprentices, in neighborhood.

Iron Mountain Stoneware, Laurel Bloomery, Tennessee
The establishment of this new pottery, one of the first large commercial ceramic plants in the U.S. in seventy-five years, makes an interesting contrast with, for instance, the Bybee Pottery, the oldest pottery west of the Alleghenies, an operation of the Cornelison family dating from perhaps as early as 1809. Bybee is on Kentucky Highway 52 not far northeast of Berea. I watched Walter Lee Cornelison (fourth generation) exercise his skill throwing milk pitchers using a local ball clay. This skill is not to be denied, but neither is the fact that there is no design to the work that hasn't been available for generations. As Marguerite Wildenhain wrote in a letter (1957) to Charles Counts at Berea: "I know those Kentucky potters, and while they are infinitely better than most as to the pure business of throwing, I also know that they are artistically and creatively quite dried up. All their shapes are old seventeenth century ones, and they have never developed since that time. . . ." The Cornelisons would probably argue, Well, what's the problem, we sell all we make and can't possibly keep up with the demand? However, this side step does not speak too well for either the maker or the consumer, this dipping of (once) tried and true pitchers into commercial glazes that look like so much blue and yellow shiny paint. This kind of parochialism is offensive, painful as that may be to say about these diligent potters who are simply not willing to face up to this new situation of the Universal Village.

On the other hand: Iron Mountain Stoneware. This venture is the creation of two individuals, Albert K. Mock, Jr., an architect from Damas-

cus, Virginia, and Miss Nancy J. Patterson, of Los Angeles, a ceramics
designer. Having formed a company in Tokyo that created jobs for 125
Japanese workers building ocean racing yachts, Mock suddenly thought of
the area of his boyhood, the handsome hill-and-valley country of southwest
Virginia and east Tennessee, where unemployment and poverty overshad-
owed the Iron Mountains and the economy was stagnant and depressive.
Miss Patterson was aware how little American stoneware could compete
with foreign work; she had had seven years training and experience with
such firms as Arabia in Helsinki, the Royal Copenhagen Manufactory, and
the Peitou Ceramic Plant near Taipei, Taiwan. So, after elaborate studies of
the ceramic markets, four-year financial projections, etc., the plant is now
operating, as of June, 1965. It is a handsomely designed and landscaped
building by Albert Mock.

Again, as in the case of the shops of Rising Fawn, Georgia, Iron Mountain Stoneware demonstrates a basic confidence in the mountain people to
learn skills and to cooperate with new designs. It is hopeful and it should
work, to judge from the industry and dedication of Mr. Mock and Miss
Patterson and of the people of Laurel Bloomery.

Perhaps all this tangle of observation will serve to indicate the richness
of a special biota—of people and places and work now under way. Few
people know even one mountain on speaking terms. There is much to see on
Mt. Le Conte alone, if you will come and look—and not just look for what
you have seen before, which seems to be the modern approach to travel. One
time you'll hear the winter wren, one time you'll see Grass of Parnassus, and
another it'll be the scarlet berries of the mountain ash. "O Taste and See!"
said King David.

Highlands, North Carolina 1965

Beauty? Beauty My Eye!
(Folk Art in Kentucky)

38

What better place to write a note on Kentucky bluegrass-root artists than here in the December shadows of Dentdale, a remote part of the Cumbrian Pennines in the far northwest of England? The saying around here is: "There's nowt so queer as folk."

Which, I think, once used to be true of folk in either place. Which, sez me (The Old Original Onomamaniac), is clear simply from the names.

Once upon a time Thomas Thistlethwaite, James Dinsdale, Cherry Kearton, Dixon Daykin, and Myles Bainbridge lived near Elysian Shades, Cowclose Hill, Green Edges, Bower Bank, Shake Holes, Nettle Pot Beck, Tongue End, Stalling Busk, Rowantree Top, Clanking Stones, Hag Worm Haw Moss, and Cluntering Gill Head. The men and the places are both very topographical in their names; and, here, in Dentdale, there is a distinct Norse ring to the names. A *thistlethwaite* would be a clearing with a thistle patch in it. A boy named Tom was once born there. What else to say about these names? They sound old and settled, very literal, very rich.

Once upon a time Red Sol Day, Aunt Tish Hays, Aunt Cord Ritchie, Jethro Amburgey, and Wilma Creech lived near Viper, Sacred Wind, Handshoe, Boreing, Hardshell, Dingus, Cutshin, Breeding, Stab, Acorn, Rowdy, Decoy, Redbush, Ruin, Load, Crum, Blue Lick, Climax, Highsplint, Flippin, Marrowbone, Furnace, Meshack, Pippa Passes, Bypro, Decay, Dwarf, Hi Hat, Neon, Science Hill, Wolf Coal, and Slaughters. Is it too much to deduce that this was a raw, untamed place, or that the people who did the naming were imaginative, humorous, Fundamentalist, realistic, even a mite paranoid, and on their own? They were, in fact, serving a life sentence of solitary confinement on a huge, new continent. Tocqueville, recall, kept being amazed by the human distance from one heart to another. It was D. Boone, was it not, who declared he did not want to hear another man's axe or see another man's fire.

The New World situation (both edenic and horrific) did something to promote Imagination amongst the Anglo-Saxons. There are those tart observers here in England today (like the journalist Bernard Levin) who are of the opinion that Imagination left these shores by the end of the eighteenth century and now even the shadow is fading away. Certainly, the eccentrics and *nouveaux riches* and characters who filled Britain with follies and grottos are extinct. And this particular savant knows very well that the malaise of *meilikhoposthoi* (vagueness of mind and cock) is a national disgrace. Sir Fancis Dashwood ("Hell-Fire Francis") had carved at Medmenham Abbey: *Fait ce que voudra.* The days when you did what you liked are gone. Eighteen bureaucrats have been invented to see that you won't, or can't.

Kentucky, to this very day, has a fair share of citizens who see "differently" with as much distinction as any "fine" artist. When it comes to making art, "the folks are as good as the people." And I say that before push comes to shove, because the winning combination in this democracy, for me, has always been high art and low life. So I have spent a number of years tracking down the extraordinary things that dot the country: Henry Dorsey's house at Brownsboro; the funeral monuments at Mayfield. It was important to sit on Father Merton's front steps at his hermitage and talk; or watch Wendell Berry tend to his place and tend to his poems; or go up to Campton to see Ed Tolson in the flesh and hear about why he makes his dolls; or know about the photographs of Ralph Eugene Meatyard and Doris Ulmann; or let Guy Mendes tell me about Sweet Evening Breeze, Cowboy Steve Taylor, and Carlos Toadvine, the World's Greatest Upside-Down Left-Handed Guitar Picker. (The latest discovery is one Carlos Cortes Coyle, 1871–1962, of Bear Wallow, Kentucky, whose bizarre paintings are at Berea College—if you can get anybody to show them to you. I have been to Berea seven times and have had to encounter the pictures in a book, *Twentieth Century American Folk Art and Artists,* Herbert W. Hemphill, Jr., published by Dutton.) If a man who lives in the North Carolina Blue Ridge and the English Pennines can find that much in fifteen years, think how full the Kentucky woods must be with other curiosities and glories. Things made by eccentrics, booger men, wierds, populists, hell-fire shake-handling preachers, end-of-the-world shouters, people in touch with the spirits, mentals, them a mite tetched in the haid, busy old ladies, and just folks, etc.

We in the South (I am speaking of the *we* who profess our book-learning in universities, or try to make art works, or mind our manners and not become either slovens or slobs) have been particular victims all our born days of the taste for Beauty and the Finer Things of Life, as defined by Nice People with plenty spondulix in the family bank. I am beginning to think that Dorothy Day may be right when she says: "The best thing to do with the better things in life is give them up." Because, sadly, Nice People are a pathetic conspiracy on the whole. They assume that all people in the world without that moola in the bank and conspicuous consumption on the brain are genuine vermin: cretins, spending their days on federal relief, swilling booze, womanizing, refusing to work, stealing, plotting the End of Civilization As We Know It, etc. One hears the gentle voices shouting for Old Black Joe to fetch them a julep, and sighing "I just love Beauty." Which sentiment, friends, is not just liberal bleating but the lament of an old-fashioned Jeffersonian democrat, who sees that those distances from one human heart to another, noted by Tocqueville all those years ago, are now bridged only by what they call in the textbooks "a tenuous pecuniary nexus." Yet, of course, Mr. Jefferson sat there on his hill, surrounded by good, landed Virginia farmers, congratulating one and all that they were far from "Europe's *canaille*." The self is selfish.

This begins to sound more like a sermon than a note on folk art, but I am saying that it is very easy to ride in on our isolation and see things in an easy, art-loving stupidity. A moralist, or a gentle person, has it worse than a dog with a ten-pound bone, for greed is a national dilemma and the Nation is dog-eat-dog. For example: my eyes grow wide and both dismayed and pleasured when in front of Edgar Tolson's whittled visions of "The Garden of Eden" in the Baptist Genesis. They are a sight to see, but are they the product of a naive, an innocent, a man with a childlike talent who can entertain us with these "dolls" of his? One would have to be very blind and callous to think so. If you go visit Ed Tolson up in Campton, Kentucky, you see a man who is a wreck, like his community, and a man treated by his neighbors as no better than a mongrel dog. *Abandonné*, as the French say— that double sense of the word, as so much of American life is now abandoned, like those corridors of rotting cars along the roads of Harlan County. People treated like curs and strays. Ed Tolson, poor old devil, sitting there with his fierce daily hangover, screaming as the youngest of his eighteen children bumps into his chair: "Somebody ought to kill that son-of-a-bitch!" Ed is into sin, and misery, and revival—in a powerful way. It's not pretty. The dolls show it. They are *sobering*. You leave Campton muttering Protestant prayers: "There, but for the Grace of God, go I." In a gallery or on a coffee table, a lot of Campton may be left behind, but I am not about to forget, listening to this wild old man telling about how he likes to sober up out in the woods, "livin' just like the injuns," with a Nehi and some baloney. Well, would he like it better if he spent an evening here in Dentdale, listening to Frederick Delius on the stereo, eating Lancashire Hotpot washed down with a bottle or two of Guinness? The self is selfish and learns how to survive. After all is said of ethnology, sociology, and politics, the fact remains he is no less an *artist* than I am, or most others.

There are other reasons besides pain and sin and idleness that will set a man's hand to shaping pieces of wood. Shakers once lived in Kentucky, and a sentence by Thomas Merton comes to mind: "The peculiar grace of a Shaker chair is due to the fact that it was made by someone capable of believing that an angel might come sit on it." But, of what use is that uncomfortable, austere, angelic chair to some gross dude of Middle America, laid back on a reclining, vibrating, plastic-covered La-Z-Boy Rocker—wolfing down the peanuts, working a six-pack, sweating out Super Bowl X in front of the box? Not much, baby.

Folk Art or Art Art or Folksy Art or Arty Folks can get your head all folked up. But do not think you can buy taste from Monkey Ward or that nice young decorator out near the country club. The Average American Living Room now looks like a lounge in a Ramada Inn—Lord, Lord, those hanging lamps, those fiberglass French Provincial accessories, that wall-to-wall muzak, those containers for Big Macs lying in trash baskets by the billion. If you go get it from the Colonel, do please consult your nearest Public Health facility. Lay aside the blinders introduced by the Franchise People from Beyond Space and let these objects here collected before you, this folk art, remind you of the days of one-to-one relationships, of things made by the hands and talents of persons with a feeling of kinship for you. There is no reason to fear that those times are all over. We are each new human beings, when it comes to that.

Dentdale, Cumbria 1975

T. Ben Williams:
January 17, 1898–May 5, 1974

39

"The only way they'll get me off this mountain is to carry me off." My father's assertion has the Blakean fierceness. He was, after all, a Celt and a mountain man. And so it came to pass in this particular Appalachian springtime, when many of his favorite things were around him: bloodroot and leucothoe, pileated woodpecker, *Franklinia alatamaha*, galax, the rose-breasted grosbeak, dogwood, Solomon's seal.

T. Ben died at "Skywinding" on an early May evening precisely where he wanted to. It was a combination of arteriosclerosis and Parkinson's. His heart simply stopped—very quickly, very quietly.

Sons know woefully little about fathers. I will say it in that laconic way, rather than emulate my townsman, Thomas Wolfe: "Which of us has looked into his father's heart? Which of us has not remained forever prison-bent? Which of us is not forever a stranger and alone?" I resist Buncombe—even cosmic buncombe. I regret that if I sometimes thought my father was stubborn as ten mules, I was undoubtedly stubborn as eleven! And, if I used to think he had stone-age politics, my distrust of the shoddiness of Modern America more than equals his—and my distrust of scoundrels in high (and low) places. He was a *very* honest man. I have never met anyone to question that. A man who stood by his word, which is what ethics has been asking for since some Chinese invented that Greek word.

It is not so curious as it might seem for Ben Williams to have had a poet for a son. Looking back at old family papers, you find he was "Class Poet" at Fruitland Academy, over in Henderson County. He had a feeling for writers he conveyed to me from the first years: Kipling's *Just So Stories,* Hugh Lofting, DuBose Heyward, Horace Kephart, John Charles McNeill, Wolfe, Joel Chandler Harris, and, especially, Roark Bradford. And he had a true feeling for the speech and humanity of his mountain neighbors and friends in Macon County. I think of Tut Burnette, Uncle Iv Owens, Hayes Bryson;

Tolliver Vinson, Steve Potts, and Leonard Webb. No airs, no nonsense. "No aires"—exactly what happens in my poems. An attempt to restore common, ordinary persons and things to the place they deserve in this careless world. The *commoner* the better. No airs: *of the earth*, hooved up into Blue Ridges. Tut Burnette used to say when he was jollified: "Lord, Lord, well, I'm tickled to death!" I can think of nothing that says it better; i.e., what my father and I felt about these ancient Appalachian hills and the folks in them.

What fascinates me about this country of ours is the fact that a man with what they call a "simple" background had not only a sparkling Ground Sense but could develop an extraordinary acuity and information about rare works of art. He, after all, discovered the lost "Jersey Service" of Meissen ware, decorated by Loewenfinck, in a department store in Atlanta, Georgia. His collection of Sevres and Nantgarw, of T'ang, Sung, Ming, and later dynasties of porcelain, remains. This speaks of the vitality of his imagination and of the region that spawned him.

These things are never completely random. My mother was always there and always lent her own remarkable flair and companionship. She is certainly no less.

James Mooney, in his *Myths of the Cherokee* writes: "The Cherokee once had a wooden box, nearly square and wrapped up in buckskin, in which they kept the most sacred things of their old religion. . . . They travelled seven days to the west until they came to the Darkening Land." In my father's box, I would like to place: (1) a curly-maple banjo that Earl Scruggs had picked a whole lot; (2) a mixed packet of seeds of the sourwood tree, the persimmon, the dogwood, and the staghorn sumac; (3) an Indian pipe he once found in a cave on Sugarloaf Mountain; (4) a copy of *Ol' Man Adam an' His Chillun (Being the Tales They Tell About the Time When the Lord Walked the Earth Like a Natural Man)*, by Roark Bradford; (5) a clump of shortia; (6) a gallon of Virginia Gentleman, with a supply of mountain spring water from Scaly; and (7) his K'ang-hsi black hawthorn ginger jar, the one with manganese brown, purples, greens & yellows, on a black ground, with magpies perched in the branches. In China the magpie is a bird symbolizing happiness.

Highlands, North Carolina 1974

Design by David Bullen
Typeset in Mergenthaler Sabon
by Wilsted & Taylor
Printed by Maple-Vail
on acid-free paper